"It's strange seeing you like this," Faith said.

"Like what?"

"All responsible. A dad."

"I'm not a dad in the fullest sense," Trent replied. "I'm Tyke's guardian. He calls me Tent. He can't say his *r*'s yet."

She chuckled. "Tyke and Tent?"

"Yup." His warm brown gaze flickered in her direction. "We're pals."

That was an interesting delineation. But there was something more settled about him now, and she had a feeling Tyke was the reason for it, because even their marriage hadn't settled him like this.

"You seem happy," she said.

"I am. Tyke came along when I needed someone to love, and he needed someone to love him, too."

Her heart gave a squeeze at that. After their divorce... Yeah, she knew what desperate loneliness felt like, too.

Dear Reader,

I hope you enjoy this new miniseries set in Amish country in an antiques shop that is bound to stir up some romance... History is like that—filled with hearts and homes, drama and intrigue. One day, our lives will be condensed down to a set of dishes, an egg beater, a pair of dress shoes we hardly wore...and strangers will wonder about us, too. I hope whatever I leave behind will inspire stories.

If you'd like to connect with me, you can find me at my website at patriciajohns.com. I'm also on social media, and if you sign up for my newsletter, you can be entered into my giveaways! I'd love to connect with you.

And if you enjoy this book, can I ask a favor? Would you leave a review? Reviews help us authors get the word out, and I'd be eternally grateful!

Patricia

HER AMISH COUNTRY HUSBAND

PATRICIA JOHNS

Harlequin

HEARTWARMING

> If you purchased this book without a cover you should be aware that this book is stolen property. It was reported as "unsold and destroyed" to the publisher, and neither the author nor the publisher has received any payment for this "stripped book."

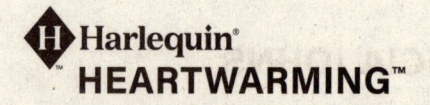

Harlequin® HEARTWARMING™

ISBN-13: 978-1-335-05154-7

Her Amish Country Husband

Copyright © 2025 by Patricia Johns

All rights reserved. No part of this book may be used or reproduced in any manner whatsoever without written permission.

Without limiting the author's and publisher's exclusive rights, any unauthorized use of this publication to train generative artificial intelligence (AI) technologies is expressly prohibited.

This is a work of fiction. Names, characters, places and incidents are either the product of the author's imagination or are used fictitiously. Any resemblance to actual persons, living or dead, businesses, companies, events or locales is entirely coincidental.

For questions and comments about the quality of this book, please contact us at CustomerService@Harlequin.com.

TM and ® are trademarks of Harlequin Enterprises ULC.

Harlequin Enterprises ULC
22 Adelaide St. West, 41st Floor
Toronto, Ontario M5H 4E3, Canada
www.Harlequin.com

Printed in Lithuania

Patricia Johns is a *Publishers Weekly* bestselling author who writes from Alberta, Canada, where she lives with her husband and son. She writes romances and mysteries set in Amish country that will leave you yearning for a simpler life. You can find her at patriciajohns.com and on social media, where she loves to connect with her readers. Drop by her website and you might find your next read!

Books by Patricia Johns

Harlequin Heartwarming

An Amish Country Reunion

The Butternut Amish B&B

Her Amish Country Valentine
A Single Dad in Amish Country
A Boy's Amish Christmas

Amish Country Haven

A Deputy in Amish Country
A Cowboy in Amish Country

The Second Chance Club

Their Mountain Reunion
Mountain Mistletoe Christmas
Rocky Mountain Baby
Snowbound with Her Mountain Cowboy

Visit the Author Profile page
at Harlequin.com for more titles.

To my husband—those vows we took changed a part of me forever. I'm yours for always.

CHAPTER ONE

OLD THINGS SEEM to hold magic all their own. Like people, the longer they've been around, the more wisdom and character they seem to possess, and the more the past seems to cling to them.

Amish Antiques was a shop brimming with interesting bits and pieces of local Amish history, and with the history came faint, whispered ghosts that clung to every item. Faith Fairchild, one of the joint owners of the shop, surveyed their domain. There were handwoven rugs made generations ago that were now worn down to the threads by countless feet but whose patterns were still visible. A bed step, the top step being the lid for a box, had been fashioned two hundred years ago and repaired several times over the years. The Amish had always created beautiful, but always functional, items. There were Amish dolls, simple little creatures with blank canvas for faces that had been kissed and loved by little girls until they were nothing but gray.

The shop also had a large selection of handwoven baskets. Some worn Pennsylvania Dutch hymnbooks were stacked on the seat of a surprisingly sturdy rocking chair—books that had guided the a cappella singing of Amish folks for a hundred years or more, their spines disintegrating, and their pages loose. The rocking chair's seat had been worn down to a nearly black finish, the rails at the bottom of the chair flat now—the chair wouldn't rock anymore. But it could still clunk back and forth a little if the person sitting in it was really determined. And overhead a fan wobbled and spun, cooling the June air of the sun-warmed shop. Another box fan set up beside the cash register improved upon the air movement.

Faith and her two sisters had inherited the shop when their great-aunt Josephine passed away a few weeks ago. It was a month after Faith's twenty-ninth birthday. Aunt Josephine had lost her twin sister when she was a young woman, and she'd always encouraged family unity. Her three favorite nieces had gotten more than one lecture from her about how much a sister would mean to each of them as the years went by. This inheritance, that insisted all three of them work together for a calendar year, seemed to be a continuation of those heart-to-heart talks.

Hope, newly married, was on her way from Pittsburgh, which was a two-hour drive. She was due to arrive anytime, but so far it was just Faith and her youngest sister, Elaine, working on getting the antiques shop ready for the grand reopening.

Elaine—her name having sadly deviated from

their mother's planned pattern due to her being hopped up on pain medication from the delivery—worked as a kindergarten teacher in one of Apfelkuchen's three elementary schools. After she finished college, she'd come back for a job here in their hometown and had been teaching full-time for the last two years. For Faith, though, this wasn't exactly a comfortable homecoming. Apfelkuchen held too many memories, and a few regrets she hadn't let go of yet.

To the English-speaking ear, the name of their town, Apfelkuchen, sounded rather harsh, but in Pennsylvania Dutch, a German dialect, Apfelkuchen had a sweeter meaning. It meant "apple pie," and there was no better apple pie than one baked in an Amish kitchen. Faith had bought plenty of them at the Amish markets. Plus, half of her ex-in-laws were Amish. So she'd had plenty of Amish-made apple pie, and try as she might, she could never reproduce their results.

Nor had she been able to reproduce the Amish results in her failed bookstore, or her short marriage. Whatever secret the Amish held for their long-lasting relationships, Faith had missed out on them. Those were her regrets, but when Aunt Josephine passed and Faith found out she was part owner of the old antiques shop, the timing had been right. She'd just been laid off her bookkeeping job in Pittsburgh—another disappointment in a string of them. Things had to start looking up—and maybe they would with a family-owned shop that smelled of moldering bookbindings and dusty memories.

"Knock, knock."

Faith knew that voice, and her stomach sank. Speaking of her failed marriage... She walked toward the front door, propped open with a brick to let some fresh air inside, and her heart clenched in her chest.

Sure enough, she knew the jean-clad man standing in the doorway, a tool belt slung low on his hips. He wore a short-sleeved blue plaid shirt that matched his blue eyes too well. He gave her a nod.

"Faith..." Trent's blue gaze caught hers, and then he looked down at his scuffed cowboy boots. They were familiar. Had he not gotten new boots in the two years since they'd split up?

"Hi, Trent."

That blue gaze came back up again. "How are you?"

"I'm fine."

"I heard you'd inherited Josephine's shop," he said.

That news had traveled fast. She'd only been in town a couple of days.

"Yes. Me and my sisters," Faith said. "I heard about your cousin's passing."

Kylie had drowned on a camping trip, and the whole town had grieved. There was a Facebook page set up in her memory, and a GoFundMe for her funeral expenses, since her parents had already passed away.

"Yeah, that was really tough for us," he replied. "Did you hear that I took in her little boy?"

"I did," she replied. "Was that temporary, or…?"

"I'm in the process of adopting him."

"Wow." She smiled, her chest still feeling tight. He hadn't wanted kids when they were together. "You're a father."

"He's my little buddy. We've got a routine now, and it's working pretty well."

"Are you doing it…alone?"

"Yeah. I mean, I was single and working, but there wasn't anyone else in a position to take him, so… I stepped up."

"That's good of you."

Things had certainly changed around here. Imagining Trent with a toddler in tow was hard to do. He'd always been a tough guy's guy. But her sister Elaine had filled her in on this new side to him.

"What's his name?" she asked.

"Tyson. I call him Tyke for short." He paused, his expression growing more distant. "So, back to business…"

"Business?" She squinted at him.

"Your aunt lined me up to do a rewire on the store a couple of months ago," Trent said.

"What?" Faith's heart skipped a beat. So this wasn't just an uncomfortable social call or Trent stopping by to satisfy his curiosity. "Are you serious?"

"I don't joke about rewires." He met her gaze

evenly. "I'm due to start this week to get it all done in time. It was an insurance issue. Had to be done."

"Where would we even find a record of that?" Faith turned back toward Elaine, who was cleaning out the paperwork from underneath the front counter. It was just one more complication on top of many in the last couple of days. There had been some outstanding debts, a plumbing issue, some customers waiting on items that they'd paid for but Faith had no idea about. Thankfully, they'd agreed to be patient while Faith sorted out details. And now a rewire of the store, and one that was apparently pressing?

"Hi, Trent," Elaine said. "Good to see you. How's the kiddo?"

"He's keeping me busy," Trent said. "How was the school year?"

"Amazing." Elaine dropped her dusting cloth and headed to the cash register. "Let me take a look in the file box." Josephine had a haphazard filing system under the till, and Elaine squatted down to look.

"Trent, no." Faith met his gaze. "I don't want to do this. You and I have history, and I don't have the emotional energy to wade through it right now."

It was the honest truth. The end of their three-year marriage had just about crushed her, and add her aunt's passing to the heartbreak of her divorce, and she had nothing left to fight with right now.

"I've got a contract," he replied.

"You made her sign a contract?" Faith demanded.

"*She* made me sign one!" he shot back. "She wanted to make sure that this store would be my priority and she'd get the work done on time. Josephine was a tough nut."

"Are you really going to hold us to that?" she asked.

"Sure am." Trent leaned against the doorframe and his gaze flowed past her shoulder into the shop. Faith took a step to the side to block his view. He was not going to sweet-talk her sister!

"Trent!" she said.

His gaze came back to Faith's face. "I've gotten a little tougher in my business practices, and I'm sorry, Faith, but I scheduled a week to do this job that your aunt contracted me to do. And from what I understand, you can't put this rewiring off, either."

"Here it is—" Elaine said, emerging from behind the till, a couple of pieces of paper stapled together in hand. "A signed contract for the work to be done, and an email from the insurance broker saying that if the building isn't up to code in…in eight days, they'll cancel our insurance."

Faith and Elaine exchanged a look. Great. It would have to be done, and in a place the size of Apfelkuchen, there wouldn't be another electrician to call. They'd have to shop around in a larger community, and that would take time that they didn't have.

"The whole building?" Faith said faintly.

"The store and the apartment above," Trent replied. "It's ancient wiring—a definite fire risk."

"And it'll take a week?"

"Yep."

She could handle that, couldn't she? They were going to do a soft open just as soon as they were able, so they could plan that for after the rewire. She felt her throat close off again with emotion and she defiantly blinked back a mist in her eyes. She was not going to cry in front of Trent! She was frustrated and tired. That was all.

"I'll let you off the hook with the contract." Trent's tone softened. "If you figure you can find someone else to get it done fast enough."

"Do you know of anyone else?" she asked, swallowing past the lump in her throat.

He shook his head. "Nope."

Shoot. Faith looked over her shoulder at Elaine, who had a pleased little smile on her face. Her sisters had always liked Trent. He'd been the charming older brother they'd never had.

"I don't see a way out of this," Faith admitted.

A smile touched Trent's lips. "Me neither."

Faith stepped back, and Trent slipped into the shop, the scent of his aftershave tugging at long-buried memories. She let the door swing shut and stood there as Trent ambled inside, swinging his bag off his shoulder.

He was still a good-looking guy—fit, tall and with a saunter that could outdo any cowboy. If Faith had a type, Trent was it. And that was a problem she was actively trying to fix. She needed a new type— one that was better for her. Trent Lantz seemed to be the same intoxicating, impulsive, going-by-the-seat-of-his-pants guy she'd divorced.

Except now, he was the guardian of a toddler. It was hard to imagine him with a little boy.

But there was one thing she was still certain of—Trent Lantz was an emotional liability.

CHAPTER TWO

THE OVERHEAD FAN whipped around, stirring the warm air like soup over Trent's head. Faith stood back, arms crossed over her chest. She was watching him with a cautious look on her face as if she wasn't sure if he'd bite or not. She'd changed over the last two years. She looked different now—her once-cropped hair was shoulder length, and she looked warier, more jaded perhaps. Weren't they all.

But it felt good to see Faith again—uncomfortably good. He'd seen her at Josephine Fairchild's funeral, of course, but he'd been in the back of the church, and Faith had been up front in the first two rows with family. He'd slipped out before they had the reception line. He'd gone to pay his respects to his departed friend, not upset his ex-wife. And maybe running out early had been for himself, too, because seeing Faith left a lump in his throat. She'd been the love of his life.

But this was business. Like he'd said, he had a contract, and he had already done a site check on the place, ordered supplies he'd need to rewire the old shop and apartment above, and done all the legwork. He hadn't been exaggerating his investment in this job already. All the same, he'd had to psych himself up to come out here. He'd known it would be tough to face Faith again, but he hadn't known that it would ache this way.

Elaine gave him a nod. "So how are you, Trent? I mean...really."

Faith and her sister looked completely different upon first glance. Faith was tall and slim, and Elaine was like a blonde fairy—petite and full of fire. But both had the same eyes and the same smile. The family similarities were oddly striking.

"I'm pretty good," Trent replied. "Hanging in there."

"How is Tyke doing?" Elaine asked. "Is he two yet?"

"Yeah, he just turned two last month," he replied. "A week after Faith's birthday. I'm going to get him into play school in September."

He glanced toward Faith again, but her expression was unreadable. He'd taken Tyke in a year after their split. In fact, he'd signed the divorce papers during one of Tyke's naps. Having someone else to take care of had gotten him through that painful time.

How hard had their split been on Faith? That was what he wanted to know, because he'd been a wreck when his wife left. Ask his family who'd stepped in to give him a shake and offer moral support—in that order.

"It was a nice funeral for Josephine," Trent said

to change the subject. "Your uncle gave a beautiful eulogy."

"You were there?" Faith asked.

"Of course," he said. "I'll miss her."

Faith's great-aunt Josephine had been a friendly constant in their life when they'd been married, and after the divorce she'd been a surprising source of compassion, too. She'd been understanding and more than once she'd told him, "I wish you'd get her back, Trent. I don't think she's happier without you."

Did that mean she had a new guy, or was she still on her own? When he asked Josephine, she'd always said he should call Faith and ask her himself. He didn't like to admit it, but the thought of Faith moving on and loving another man did hurt. Like a gut punch.

"Well... It's nice to see both of you again," Trent said, sparing a nod for Elaine, too. "I know it's a bit awkward, but I'm sure we can find some way to get along while I work."

Trent dropped his tool bag next to the counter. He pulled out a copy of his estimate, which he and Josephine had signed, and pushed it across the counter. It was fair. He wasn't charging a penny more than he needed to charge.

Faith tucked her fingers into the back pockets of her jeans and sighed. There it was—that certain unnameable thing that had changed. Faith *was* different. She looked sadder, thinner and...a little defeated. Faith had been many things—stubborn being one of them—but she'd never looked this tired before that he could remember. Ever.

"Faith, can we talk privately?" he asked.

Faith looked up. "Sure."

Elaine turned her attention to the estimate, and Trent angled his head toward the window where a fly buzzed, bumping up against the glass. Faith followed him over there, winding their way around some displays of antique postcards, greeting cards and old newspapers.

Faith looked up at him when they stopped in the pool of warm sunlight at the front of the shop.

"First of all, I'm going to do the job as quickly as I can and get out of your hair," he said. "But it'll be a job well done. You can be sure of that."

"I'd never question your ability," she said with a faint smile. "You always were a good electrician."

Just not a good husband, apparently. But she'd blamed him for things outside his control, and that hadn't been fair.

"Good. I'm glad. And secondly..." This was where it was a bit dicey. He hadn't thought it through, and he didn't know why he was putting it out there now, but seeing her again was rattling loose all sorts of feelings. "How can I help?"

Faith ran a hand through her hair, tugging it away from her face.

"You can't," she said, shaking her head. "Trent, we're divorced."

"You look like you could use some compassion about now," he said.

She smiled faintly. "That's a bit backhanded. Do I look particularly tired? Have I aged?"

"That's not what I meant—if I can help, let me know. That's all I'm saying."

"We'll be fine," she replied. "Aunt Josephine left the shop to us on the condition that we three run it together for a year. Then we can sell it and do whatever we want with it. So we're doing just that."

"The plan is to sell?" he asked.

"That's what we've decided upon. The minute we can."

"And then what?" he asked.

"And then I'll use my part of the money to open another bookshop—a used bookstore this time. I'm ready now. I've got it all planned out."

So Faith was focused on leaving again. Good to know. Before she died, Josephine had asked him to make peace with Faith. *Talk it out, Trent.* That was what she'd said. She'd meant well, but she also hadn't understood their relationship very well.

Trent nodded toward his bag. "I'd better get my ladder and some more equipment from my truck, and get started on that wiring. I'll have to flip the breaker. That means no electricity while I'm working. You okay with that?"

"We'll survive," she replied. "I should probably give you my number in case you need to reach me...for work-related things."

"Good idea." He typed her number into his phone, and she did the same with his. Strange—exchanging new phone numbers with someone he used to be married to.

"Thank you for doing the wiring," she said as she pocketed her phone again.

And for keeping his nose out of the rest of her business, it would seem. The frustrating part was, if she wanted antiques, he had all sorts of family connections in the Amish community. But she didn't want his help.

He headed for the door, thinking about her first bookstore. It had been a cute shop—floor-to-ceiling bookshelves and lots of potted plants. If any space had been Faith's, heart and soul, it had been that shop. He'd been gutted when it failed, too.

Trent paused at the door and looked back.

"Faith, what will you call your next shop? Will it be another Bumblebee Books?"

He wasn't sure why he wanted to know. Maybe it was just to remind himself that her future was somewhere out there, away from him.

"I'm calling it Second Time Around," she replied.

He gave a nod and strode back out into the summer sunlight. It was appropriate. Fresh starts, new beginnings... She could manage that in the city. But for a guy like him there was no such thing as a fresh start.

He'd have to create a future for him and Tyke here, and just keep plodding forward. Faith might be part of his past, but their marriage was still a piece of him.

There was no clean slate for Trent. Maybe Josephine had been right, and he'd need to make his peace with his deepest regret—the ending of his marriage.

CHAPTER THREE

As she propped open the front door and then the back door in hopes that they'd harness a breeze, Faith tried to keep her gaze from moving back to Trent. With the electricity turned off, the fans were still. Trent leaned his ladder against a wall and started walking around the store with a flashlight and a clipboard, taking covers off of light switches and electrical sockets and making notes as he did so.

It had been less than an hour since he'd waltzed back into her life. And that man had not changed a bit, and that was both a relief and an annoyance. Because he was still a distraction, but it also meant he was still the same guy who'd been so impossible to live with. That still twanged at a sore spot in her heart, though. Because when she'd fallen for Trent, she'd fallen hard.

What she should be thinking about was their budget for the Amish Antiques Shop reopening. Aunt Josephine had left behind a small operating fund, but it was very modest, and Faith wasn't exactly in a position to get a loan after her humiliating bankruptcy. She couldn't ask her sisters to put in more money than she could, either, so that left them working with very little indeed.

She looked down at her phone, checking for emails. She should hear back from the Philadelphia Small Business Enrichment program soon. They'd be announcing the winners of a small business bursary meant to build up struggling communities in the city—and Faith had her eyes set on a location that would be ideal for her used bookstore. Her chances of even getting the bursary were slim, but if she did manage to snag this prime opportunity, she was determined to work both places until the year at the antiques shop was up. She'd be exhausted, but it would be worth it in the long run.

A second chance to prove that she did have what it took to make her dream of a bookstore come true. And maybe, just maybe, she'd make the cut for that bursary.

A white Lexus coupe pulled to stop in front of the store, and it took Faith a beat to realize this was Hope's vehicle. She'd recently married a man who did rather well in sales, and Hope now lived a cut above the rest of them.

Hope was short and curvy, and she wore her shoulder-length brown hair back in a ponytail. Her summer dress was cotton with what looked like a floral pattern from a distance, but up close the flowers had little pug dog faces poking out amid the blooms—a testimony to Hope's buoyant personality. She hauled out a suitcase after her, then a second. Faith raised her eyebrows as a third smaller bag landed on the sidewalk next to her. She lived an hour and a half away, but she'd insisted on coming to stay, which was strange.

The apartment above the shop had two bedrooms, but those bedrooms were tiny, and it looked like Hope hadn't been packing light. Her wedding ring set sparkled on her left hand—her husband, Peter, had spared no expense.

Hope turned, and Faith came out to meet her on the sidewalk.

"You made it," Faith said, and she gave her sister a hug.

"I made it," Hope replied, and squeezed her back. "How are you doing?"

"Me? I'm fine," Faith said. "How long are you staying?"

"Peter's traveling for the next six weeks," Hope said, "and I'm tired of being lonely back in Philadelphia. I know I was only going to stay for a week, but I thought I might as well help out here until Peter comes back, and I don't want to commute that far every day."

"That's a good idea," Faith said. "It'll be nice to have the three of us back together again."

Hope grimaced. "If we can get along that long."

"We're adults," Faith said with a grin. "We're capable of getting along."

But Hope had a point—the three of them had never seen eye to eye on anything.

Hope's gaze moved over to the shop, and she

scanned the front of the store. "It's just like I remembered..."

"Yeah, we're cleaning out a lot of junk," Faith said. "And we just found out that the whole place needs to be rewired—the store and the apartment."

"What? Why?"

"An insurance issue," Faith replied. "So Trent is doing it."

"Trent?" Hope's eyes widened. "As in...*your* Trent?"

"He's not *my* Trent anymore," Faith said. "But yes, Trent Lantz, the one and only."

"Ah." Hope's lips turned up in a faint smirk. "It didn't take him long."

"Aunt Josephine contracted him to do the work," Faith said. This was one of the points on which they didn't always get along. Hope and Elaine liked to think they knew better than she did about her own life, and if a divorce didn't put Trent solidly in the past in her sisters' eyes, she didn't know what would.

Hope's phone pinged, and some of the sparkle went out of her eyes as she glanced at it.

"Who's that?" Faith asked.

"Peter." Hope sighed. "He's just saying that he'll be busy until late tonight. He'll call me then."

"So, you've got a call to look forward to," Faith said, trying to lighten her sister's mood.

"Yeah..." She tucked her phone back into her purse and reached for a suitcase and the smaller bag. "It's always the same. He works so hard. Sales is like that. Whoever is in front of him has his undivided attention, and with him traveling for work, that's seldom me."

"You miss him," Faith said.

"I do. But I'm also getting just a little bit tired of always coming in last. When he's home with me, he's fielding calls and emails from clients. When he's traveling, he's doing the same thing."

"That's what it takes to make that income, I guess," Faith said. And Peter did make a great income.

"I know." Hope gave a tight smile, and she glanced back at the car. "I'm not ungrateful. I'm very comfortable... I just miss him."

Faith grabbed the other suitcase, and they headed into the shop.

"Hope!" Elaine came around the counter and swooped in to give their sister a hug. "You look fantastic. Where did you get this dress? It's adorable!"

"A little vintage shop in Philly," Hope said. "I have another one that's got a T-Rex print—just tiny roaring T-Rexes all over it."

"That sounds cute," Elaine replied. "My students would love that. I should go find that store one of these days."

Trent stood up from where he'd been squatting next to an outlet, and he shot Hope a grin.

"Hey, Mrs. Taylor," Trent said. "How are you?"

"Trent!" Hope put down her bags and went over to give Trent a quick hug. "Faith said you were rewiring the place?"

"Sure am," he replied, and his gaze slid past Hope toward Faith in a way that felt rather familiar.

Hope giving Trent a hug shouldn't annoy Faith, but somehow it did. It was like the divorce and the last two years hadn't happened when they all smiled and hugged like they were still family. She pushed back the resentment, though. That was Apfelkuchen for you—a place so small that avoiding your ex was downright impossible. Besides, Trent had always gotten along with her sisters. Family tensions had never been the problem in their marriage.

"Let's get your bags upstairs," Faith said.

There was an echoing wooden staircase that led up to the front door of the second-floor apartment, and Faith and Hope each took a big suitcase, Elaine following behind with the smaller one. Faith's muscles were burning by the time she got to the top of the stairs and opened the door.

"How much did you pack?" Elaine asked as they pushed into the sitting room. It was a small living space, but there were three tall windows along the front that let in a generous amount of daylight.

"I'm staying for a while," Hope said.

"Why?" Elaine asked bluntly. "You're a newlywed. How long have you been married now...four months?"

"Peter is on a work trip."

"Why not go meet him there?" Elaine asked.

Hope pressed her lips together. "Because I'm not, okay?"

Elaine had a good point, Faith thought. Why not go meet her husband wherever he was and spend some time with him? Hope wasn't working right now. She'd quit her job managing a retail store when she got married, and while she'd insisted she'd look for a position she liked better now that money wasn't a problem, she hadn't. So she could very well go see her husband on his trip. There were no work obligations holding her back.

Faith and Elaine exchanged a silent look.

"Cut that out!" Hope said. "Peter doesn't like it when I go see him while he's on a work trip. He's not vacationing, he's selling speedboats. He likes to focus. He's a different guy when he's in work mode than he is with me, and the sweet, soft Peter I get to see wouldn't be able to sell a thing! So... I let him work."

Hope looked between the bedrooms.

"That one—" Faith pointed toward the second bedroom. It was a little bit smaller, but since Faith was going to be living here all year, Hope could make do.

Hope hauled her suitcase in that direction and disappeared into the small bedroom.

"Why not surprise him?" Elaine called, raising her voice to be heard. "Just...show up dressed in something cute!"

Hope emerged again. "Because we don't do that."

"Why don't you do that?" Elaine asked. "For crying out loud, Hope, you're his wife! If you can't just show up, what's he hiding?"

Hope's expression darkened, and she held up a finger. "I am a married woman, and how Peter and I function in our marriage is none of your business. He isn't hiding anything. If I didn't trust him, I wouldn't be married to him. Period."

Elaine shrugged but stayed silent, and Faith handed off the next suitcase to her sister.

"You've been married before," Elaine said, turning to Faith. "Am I right that this is weird?"

"I'm staying out of this," Faith replied.

"Oh, come on!" Elaine said. "If you can't trust your own sisters to tell you the truth, then who can you trust?"

"I *have* been married before," Faith said. "And I know enough to keep my nose out of her business."

Besides, none of them really knew Peter. Hope had met him at a dinner club, dated him briefly and they were married only a few months later. Faith and the rest of the family had seen him all of twice before the actual wedding. It was easy to distrust a man they'd seen so little of, but he was now Hope's husband, and if only for Hope's sake, they needed to give him some benefit of the doubt.

"Thank you, Faith," Hope said, emerging from the bedroom once more. "I appreciate that."

"You see?" Faith said. "We can afford each other a little respectful privacy."

"Oh, you aren't off the hook, Faith," Elaine retorted. "You've got your ex-husband down there."

Faith rolled her eyes. "Speaking of whom, we now have to pay him for his services, which means we'll have even less money in that operating account to float us if sales are soft when we reopen. So I don't know about you, but I want to get things organized down there. I'm going to go get some work done."

Hope's phone blipped and she pulled it out to look at it. When she looked down at the screen, Faith almost thought she'd cry. Faith might believe in staying out of her sister's marriage, but Hope didn't look like she was a blissfully happy newlywed right now.

"I'm going to unpack," Hope said, and she turned back into the bedroom again.

Faith looked over and silently met Elaine's gaze.

"See?" Elaine whispered. "Something's wrong."

Faith hated to admit that Elaine was probably right, and the realization stirred up a tumble of memories of her own marriage. She'd felt that way, and they hadn't been able to fix it.

Faith and Elaine headed down the stairs together and back into the dim shop. Trent had moved a couple of shelves at the back of the store, and he was crouched down with his clipboard again.

"She's not happy," Elaine said.

"She's dealing with something. It's between her and Peter," Faith replied.

"Has it never bothered you that he basically scooped her up, married her, dropped her into that gorgeous penthouse condo with a padded checking account and then disappeared?" Elaine demanded. "They've been married four months! Where is he?"

"He's doing the work that pays for that lifestyle," Faith said. "Elaine, I get it. It's not my ideal, either, but he's her husband, and she loves him. So they'll have to sort this out."

"She's back in Apfelkuchen with enough clothes to move here indefinitely and clothe me to boot," Elaine said. "I think you're giving him more grace on this than she is!"

This was how their sisterly dynamic worked—Faith was always the one who had to calm everyone else down. Not everything was the end of the world.

"Don't read too much into it," Faith said.

"Do you think she's happy?" Elaine asked pointedly.

Faith glanced up at the ceiling, her mind conjuring up an image of their sister's face when she'd been looking down at her phone. No, Hope was not happy right now, and her arrival with all that luggage did seem a little odd. Why not stay in the city with the comforts Peter provided? It wasn't that far away.

"She's lonely," Faith said.

"Bingo." Elaine headed toward the front door. "I'm going for coffee. But you know what, Faith? You're always trying to keep Hope happy—agreeing with her and never telling her straight what you really think. Well, maybe she needs to hear that she's worth a whole lot more than this. Peter can't just wrap her up in money and take off like that. If money were enough for her, she wouldn't be here right now."

Elaine headed out the door, leaving Faith standing next to an antique quilt. She looked down at the pattern, made by a mother of fourteen children, according to the little piece of paper pinned to one corner. Somehow, the Amish made marriage and family look easy, but they were just people, too. Was it just as complicated for the Amish to find the kind of love they wanted? Or were things easier for them?

"Elaine's got a point, you know," Trent said.

Faith startled. She'd forgotten he was there. He backed down a ladder and tossed something into his toolbox.

"It's a careful balance with my sisters," Faith said. "You know that better than anyone."

"Maybe so, but it does seem kind of early for this kind of distance between Hope and her husband," Trent said. "Elaine's right."

Faith shot him an annoyed look. "You don't even know him."

"Do you?" Trent asked.

"How do you know so much about Hope's husband?" she asked, avoiding his question.

"Elaine has kept me up-to-date on it," he replied with a small smile. "And before you get upset with me, we were just chatting, and it was around the time that Hope was getting married, so it was the big piece of gossip that Hope was marrying some rich guy she hardly knew."

"Well, I know my sister, and unlike you, I've actually met Peter. He adores Hope—as he should."

Except that for a newly married guy, he sure was traveling a lot. And what was Elaine doing sharing family gossip with Trent, of all people? She couldn't help but feel just mildly offended with that. But again, with a place the size of Apfelkuchen, people talked. And while Faith and Trent had split up, there were no hard feelings between her ex-husband and her sisters, apparently. She halfway wished there were.

"I'm going for a walk," Faith said.

Trent didn't answer, and Faith headed for the front door.

"Are you mad at me now?" Trent called after her.

Faith turned back at the door. "These are my sisters. I know them better than you do."

She didn't wait for an answer, heading out into the fresh air. They had a big sign in the window saying they were temporarily closed, under new management and would be reopening soon.

New starts…grand openings… It wasn't as bright and shiny as it looked from the outside.

What had Aunt Josephine been thinking, pushing the three of them to work together? Sometimes sisters needed space. This would either work or the three sisters would kill each other. Faith wasn't sure which way it would go yet.

But there was one life lesson that Elaine hadn't learned the hard way yet: love wasn't easy. Faith and Trent had been an excellent example of that, and no one had loved a man as much as Faith had loved her husband.

No one.
So maybe Hope deserved a little time to get her balance in this new marriage.

CHAPTER FOUR

Trent watched Faith disappear out the door, and turned back to the electrical map of the store. These sisters had always defended each other as passionately as they'd fought each other. That was the nature of sisters, he supposed. Sort of like him and his brothers.

He idly wondered if Tyke would feel like he'd missed out if he never got any siblings to tussle with. He remembered how Faith used to argue with Hope and Elaine about everything and nothing at all. They'd never seemed to be able to agree on anything. And he'd had to take Faith's side, because that's what husbands did. But this time? Faith was wrong.

A newlywed wife left on her own like this? Trent had to wonder what was going on there. Besides, even if this Peter fellow was honest as a Boy Scout, there was the fact that Hope seemed lonely and deflated. Her happiness mattered, too. That irony might be pretty rich, considering that Trent hadn't realized how deeply unhappy his own wife had become, but as an outsider, it seemed pretty clear to him.

Not that it was Trent's business anymore. Still, he found his gaze moving out toward the window again—no one visible on the street, but his mind kept going back to Faith all the same.

She was going to open another bookstore... That thought kept coming to the surface. She was going to get back to the one goal that had mattered most to her. Good for her. Right? Good for her! He'd done what felt right in his own life, and she was doing the same.

Trent forced his attention back to his sketched electrical map, his gaze moving over the outline of where wires would connect to the panel box, then to the electrical grid. Moments later, he heard footsteps in the doorway and he looked up again to see Eddie, his new apprentice, standing there with his tool belt slung over his shoulder. He was all of twenty-one, and he had a mop of rust-colored hair and a sprinkling of freckles over his face making him look even younger than he was.

"Hey, Eddie," Trent said. "You made it."

"Yeah, I'm here." Eddie came into the store, looking up around the room, his gaze stopping at the now motionless ceiling fan, then moving to light fixtures. He was assessing, too.

"How was your day off?" Trent asked.

"Good. I had a really good time at your uncle's farm. He was showing me the cattle and all that. It's impressive. I'm sure you're familiar with his farm, but I've never gotten an up-close-and-personal look at how the Amish do all that work without the farm machines we use, you know? It's smart—and a heck of a lot cheaper than spending all that money on gasoline and tractors."

Trent and Eddie had been having lunch one day last month when Trent's Amish uncle had happened by. Eddie was enthralled with Amish farming, and Trent's uncle Albrecht had offered to show him around the farm. A good number of Trent's family were practicing Amish, but it was amazing for a city kid who didn't personally know any Amish folks.

"How long did you stay?" Trent asked.

"All day," Eddie said. "They asked me to stay for lunch, and then for dinner. Then they brought out this card game—Dutch Blitz?"

"Yeah, that's a fun one," Trent chuckled. "So you had a good time."

"Yeah." Eddie's face colored a little bit. "I really did."

"It sounds like Albrecht likes you. He likes showing Englishers how the Amish do things," Trent said. "I'm glad you enjoyed it."

"I really did. Your aunt is an incredible cook. And your cousins are fun guys. Sarah made this pie that was amazing—I mean, I've never tasted better."

"How do you know Sarah made it?" Trent asked, turning his attention back to his clipboard.

"She told me she did," Eddie said. "She wanted me to try it, especially, since she'd made it."

Trent looked up then. Getting a guy to try her pie? That was some pretty open flirting for an

Amish girl. Had she done that in front of her parents? Because Trent had a feeling that Uncle Albrecht and Aunt Mary wouldn't approve of that one bit. Trent would probably get an earful about it from his grandmother. Trent's grandma Trudy had been born into the Amish faith, although she'd left as a teenager and married an Englisher guy, Trent's grandfather. All the same, she stayed close to the Amish side of the family. She passionately defended their right to live by their conscience.

"They do have good pie," Trent said, trying to make light of it and move on. "Glad you had a good time."

"Your uncle said to tell you that they're expecting you to come by and visit," Eddie said.

"Right. Message received." Trent's mind was turning back toward work again. "Anyway, back to the job at hand, like I said, this is a complete rewire. This is all original wiring from the fifties, so it has to go. On this level, we've got a store, a bathroom, a storage area…and then there's a basement downstairs, and upstairs a small, two-bedroom apartment. So we're rewiring all of it and replacing everything. We're starting from scratch—new wires, new panels, everything."

For the next few minutes, Trent took Eddie through the store area and the basement. The upstairs apartment would be finished last, so it could wait for now. He'd have to give Faith and her sisters some warning before going in there. Still, he'd already surveyed the area for Josephine, so he knew what they were working with.

"Uh, can I ask you something?" Eddie asked.

"You bet."

"It's about Sarah."

"My cousin?"

Sarah was around Eddie's age, but she was past her Rumspringa. The Amish's "wild time" for their teenagers gave them a chance to see what life was like outside the Amish fold. And afterward, they normally made a decision for the Amish faith. Like Sarah already had.

"Yeah."

"What about her?" Trent asked.

"Is she single?"

Trent's stomach squeezed. Working on his ex-wife's new store with her sisters wasn't going to be easy, and adding in some drama with Eddie nosing around his Amish cousins? Not happening! Trent didn't have any more emotional energy for this garbage. "It hardly matters, Eddie. She's Amish. She's off-limits for you."

"Says who?" Eddie demanded.

"Uh...everyone?" Trent shook his head. "Let me explain this. Sarah is past the point of being allowed to nose around outside of the Amish boundaries. She's already joined the faith. That means she's expected to live Amish. If she were to go against that, she'd be shunned. That's a very big deal. It would break her heart. She's not going to risk that."

"I'm not asking her to change anything, or go against her way of life," Eddie said irritably.

Trent rubbed a hand over his eyes. Someone had to explain this to Eddie. It might as well be Trent. "She *can't* date an Englisher guy. That's what they call the rest of us—Englishers. You are not Amish."

"But I'm not like the other guys. I'm not asking her to go to movies with me, or even drive in my car. I'm just wanting to get to know her. Respectfully. Her family liked me. I can sit in the sitting room within earshot of her old man, and we can talk. Like I said, I'd be respectful."

"Well, then, respectfully back off," Trent replied a little more curtly than he'd intended. But he didn't have the energy for this. "You can't do it. She's Amish, and the Amish date with the intent to marry. And you can't marry her. Period. There is no way around this, and her parents would never support it. It's impossible. Don't waste your energy. Or, more importantly, mine."

"Oh." Eddie nodded, and he pressed his lips together. He looked hurt. But right now, Trent didn't really care.

"Are you ready to get back to work?" Trent asked.

"Yep." But the guy's voice still sounded a bit tight.

Trent sighed. "Eddie, I'm sorry to be so blunt about it. It's just… You aren't the first guy to turn his eye toward a sweet Amish girl, but the facts remain. It can't work. You're better off forgetting her and finding someone you have more in common with."

"Yeah, I hear you," Eddie replied. "Let's get to work, then."

The front door opened, and Trent looked over his shoulder to see Faith coming back in. She had a bakery box balanced in one hand—that was Marta's Bakery, an Amish-run place on Third Street. She glanced around, then gave Trent and Eddie a nod.

"Hi," Trent said.

"Has Elaine come back yet?" she asked.

"Not yet," Trent replied. "Is that a peace offering?"

"Yep." She smiled faintly. "My sisters and I are squashed into close quarters. We can't afford to argue. I'm buying them off with doughnuts."

"Doughnuts, you say?" Eddie asked hopefully.

"Touch them and die," Trent muttered.

With the tension he'd seen in the store this morning, those doughnuts were needed. He cast Faith a smile.

He'd missed Faith, he realized in a rush. Really, really missed her. And that wasn't going to make this job any easier.

If Eddie was smart, he wouldn't play around with hearts. They didn't bounce back as fast as people claimed they did. Sometimes, a heart just stayed tattered and bruised. He knew that better than anyone.

CHAPTER FIVE

THE NEXT AFTERNOON, Faith watched as Trent squatted next to an outlet with a small electronic tester in one hand and that clipboard in the other. He had his assistant, Eddie, who was in the basement on his cell phone, as they mapped out the old wires in the walls—what connected to what. They'd been at it all day.

It was all Greek to Faith, and she had to admit, it was rather impressive watching Trent at work. He was knowledgeable and patient with the younger man who was obviously learning the trade. And he'd assured her that he wouldn't have to rip out the drywall, though it would take a bit longer. He might have to cut a few holes, but he'd fix those when he was done.

Being Trent's customer was entirely different from being his wife. As the electrician working on their shop, Trent was patient, explained things thoroughly, made sure she felt comfortable with the work he was about to do… She could see why people liked her ex-husband so much. As an electrician, he was a gem.

She left it at that. They hadn't worked out so well as a couple. They'd butted heads about everything, especially finances. Then on their second anniversary, he'd surprised her by leasing a store for her. It had been a generous gesture, but it had been too soon. She knew they weren't ready for this step, and he hadn't understood why she hadn't been excited at the possibilities.

By the end of the year, after a lineup of unexpected expenses, Bumblebee Books was out of business.

Faith turned back to the box of books she'd been sorting. Books had been her happy place for as long as she could remember. They soothed her. They made her feel like every bump in her life was just part of a plot that hadn't come together yet. They gave her hope, and she felt like she could reach across decades, across centuries, and connect with another person who had put pen to paper. There was comfort in being able to read the deepest thoughts from a nun writing in an enclave hundreds of years ago, or a lady writing her memoirs from the Scottish moors… Whatever separated them—time, geography, culture—more always connected them. Like antiques, books held their own dusty magic.

When she'd lost her bookstore, it had hurt her more deeply than anything else in her entire life. Her lifelong dream had dissolved before her eyes. And somehow it had driven her and Trent even further apart. She wasn't sure how…

Faith had found the box of old hardback editions in the back of a closet with a flashlight, but it was dark and there were spiders, so Faith had left Eddie to battle the cobwebs, and she had hauled the box out to sort through. There were three editions of *Black Beauty* in excellent condition, several *Farmer's Almanacs*, a few different farming manuals on the use of windmills, crop rotation and setting up watering systems for small farms. There were a few history books that looked like they were wildly outdated in their interpretations of a few major historical events. Those might be of interest to an academic history buff. And then there were about fifteen old Nancy Drew books in their yellow hardback covers, and Faith had to assume those hadn't belonged to an Amish family. At the bottom of the box was a solitary Anglican prayer book. She picked it up and turned it over in her hands. This prayer book had either been an Amish scandal or had belonged to another family. The thought of the Amish scandal made her smile, though. Maybe they should be selling these items with a backstory attached... It was the story that made items precious.

"All right, I'm making a label for this wire," Trent said into his cell phone. "We can pull it first thing in the morning. At least we know where we're starting. You might as well come up."

Trent hung up his phone, and he glanced over his shoulder.

"Find anything you like?" he asked.

"The books?" She pulled out one of the *Black Beauty* tomes and looked at the publication date. "Yeah, these are some earlier editions, and in great shape. If they don't sell here, I'll buy them and use them in my bookstore when I open it."

Trent gave her a half smile. "My grandmother has a little pile of books she set aside for you."

"Mammi?" The old familiar name for Trent's grandmother, Trudy Lantz, popped out before she could stop it. "She was still saving books for me, even after…?"

She didn't finish the thought. Even after the divorce, was what she'd meant.

"She didn't see why a divorce should change that," Trent said. "And she kept coming across those murder mysteries you liked in the old church secondhand shop, and she'd buy them for fifty cents apiece and tell me that I needed to give them to you."

Mammi had always been a quirky old lady, and that she'd still been setting books aside for Faith was a sweet thought.

"She's always putting books aside for Tyke, too. He's big into trucks right now, and whenever she finds a toddler book with a truck on the cover, she nabs it."

Trent's face softened when he mentioned his son. This was definitely a new side to him…one she'd longed to see with children of their own when they were married.

Eddie came back up the stairs, and Trent deposited his clipboard on top of the sales counter.

"So let's meet up here tomorrow at nine," Trent said to the younger man.

"Sounds good," Eddie said, looking at his watch. "I've got dinner plans."

"With who?" Trent asked, just a little too tersely, and Faith shot him a surprised look. What was going on there?

"You probably don't want to know," Eddie replied with a grin. "But I don't want to be late. I'll see you in the morning."

Trent muttered something under his breath and shook his head. Eddie looked cheery enough, though. Was this some jealousy? Competition between men? Was there a woman Trent was interested in? That thought felt like lead in her chest. It shouldn't—he was a single man. He could date.

Faith turned her attention to the books again, trying to school her own emotions. This was ridiculous. Seeing Trent again was bringing up some complicated feelings, and it was best to just get past it.

"Have a good night, Eddie," Trent said.

"You, too, boss!" Eddie gathered up his tool belt, a hoodie and his lunch bag, and headed for the door.

Trent's phone rang and he picked up. Faith pulled out the Nancy Drews and flipped through the selection. She opened the front cover of the first book and there was no name, no explanation of whose books these had been. She carried them over to that walnut bookcase and slid them into place.

"Wait… Slow down, Mammi. What's going on?"

Trent said, his voice rising. "Is it a burst pipe, or is it the hot water tank downstairs?"

Faith looked over at Trent, who was frowning, his phone pressed up against his ear. She couldn't make out words, but the panicked jabber of his grandmother's voice made it clear enough that something was wrong.

"Okay, I'm on my way. Turn off the water, if you can. I'm coming," Trent said, and he hung up and looked over at Faith. "She's got a burst pipe or something, and I'd better get down there before she's completely flooded."

"Of course!" she said.

"You want to come?" he asked.

Faith blinked at the invitation. Was he really inviting her along to see his grandmother? He seemed to realize his mistake, too, at the same time, because as he unbuckled his tool belt and tossed it over his shoulder, he gave her a rueful smile. The tips of his ears turned red.

"Sorry," Trent said. "Old habit, I guess. But if you do want to come, I could use an extra pair of hands getting the water turned off and everything. Up to you, but I've got to get moving."

"Uh—" Her gaze flew toward the ceiling, her first thought being of Hope upstairs—Elaine had already gone home—and then she shrugged. "Sure, let's go."

While this was probably a bad idea, it was simpler to say yes than to think it all through. She could berate herself for it later. Plus, if Mammi's house was being flooded, she wanted to help.

Trent led the way out of the store, and Faith grabbed her purse and her keys, then locked the front door after them. The sun was low, and the breeze had a comfortable coolness to it now. She looked up at the windows above the store, but she couldn't make anything out from this vantage point. She pulled out her phone and shot off a text to Hope as she walked briskly next to Trent.

Heading out for a bit. I'll be back. Store is locked.

She had to wonder what Elaine would have to say about this. She'd have strong opinions, no doubt. She could just hear her now... *I think you still have some lingering feelings for your ex-husband, Faith.* And she wouldn't be wrong.

Trent's truck was parked along the street—a dusty pickup with a ladder rack on the top, and a bed cover that locked. The doors unlocked with his key fob, and he jogged over to the passenger side, pulled the door open a few inches and then continued around to the driver's side. It was a gentlemanly gesture, and she tried not to let her emotions soften.

Faith hopped up into the passenger side, slammed the door and put on her seat belt. There was a car seat in the back seat, and a tub of Cheerios in a Tupperware container. Things really had changed around here. Trent put the truck into gear, leaned forward to shoulder-check and pulled out into the street in one fluid motion.

"She's eighty-nine this year," Trent said. "And when things go wrong, she can't exactly take care of it herself. Everyone wants her to go into an old folks' home, and she doesn't want to. And apart from big things like this, she doesn't need to yet, either. So I told her to call me if she needs anything. I won't pester her about leaving her house."

That didn't surprise Faith in the least. Trent was probably at the top of a lot of people's lists of who to call in an emergency. But his grandmother was special. Faith had really loved her, too.

Trent cast her a smile. "You're a good sport to come along."

"I was always a better sport than you gave me credit for," she retorted.

Trent chuckled, not letting himself be baited. She wished he'd bicker with her. Ironically, it would be easier. Trent on his best behavior was a little too charming.

"So what's Eddie up to tonight that you hate so much?" Faith asked. That should put things back into balance for her—a reminder that Trent had a romantic life.

"He's eating at my uncle's place."

That wasn't what she expected.

"Your uncle's place?" she said. "Which uncle?"

"Albrecht."

"Why is he eating there?"

"He's got a crush on my cousin Sarah. You remember her."

When Faith had known Sarah, she'd been in her teens, but she must be around twenty now. Faith remembered her as pretty and very sweet. But Amish girls dated and quickly married Amish men. Plus Trent's uncle Albrecht was a serious, stoic man who wouldn't appreciate an Englisher's interest in his daughter.

"Does Eddie know he has zero hope with her?" Faith asked.

"Thank you!" Trent shot her an exasperated look. "I tried to tell him, but he's determined to have his heart broken, I guess."

That would be complicated...and probably messy. Eddie wasn't going to get out of that unscathed, she was sure. She knew how the Amish worked, and they didn't take kindly to outsiders stealing their daughters' hearts.

"Are you going to warn your uncle?" she asked.

"Nah." Trent shrugged. "I tried warning Eddie, and if I step in, I'll only get my assistant mad at me. There isn't really any threat, just an annoyance to my uncle."

"And to you, apparently," she said.

"I'll survive. Trust me—he's not getting anywhere with Sarah. It'll be more disruptive to my life if I lose my apprentice."

As they zipped past Oak Street, she couldn't help but look down that familiar old road. That was where they'd started out—renting a little one-bedroom shoebox of a house that probably had been built back when the antiques store was constructed. Faith pushed back the nostalgia.

"Where are you living now?" Faith asked, mostly to distract herself.

"Our place. Uh—" Trent's gaze flickered toward her. "I mean, the same house."

Her heart skipped a beat. That was a detail no one had mentioned to her...

"You didn't move?" she asked.

"The new owners bought it for an investment property, and they let me stay on. The rent's good." He shrugged, but when he looked over at her, his eyes held a sadness that she understood.

"Do you have...a girlfriend?" Faith tried to sound casual, but it sounded strangled in her own ears.

"Nah," he said. "Not right now."

That was a relief to hear, and she knew it meant all sorts of bad things about her own emotion equilibrium, but she was glad he was just as single as she was. At least they could be on equal footing there.

"What about you?" Trent asked.

"No, I'm single," she said.

"That surprises me," he said. "I figured you'd have me replaced by now."

His gaze flickered toward her again, but she couldn't read his expression. Was he gloating a little?

It had turned out that Trent was harder to replace than she'd imagined. She knew what she wanted—a man who was good with money, who was secure, loyal, stable, kind—and there weren't an overabundance of guys just like that. Besides, she'd met exactly two of them since her divorce—one was still hung up on his ex-girlfriend, and the other just didn't have the spark. Dating was not easy.

"Nope, not yet," was all she said.

Trent didn't need to know the rest of it.

CHAPTER SIX

FAITH WAS STILL SINGLE. Trent tried to dampen his interest in that fact, but he couldn't help a little surge of satisfaction. Maybe he didn't want to be so easily replaced, because he'd done his best by her, even if it wasn't enough. And besides, even though he'd been angry when she left and determined to prove that he'd be just fine, she wasn't easily replaced, either.

Tyke definitely kept him busy and gave his heart someone to wrap around, but Faith wasn't erased from his thoughts. Even if forgetting her would have made everything easier.

Trent took the next turn onto a side road and followed it out of town toward his grandmother's place. She lived in an old farmhouse—most of the surrounding land having been sold off to the neighboring farm, so that it was just Mammi, her garden and an old chicken coop that was no longer in use.

Trent drove as fast as he dared on these back roads. The cops liked to camp out and stop speeders, but more than that, the gravel could be slippery and send a truck into the ditch if a guy wasn't careful.

He slowed when he came to his grandmother's drive and pulled in. Mammi stood on the porch in an old apron, her small, shaggy dog yapping at her ankles. Was Faith going to be okay here? He'd kept up with her side of the family because in a place this size, there was no choice. But she'd been in the city, and his family hadn't been foisted upon her. He pulled to a stop next to the house, and looked over at Faith.

"You okay?" he asked.

"Fine," she replied. "Let's go."

She wasn't easily spooked. He'd always liked that about Faith.

"Hi, Mammi!" he called as they hopped out of the truck. "Where is the water coming from?"

"It's in the kitchen—" his grandmother began, and then her gaze moved behind him and her white eyebrows went up. "Is that our Faith?"

"Hi, Mammi," Faith said. "Trent was at my shop and I heard your call, so I tagged along."

"Was he, now?" Mammi's gaze turned back to Trent, and he felt his face heat. She could read a thousand things into this—it was Mammi's talent.

"The water?" he prompted.

"In here—" Mammi hurried through the side door, and he went past her into the kitchen. There was about an inch of water on the floor, an overflowing sink and a broken tap that was spraying water like a fountain. The last of the sunlight through the kitchen window made a rainbow in the fine mist.

But Trent was already looking for the water turn-off, and he hauled open the cupboard doors at the bottom of the sink, swept aside the array of bottles down there and found the knob. It seemed to be stuck, and he gritted his teeth and turned with all his strength. It loosened, and then turned with a stubborn squeak. The spray of water overhead stopped and left just the sound of dripping water from the counter onto the floor.

"There..." Trent crawled out again. His hair was wet, and his pants and shirt were soaked through. Faith appeared with some bath towels and she was putting them on the floor next to the cellar stairs to block that exit for the water. That was smart.

Mammi had a broom and was brushing the water out the side door as quickly as she could, which wasn't very fast.

"Here," Trent said, taking the broom from her hands and taking over. "Where is the mop, Mammi?"

"Oh, that's in the closet. I'll get it," Mammi said. "Thank you for coming, Trent. I don't know what I would have done if you hadn't come! I would have drowned, most likely."

Faith laughed at his grandmother's little joke.

"I'll get you a new tap and install it for you tomorrow," Trent called after her. "The hardware store isn't open this late, so I'll do it in the morning."

He glanced over at Faith. "Do you mind if I get in a bit late?"

Faith shook her head. "Of course not. This can't be helped."

Getting the water out of the house was the most time-consuming problem, but between Trent and Faith, they managed to clean it up. Trent carried piles of heavy, sodden towels into his grandmother's laundry room and he started a load of towels for her, and when he came back to the kitchen, he found Faith wringing out the old mop. The floor was damp but now free from standing water.

"My goodness…" Mammi said. "What a mess that was. I don't know what happened to my old tap. It had started spraying a little bit of water last week, but I thought it would be okay."

"If anything starts spraying water, tell me right away!" Trent said.

"But you're so busy, Trent," Mammi said. "You work so hard, and Tyke needs you, too."

Maybe so, but if a tap was spraying water, it was only a matter of time before the whole thing busted open, like what had happened tonight.

"If you don't call me, this is what happens," Trent said. "Okay?"

His grandmother nodded. "I meant well."

"I know, I'm not upset," he said, softening his tone. "Just don't feel bad about calling me, okay?"

He looked around the little house. How was she doing on her own? He knew he was her one champion for staying in the house, but he did worry. A bag of dog food looked like it was soaked through. He'd have to get her more—and maybe a sealable plastic container to keep it in. He went rummaging for garbage bags, and when he turned back to the women, he saw his grandmother and Faith smiling at each other.

"How are you, dear? I'm sorry about your Aunt Josephine's passing. She was a treasure."

"I'm really good, Mammi," Faith said. "And thank you. We miss her a lot."

"It was such a shock," Mammi said. "She was perfectly spry and healthy."

"I was stunned when my sister called me," Faith said.

They talked a bit about Josephine, the shock of it all, what the doctors said had happened—a stroke, they thought... And while they talked Trent got the heavy, soaked bag of dog food into the garbage bag. It was already smelling pretty strongly. He managed to scoop out enough dog food that was still dry to last a couple of days. It was something.

"So Hope, Elaine and I are running the store. I'm sure you heard?" Faith was saying.

"News travels," Mammi said demurely. His grandmother was part of a web of shameless gossips. She'd probably heard before Faith had.

"And here you are with Trent," Mammi said. "I'm delighted to see it. I always thought you two should get back together again. You were such a nice couple. I often thought that poor Trent on his own was just the saddest sight. He's a miserable cook, and he can't make his clothes match properly if his life depends on it..."

Trent shot his grandmother a look of alarm. Way to make him look pathetic! And what was wrong with his clothes? He looked down at his own soaked jeans and T-shirt.

"Mammi, we aren't back together again," Trent interjected.

"What?" Mammi frowned. "You aren't? I thought that if Faith came with you tonight—"

"It was just—" Yeah, how exactly did he explain that one? "I'm doing the rewiring at her shop. I was getting ready to leave when you called, and... Faith just came along."

Faith shot him an annoyed look then. Okay, that hadn't come out quite right, either.

"I *invited* her along," Trent amended. "But this isn't what you think. This is just two exes being civilized and getting along."

That covered it, didn't it? Faith looked like she agreed, at the very least. And there was no need to tell Faith that he'd been a mess when she left. He was doing just fine now, thank you very much.

"Oh." Mammi looked disappointed. "Well, I have some books for you, all the same, Faith. Let me see if I can find them. Trent, would you help me?"

Trent winced. Mammi was trying to get him alone, clearly.

"I'll just clean up your counters," Faith said, pulling a sponge from under the cupboard.

He met Faith's gaze and she gave him a mildly amused little smile. She probably saw what was coming, too.

Mammi shuffled down the hallway toward her bedroom. The water hadn't gotten that far, thankfully, and she led Trent inside. Her bed was neatly made, but the top of her dresser was a clutter of bottles and pictures, pillboxes and tubes of cream. She went to a bookshelf at the foot of her bed and pulled out three hardcover books.

Then she turned to look at Trent thoughtfully.

"Just say it, Mammi," he said.

"You need to get her back, Trent," she said.

"We're divorced, remember?" he said gently. "She left me."

"I'm not senile yet!" she said. "I remember exactly what happened. And it was heartbreaking. You two loved each other, and I think that three years of marriage isn't much of a go."

"I'm not the one to lecture," he replied. He'd loved Faith dearly, but they'd never really understood each other well enough. Hearts shouldn't have price tags, in his humble opinion, but when she lost her store, she left him. It was the last straw, he supposed. They'd been arguing so much, and...

"It takes two to make it work, and two to ruin it," Mammi said. "You are not off the hook, young man. You need to get her back."

"Things have changed," he said. "I'm not the same guy from two years ago. Taking Tyke in changed a lot of things for me, including my willingness to jump into a relationship."

Mammi's eyes softened, and she reached up and patted his arm.

"You're a good dad," she said. "But Tyke might like having a mom, too, you know."

"I agree," he said. "And you're right that I miss Faith a lot, but Mammi, I can't see where things would go with her. The ironic part is, Faith used to hate how spontaneous I was, but now I'm the one who can't just go jumping after my feelings. Tyke needs stability. He lost his mother, and I know that deep in his little heart, he's still grappling with that. I'm not bringing a woman into his life just to have her leave. Heaven knows how much that would damage him."

Heaven knew how much it had hurt Trent.

"In Amish families, we'd bring two lonely people together to make sure there were two parents in the home," Mammi said.

"True, but I'm not Amish, and neither is Faith."

"So you don't think there's any hope for the two of you?" she asked sadly. "Even after those vows? Even after three years of marriage?"

He sighed. "We tried hard, but it didn't work. We're too different, and if she could leave me once, she could leave me again. I know that I'm the guy who would have risked it before, but..."

"But Tyke," Mammi said softly.

"But Tyke. Exactly."

For the first time in his life, Trent had a small, vulnerable person relying on him. He'd held Tyke as a baby as he'd wailed for the mother who couldn't come back. She was dead. She was gone. Trent had stayed up nights with Tyke, and earned his trust.

He'd had to drop him off at a day home when he went to work, and picking Tyke up again was the happiest part of his day. Tyke needed some rock-solid stability, and he wouldn't have that if Trent was struggling in a romantic relationship. Trent wasn't the same guy Faith had left.

Tyke changed everything.

CHAPTER SEVEN

As Trent drove back them back to town, Faith listened to the rumble of the truck engine and let her gaze trail over the barbed wire fence line. The late afternoon sunlight was bright and golden, warming the fields into the aroma of grass, wildflowers and cattle. Most of the Amish farms around here raised cows, though there was one chicken farm a few miles from here, and chickens were a surprisingly aromatic animal to farm. They stunk from quite a distance.

She noticed Trent check his watch.

"Are you late?" she asked.

"A bit. I have to pick up Tyke from the day home," he replied.

Just as responsible with childcare as he was with his job. When they were newly married and Trent had been late to just about everything that wasn't work-related, she'd wondered what kind of father he'd make. And here he was—blowing past all of her expectations with the little guy in his care.

"It's strange seeing you like this," she said.

"Like what?"

"All responsible. A dad."

"I'm not a dad in the fullest sense. I'm Tyke's guardian. He calls me Tent. He can't say his *r*'s yet."

She chuckled. "Tyke and Tent?"

"Yup." His warm brown gaze flickered in her direction. "We're pals."

That was an interesting delineation. But there was something more settled about him now, and she had a feeling Tyke was the reason for it, because even their marriage hadn't settled him like this.

"You seem happy," she said.

"I am. Tyke came along when I needed someone to love, and he needed someone to love him, too."

Her heart gave a squeeze at that. After their divorce. Yeah, she knew what desperate loneliness felt like, too.

"I didn't expect to hang out with you again," he added.

"Me, neither."

She'd expected to avoid and privately resent him, quite honestly. But her sisters would never have let that continue for long. They would have insisted upon civility.

"Look, I should probably warn you," Trent said with a wince. "My family doesn't really know how to deal with divorce—at least not the Amish side. Mom's side of the family knows the drill, but the Amish side have their way. If you know what I mean."

"I don't," she said. "Spell it out, Trent."

"Well, as you know, the Amish don't have divorce," he said. "It's flat out not allowed. They understand the concept and all that, but they don't know how to deal with it on a practical level. They, um—" his face colored slightly "—still refer to you as my wife and ask how you're doing, as if you're just traveling, or something."

"That's very awkward for you, I'm sure," she said with a little smile.

"Yeah, well, it'll be awkward for you, too, when you see them," he said and shot her a downright villainous grin.

"I'm sure they'll get used to it," Faith said. They weren't her family, after all.

He shrugged noncommittally. "I wouldn't count on it."

"Your *mammi* is different, though," Faith countered.

He winced again, but didn't answer.

"What? Your *mammi* left the Amish life. She understands!"

"She left the Amish life and raised her kids English, and she understands that you and I are split, but she's still got her heart set on bringing us back together."

Faith's heart skipped a beat. Divorce and all that regret was hard enough without people poking at old wounds.

"The thing with my grandmother is that she has this belief in marriage vows. She always said that they tie two people together in spite of themselves."

"There's a whole lot of choice in the matter," Faith countered.

"I know. You don't have to argue with me on this. I'm just telling you how she thinks."

"Did she say anything about us today? I mean beyond when we first arrived and she figured we were together again?"

"Yup." His gaze flickered toward her again. "When I helped her get the books from her room. It's okay. I set her straight."

That stung more than it should have. Maybe there was some small part of her that wished that Trent was tempted at the thought. "Good. I mean, I know it's not their culture, but—"

"They loved you," he said gruffly. "And when they love, they don't stop."

"Oh..." That was a little harder to argue, and she felt herself softening. Her in-laws had been loving and supportive, and she'd always felt grateful for that. When other women complained about their in-laws, she had nothing to contribute to the conversation.

"Anyway," Trent said with a sigh. "I thought you deserved some warning."

"Thanks."

And maybe that warning was a good thing. At least she'd be prepared for it. She was going to be here in Apfelkuchen for the next year, after all, and there was going to be no avoiding them, any more than Trent could avoid her family.

Trent signaled and slowed for the turn that took

them back into town. They passed the trailer park with the old sign that read Treasured Estates over the entrance, and passed the recycling center next to it, then the auto parts shop with its old graveyard of cars out back. Then they were in the town of Apfelkuchen proper, the old highway turning into First Avenue, and the little shops and restaurants clustered close together.

"What are you up to tonight?" Trent asked.

"Dinner with my sisters at Elaine's place," she replied.

"That sounds like fun," he said. "I know this is all really awkward and uncomfortable, but I'm glad you're back for a bit. It's nice to see you."

"Do you mean that?" she asked.

"Of course I mean it. Maybe I need this—a chance to see you again and see how far we've both come."

Maybe she did, too, for that matter.

Trent pulled to a stop at the corner, right in front of Amish Antiques, then he shot her a grin. "See you tomorrow."

"See you."

Faith hopped out and slammed the door shut, and the truck immediately pulled away from the curb. But he did lean forward to meet her gaze once more before he was out of sight. On his way to pick up Tyke.

Faith rummaged in her purse for the key and let herself into the front door of the shop. Trent's life had moved on a whole lot more than hers had—

even if he didn't seem to realize that yet. Sure, she'd had a good job and had plans for her own bookstore again, but her heart hadn't recovered quite so easily.

Good for Trent. She should be glad for him, not wish pain and misery on him. Divorce meant they went their separate ways, and if they were mature, they wished each other well.

Maybe she wasn't quite as mature as she liked to think, because while she did wish him well, it was not without a pang of her own sadness. And she kind of wished that he carried the same amount of regret that she did. It would only be fair.

CHAPTER EIGHT

Faith was frustratingly beautiful.

That was the thought that kept rattling around in Trent's head as he drove through town. Faith was just as pretty as she'd always been, but somehow the last few years had deepened that beauty, and he couldn't help but notice. It would be easier if somehow their time apart had swept away his feelings and made it so that he no longer felt that tug toward her. They'd tried marriage, and it hadn't worked.

So why was he still doing ridiculous things like getting her to go with him to his grandmother's place? He was acting like she was still his, somehow, and she wasn't. She wasn't his wife. She wasn't his girlfriend. She wasn't even a woman he had any kind of possible future with. She was his ex! Why couldn't he get that through his own thick skull?

When Trent pulled up in front of the little house where Abigail Turner ran her day home, the screen door opened and Tyke came powering outside on his sturdy little legs with an excited grin on his face. This was how Tyke greeted Trent every day at pickup time, and he couldn't help but grin back.

He hopped out of the truck and waved at Abigail, who came out the front door after Tyke.

Abigail, a pleasant woman in her forties, wore a pair of jeans, a T-shirt and a tired smile.

"Hi, Trent!" she called.

Tyke collided with Trent's legs, and he bent down to pick the toddler up. Every day, the kid seemed a little bit heavier.

"Hey, buddy," he said.

"Tent!" Tyke said, and he reached up with one grubby hand to pat his face.

Trent made a face.

"Sorry, he was playing on the sensory table just now," Abigail said. "It's only garden dirt."

"How was he today?" Trent asked.

"Tyke was very helpful, weren't you, Tyke?" Abigail said. "He helped us clean up our toys, and he helped Lily finish eating her yogurt, too."

"As in he stole Lily's yogurt?" he asked ruefully.

"She was done with it." Abigail chuckled. "He had lots of energy today, and he played on the slide outside a lot. Lily's got a sniffle, so that might pass around. We'll see."

"Sounds like a great day, Tyke," Trent said. "Thanks, Abigail. See you tomorrow."

"Actually, I've had a bit of an emergency come up," Abigail said. "Oh—you've got a bit of dirt on your face now—"

Trent wiped at the side of his face that Tyke had been patting.

"You got it," Abigail said. "Anyway, I've had a

pipe burst, which is causing all sorts of trouble. Zero water pressure, the toilets won't flush. The plumber is coming later on this evening, but it'll be a couple of days before everything is fixed. Would you be able to find some other arrangements for Tyson until then?"

Burst pipes were going around, too, it seemed. "Yeah, I'll have to," he replied. "No problem."

Although it was a bit of a problem. He couldn't exactly bring a toddler with him while he worked with electricity and wires. And he couldn't just take a couple of days off, either. Faith needed him to finish this on time—their insurance was riding on it. And she might be his ex, but he owed her this much, just as her electrician.

But there was the possibility someone in the family would help him out...maybe his cousin Sarah? She didn't have a job right now... His mind was clicking ahead to some short-term solutions.

"I'll text you and keep you updated," Abigail said. "I'm really sorry about this."

"Can't be helped. Don't worry about it," he replied. Trent would have to figure out something.

Trent got Tyke buckled into his car seat in the back seat of his truck. Tyke twisted himself like a little corkscrew, trying to get back out again, but after a few tries, Trent got him properly buckled in and gave him his plastic car to hold on to. Tyke immediately chucked it against the back of the driver's seat. Trent picked it up and gave it back to him.

"If you want to hold it, you'd better not throw

it," Trent said. "Because once I'm driving, I can't get it for you again."

Tyke seemed to ponder this for a moment, then threw it again, letting out a loud cackle, and Trent shook his head and then closed the back door.

"Tuck!" Tyke said as soon as Trent got back into the driver's seat. That was how he said "truck," and by "truck," he meant pretty much any vehicle with wheels. Motorcycles were trucks, cars were trucks, buses were trucks...

"You threw it," Trent said.

"Tuck!"

Trent sighed, got back out, opened the back door and got the plastic car off the floor. He held it out to Tyke, who accepted it and this time held on to it. Trent got back into the driver's seat, put the truck into Reverse and started to back out. He felt the thunk of the plastic car hitting the back of his headrest.

Trent pulled onto the street and started back toward home. It was only a few blocks away, and he was thinking ahead to what he could make them both for supper. Tyke was surprisingly good about eating pretty much anything Trent put in front of him, so long as he cut it up into finger-food-sized pieces. That meant soup was out, but chicken nuggets, toast, meat, cut veggies—those were all options. Did he have any nuggets?

"Tuck!" Tyke called from the back seat.

"You threw it, buddy," Trent replied. "Sorry."

"Tuck!" The waterworks started then, and Tyke

began to wail. He was tired. It had been a long day of playing with garden dirt and stealing other children's snack food.

"Hey, Siri—" Trent said. His phone didn't respond. "Hey, Siri!"

The phone blipped into listening mode.

"Play Preschool Playlist on YouTube."

A moment later, "Baby Shark" blasted out of the speakers and Tyke calmed down. He loved "Baby Shark." Next would be "Wheels on the Bus," then a little ditty sung by Elmo... He knew this playlist backward and forward now, and he even caught himself humming it when he was working, much to Eddie's amusement.

He signaled a turn. Tyson's mom, Kylie, had stipulated in her will that she didn't want her son being raised Amish. Trent could understand that, actually. The Amish he knew were wonderful people who loved each other and lived wholesome lives, but they only went to school until the eighth grade, and Tyke's opportunities would be very limited. But with Tyke's dad out of the picture and the day home unavailable, he couldn't think of anyone else who might be home during the day for emergency babysitting.

So Tyke was not going to be raised Amish, but maybe he could have some good old-fashioned Amish babysitting for the next few days.

Trent pulled into his own driveway and turned off the engine, pondering his problem. The problem with Amish family was that while they did have phone service that they could check from a community phone hut, he couldn't just call them and get an answer. Leaving a message was hit or miss for them even getting it, but it was the best option. Heading over there tonight with a tired toddler in tow to talk in person wasn't a great idea.

So he'd leave a message tonight and if he didn't hear back from them, he'd stop by tomorrow morning with cap in hand and ask for a favor. He didn't think his aunt or cousin would turn him away in his hour of need. And he had to finish the wiring for Faith.

That was a perk of having Amish family—they believed in helping out, even when it wasn't convenient. And right now, he was deeply grateful for that.

"Come on, Tyke," Trent said. "Let's go inside and find some supper. What do you think?"

He had determined to start cooking more nutritious meals for them, so he'd been buying a lot more fresh produce and meat. But that said, he was tired tonight, and he was pretty sure he had chicken nuggets in the freezer somewhere…

CHAPTER NINE

Elaine lived in an apartment building just down the road from Bluebird Elementary where she taught second grade. As Faith and Hope drove past, Faith noticed the wooden sign by the road that read, "Have a great summer, Bluebirds!" That was what they called the students there—and it was rather sweet. This was the newer school in town, and Elaine had been thrilled to secure a position there when she'd graduated from teacher's college.

Elaine's apartment building was only four floors, and there was one section of visitor parking that was always full with residents' second vehicles. So Faith parked on the street. After the visit with Mammi that afternoon, she needed this—time away from the shop, away from Trent and his family, and with people who loved her for her. Her sisters might tell her bluntly when they thought she was wrong, but there was currently no one on the planet, save their parents, who loved her quite that much.

"I'm starving," Hope said. "I hope Elaine made cabbage rolls."

Their sister was great at making German cuisine.

"I wouldn't complain," Faith agreed. "This is nice, isn't it? Just us sisters?"

Their parents were traveling right now—taking their RV through as many states as possible, and recording their progress on Facebook for all their friends to enjoy. There were a lot of pictures of their father wearing shorts that exposed his knobby knees and their mother squinting in sunlight. Right now, they were in California, and seemed to be lingering on the beaches.

They headed into the building and took the elevator up to the fourth floor. Elaine's unit was at the far end of one hallway. They knocked at her door, and at her call from inside to come in, they let themselves inside. The apartment was small but neatly furnished with Elaine's romantic style. She'd acquired a new painting that hung over her couch—a scene of an incoming storm boiling over a prairie wheat field.

"You're here!" Elaine said from the kitchen area. "I made pierogis."

Faith and Hope exchanged a grin.

"Sounds great!" Faith said.

"We'll eat on the balcony," Elaine said.

The balcony door was open, letting in a generous, warm breeze. A small folding table was set out there, and Faith knew that the view overlooked some green space, some meandering walking paths and a man-made pond that attracted a lot of birds year-round.

Elaine brought a platter of her plump, potato-filled dumplings outside where she had toppings already waiting. There were caramelized onions, a tub of sour cream, bacon bits and a little dish of sauerkraut. In the middle of the table sat a jug of meadow tea—an Amish drink that was popular in this area. It was basically a mint herbal iced tea, and it was very refreshing.

"So how is Trent?" Elaine asked as they all took their seats.

"He's fine," Faith said. "His grandmother had a burst pipe, and he asked if I wanted to go along with him to fix it."

"Right. Of course." Elaine shot her a coy little smile.

"It's not like that," Faith replied. "I know how it looks. Even his grandmother was thinking something was going on between us, but it really was just a spur-of-the-moment thing. Trent and I aren't used to being in town together. That's all. A lot has changed."

For being as bad of a couple as they were, they seemed used to belonging together. That would change—it would have to.

Hope reached for the serving spoon and dished some pierogis onto her plate, then handed the spoon to Faith, who followed her example.

"I still like Trent," Elaine said.

"He's a likeable guy," Hope agreed. "But he was tough to be married to, if I recall. Right, Faith?"

"Thank you," Faith said, and she felt her earlier happiness waning. She served herself and added a dollop of sour cream and a healthy sprinkle of bacon bits. "Trent could be fun and sweet... But we were never on the same page about anything. If I wanted a quiet Thanksgiving, he was accepting invitations to three different relatives' festivities. If I wanted to take a vacation and reconnect with him, he was pouring himself into his work. If I needed to save more to be ready to open my own bookstore, he was signing leases to surprise me. He just didn't listen. He didn't hear me. And maybe in his defense, I didn't hear him, either. Regardless, we were at cross purposes most of the time."

"You were very different people," Hope agreed.

Faith put her fork down and waited while Elaine finished dishing herself up a plate, too.

"The bookstore was the last straw for you, though," Elaine said. "When it failed, I mean."

"We weren't ready to open a store! I knew that, but again, Trent hadn't even asked. Anyone on the outside of our relationship thought that it was the sweetest, most romantic gesture. But it wasn't. It was just Trent jumping the gun, yet again. And it was my dream on the line—*my* bookstore. This was something I'd dreamed of since I was a girl, and I knew how I wanted to do things to give me the best chance of success. I mean, if he wanted to get me a sweet gift, had the man never heard of flowers?"

Hope and Elaine both chuckled at that, and they tucked into the meal. Elaine's pierogis were delicious—stuffed with sharp cheddar and mashed potato.

And while Faith was making a joke of it for the sake of keeping this meal enjoyable, it wasn't a joking matter to her. When her business had failed, so had her confidence. And it hadn't been necessary! If she'd been able to just hold off until she'd felt sure they were ready, she might be running her own bookstore right now…and possibly still be married. Or maybe not. That was a dangerous thought to even entertain. Maybe she'd have the bookstore, but she and Trent would have split over another "last straw."

"You two fought a lot," Elaine said. "No one could get under your skin like your husband could."

"We drove each other up the wall," Faith agreed. "Looking back on it, I still get frustrated. We were just aiming at different things, I guess."

Because it hadn't been about the money or the financial stress. Those things hadn't helped, obviously, but it had been about that gap between them—the one that existed even when her husband had been doing his best to be wildly, extravagantly romantic. Because that failed business had hurt her in a deep place of her heart that Trent never understood. She'd gone from feeling like she could achieve her dream with some thought and preparation, to feeling like perhaps it wasn't possible after all. And she'd never felt emptier in her life.

"How's Peter doing?" Faith asked, mostly to change the subject away from herself.

Hope swallowed. "He's good. He misses me."

"That's a good thing, right?" Elaine asked.

"It's very good." Hope smiled faintly, but it didn't quite reach her eyes. "Look, I'm not a fool. I knew about his traveling for work when I married him, I just didn't realize how tough it would be. But I'd rather work this out with him than find someone else."

"That's a good perspective..." Elaine said.

"But?" Faith asked.

"But I don't think that all this travel is going to work for me, after all," Hope said. "And I know that's unfair! I do! I just... I miss him so much, and I see friends who have their husbands with them every night, and I feel so envious."

"Can I give a little piece of advice?" Faith asked.

"Sure..." Hope sighed.

"If you ever start thinking of finding a new guy instead of Peter, you aren't going to be able to just transfer your feelings for Peter over to someone else. You're going to keep on loving Peter, regardless. So unless the situation is truly impossible, work through it."

Hope and Elaine both turned and fixed her with surprised looks, and Faith shifted uncomfortably in her seat.

"What?" Faith asked.

"You're still in love with Trent?" Hope asked.

"I said that *you'll* keep loving Peter," Faith said. "All I'm saying is that divorce really hurts. It hurts even more than you think it will."

"Do you still love him, though?" Elaine pressed. This was getting out of control fast.

"Do you realize that Trent warned me about this?" Faith said. "The Amish side of his family don't know how to deal with a divorced couple because their religion doesn't allow for it. So he says they still refer to us as if we're still married. They just can't bend their minds around it. I thought that was a strictly Amish problem."

"I don't know..." Elaine chewed and swallowed. "It's hard for me, too. Trent was like a big brother to me, and I got attached. I guess I can understand where they're coming from."

"I need my sisters to be on my side in this," Faith pleaded. "It's hard, okay? It's hard seeing him, and knowing that he's still a good guy, just not good for me. That's really hard. And I can't sort myself out and fight off two families at the same time. Do you get that?"

"We aren't trying to meddle," Hope said. "But it's nice to see Trent again, all the same. I guess I missed having a brother, too."

"Then Elaine can get married and give you the brother-in-law you want so badly," Faith said with a laugh. "But seriously... We're sisters. I know we don't always get along and we have really different opinions on just about everything, but when it came to boyfriends, we had each other's backs, right?"

Elaine and Hope both nodded. It was true. Heaven help the guy who messed with a Fairchild sister—he got all three of them infuriated with him!

"So, let's have each other's backs with husbands and ex-husbands, too. It's just a new phase of life."

"Of course we're on your side," Hope said. "But life can get complicated. And if you decided that you did have feelings for Trent still—"

"Hope, stop it!" Faith felt some tears rising in her eyes, and Hope immediately reached out and caught her hand.

"I'm sorry!" Hope said. "I'm not joking around. I just mean that we'll be on your side whatever you choose. Is that better?"

Elaine remained silent, her blue gaze locked on Faith, and she just looked sad.

"That's better," Faith said. "I'm over him." Or she would be. Soon. "I'm not moving backward in this. I need to move forward."

How had this suddenly become all about her? Faith sighed. She didn't want tonight to be about her, about her disappointments or her regrets. She pulled her hand back, and put her attention into her food on her plate. For a couple of minutes, they were all silent, eating the meal with significantly less enthusiasm.

"Elaine, these pierogis are delicious," Faith said, forcing some cheer into her voice. "You get better and better at making them. I have never had pierogis as good as yours anywhere else."

Elaine smiled then. "Thanks. I thought we could all use a little comfort food. Pierogis are pure carbs."

Faith took a sip of her meadow tea and Elaine launched into a story about one of the teachers at

Bluebird school who tried to cut carbs out of her diet completely cold turkey. It was humorous and Faith and Hope both started to laugh at Elaine's tale.

Life hadn't turned out like any of them expected, but this evening spent together with her sisters felt right—just her and the women who knew her better than anyone. Family was who was left when everything else fell apart.

CHAPTER TEN

FAITH BENT OVER a double-sized quilt, needle and thread in hand, as she stitched up a torn seam in a splash of midmorning sunlight that came angling in from the front window of the Amish Antiques Shop.

The quilt was a little yellowed with age, but it was done in a pattern she didn't see anymore—a diamond on top of a square. Very simple, and the colors were completely plain—no pattern on the fabric, not even on the backing. A little note in Aunt Josephine's handwriting was pinned to one corner. It read, 1948. Rose Lapp.

Who was Rose Lapp? Had she been young or old? Had she been married? And whom had she made the quilt for? Because this one had hardly been touched, by the look of it. Had this quilt been made to sell in an Amish mud sale? Those were Amish auctions set up to raise money for things like an Amish school or the community medical fund. They were held in the spring, normally, which made the parking area particularly muddy. Somehow, the nickname "mud sale" had stuck. Or maybe this quilt had been carefully tucked away in memory of Rose after her passing…

If only there was a way to find out. But every last antique piece in this shop was the same—an item standing alone, outside of time, with a history that Faith could only wonder about.

"We have a lot of silver teaspoons," Hope said from where she sat perched on the edge of a stool. "I don't even know what these are worth."

Faith looked over her sister's shoulder at the cardboard box she was inventorying. All were tarnished, and some were in little plastic boxes for display. Faith picked up one that had a little black-and-white oval picture of President Calvin Coolidge on it. Another had some intricate-looking details—a man, a tree, lots of scrolling and, in the basin of the spoon, the date 1910 was etched. She looked closer at the detail on the handle and could make out a banner with the word *Illinois* written across it.

"I wonder if we could find matches for these online somehow," Faith said. "We need to learn about the antiques trade fast. Maybe we can reach out to some antiques dealers and see if they might be willing to coach us on a few things."

All three of them had worked in Aunt Josephine's store when they were teenagers in the summer, so they did have some limited experience in the trade.

"That's not a bad idea," Hope agreed. "I'll do some research on antiques dealers in the area and see if I can feel out someone who might help us."

Hope would be the best one for that task—she

was likeable and sweet. People tended to be eager to help her.

"We should have a website where we can take quality photos of each piece and list them," Elaine said. "It would open up our clientele to people who don't live around here."

That was a smart idea, Faith had to admit.

"You should definitely do that," Trent's muffled voice came from above.

Trent was up a ladder, disappearing into the ceiling, and Faith's gaze followed his legs and torso up to his chest—the rest of him was in the attic. Eddie had left early for an appointment of some sort, leaving Trent to finish up for the day alone. It had been rather comforting to have him around today, and Faith hated to admit that to herself. But he'd just been...around. And she'd liked being able to look up and see him working on some outlet. Right now, all she could see of him were his legs and half his torso.

"What's that?" Faith called.

"A website," his voice came back. "That's a good idea."

"I have to agree," Faith murmured.

"What?" Trent called.

"I said I agree with you!" she called back, and Hope snorted back a laugh.

Faith rolled her eyes at her sister. Hope and Elaine seemed to like any kind of comfortable chatting between Faith and Trent far more than they should. They were being civil...right? Wasn't this how mature, divorced people acted? What did she know? Faith leaned back into her repair of the split seam, working carefully and slowly.

"We need to find a way to get this store to be more profitable," Faith said. "I like the idea of the website—that would definitely help us. We need to get onto social media, too. That might help spread the word about our existence."

"I could do that," Elaine said, and she picked up her phone and snapped a picture of Faith.

"What are you doing?" Faith asked.

"Getting started." Elaine shot her a grin.

"Show me that picture," Faith said with a laugh.

"I'll only show it to you if you promise to let me take some pictures with you in them. People will want to see the faces behind the store."

"Fine," Faith said. "Let me see it."

Elaine turned her phone around, and the photo was surprisingly good. Faith was bent over the quilt with a look of concentration on her face, but nothing terribly unflattering.

"Okay, you can use that one," Faith said.

"See?" Elaine pointed her phone at Hope, who immediately straightened and smiled.

"Quit posing," Elaine said. "We want natural."

"Do we?" Hope grimaced. Elaine took the photo and let out a whoop of laughter at the result. Faith peeked over Elaine's shoulder and smirked.

"Elaine, you'd better not post that," Hope said.

"I won't, I won't… But you've got to ignore me while I go around taking pictures. Deal? Because the sooner I can put together some pages on social media for the store, the sooner we can start getting some word out about our existence. These days if it isn't online, no one will find it. Period."

"Well, not no one, exactly," Faith said. "There are locals."

Elaine arched an eyebrow at her.

"But your point is made," Faith added. "Work your magic, Lainey."

The sound of a phone ringing rattled through the store. Not a warbling ringtone…an actual landline with a clanging bell inside it. All three sisters straightened and looked at each other in surprise. Had Aunt Josephine left behind a corded telephone? Ever since Faith had arrived for the funeral, no phone had rung.

"Where is it?" Hope set off toward the front counter, and Elaine spun in a full circle, looking around.

Faith followed Hope, and she moved aside a pile of old newspaper, then looked under the till. The jangling ringing came from a black, 1950s-styled telephone with a rotary dial. She picked it up on the sixth ring.

"Hello, this is—" She stopped for a second, her mind spinning for an appropriate greeting. "This is Amish Antiques, Faith speaking."

"Hi, Faith, this is Esther Norman. I'm looking for Josephine Fairchild?"

"I'm sorry to tell you that she passed away a few weeks ago," Faith said. "But I'm her great-niece and I'm one of the new owners. Can I help you with anything?"

"Oh, I'm so sorry for your loss," the woman said. "I actually didn't know your great-aunt, but I was given the number for her—for your—shop by a friend of mine. I'm looking for some authentic Amish antiques."

"Oh..." This was promising. "Are there any specific items you're looking for?"

"I have an antique, Amish-made dining table," Esther said. "The table belonged to my family generations back when they were Amish. It used to have fourteen chairs, and I now only have five. If I could find three more chairs, it would be enough for my needs, and I'd like something as close to my originals as possible, something made in the early 1900s. Is there any chance you have something like this?"

"Could you text me a picture of one of your original chairs?" Faith asked. "I'll give you my cell phone number."

Faith looked at the picture that Esther texted. She hadn't seen anything like that around this shop, but it did look familiar. She was sure she'd seen chairs like this around before, she just couldn't put her finger on where.

"I don't have anything like that specifically, but we're just getting organized after taking over the store, so I might come across something similar yet. Can I take down your contact information just in case I find something?"

Esther was happy to oblige, and Faith added her name and phone number to the contacts on her phone and attached the photo of the chair. When she hung up, she found her sisters and Trent, now on the ground again, looking at her expectantly.

She explained the situation, her gaze flickering toward Trent, who was watching her fixedly.

"We can keep an eye out for something like that," Hope said. "Maybe an estate sale?"

"It would have to be an English estate sale," Elaine said. "The Amish don't sell their things that way. Do they, Trent?"

Faith looked up at Trent again, and he dropped his gaze and knocked the stays up on his ladder to fold it together.

"No, they don't do estate sales...not in my experience, at least." Trent balanced his folded ladder against his shoulder. "You'd find old chairs and such up in an attic."

A lot of good that did them, though. But maybe they could pass out flyers telling the local Amish that they were willing to buy select antiques for a fair price. As if they had the ready money for that right now...

"I was at my uncle Albrecht's place this morning," Trent said. "Tyke's day home is closed today, so I had to ask if Sarah could watch him. As it turns out, Uncle Albrecht was clearing out the attic today—just emptying stuff, decluttering."

Faith's heart skipped a beat. "Did you see chairs like those?"

"No, he hadn't started yet," Trent replied. "But it did occur to me that he might have some antiques up there he might be willing to part with. I mean, you'd have to look at what he had."

"It's a great opportunity," Hope said. "Faith, you should go check it out. You know Albrecht and Mary a little bit."

So did Hope, but Faith didn't bother bringing it up.

"How much are we willing to spend?" Faith asked, turning back toward her sisters.

"It would depend on what you find," Hope said.

"Okay, let's just stop and do the math here," Elaine said.

Trent discreetly carried his ladder out the front door, and the sisters turned their attention to the ledger with their bank account balance. They discussed upcoming bills and how much cushion they'd need, and decided upon a modest amount they could part with.

"I'll stop by the bank on the way," Faith said. "And with some luck, maybe we'll be able to rustle up some of those dining room chairs, given time."

Trent came back and stopped in the doorway, leaning against the jamb.

"So what did you decide? Do you want to come check things out?" Trent asked. "Because I'm leaving now. I can give you a ride. My truck has plenty of room in the bed to carry stuff back for you."

It was a kind offer, and one very much needed. All of their cars were far too small to start carting around pieces of furniture. That was something to keep in mind for the future.

"Thank you, Trent," Faith said. "I really do appreciate the offer. I can leave now—" She looked back at her sisters.

"Yeah, definitely," Hope said. "I'll make some dinner. It'll be ready by the time you get back. How many am I cooking for?"

"Not me," Trent said. "I've got a toddler who'll need to get home. Trust me—at that time of day, you don't want to be entertaining us."

Hope shrugged. "No problem. Am I cooking for you, Faith?"

Faith heard the silent question—how late would she be?

"Yes, please cook for me, too," Faith said, and she caught her sister's gaze with a rueful smile. No, she wasn't going to be lingering late with Trent. Those days were long past.

This was strictly business.

CHAPTER ELEVEN

TRENT PULLED OUT of the bank parking lot and into the afternoon traffic, which consisted of about six cars and two Amish buggies. He recognized the Amish man passing him—he was a second cousin—and Trent gave him a wave and a nod. The man did a double take, leaning forward to see the woman in his truck next to him, and Trent pretended not to notice. Yeah, he'd have to explain that at the next family gathering he attended. The Amish prided themselves on not being gossips, but how else was a family supposed to know what was happening with each other if they didn't pass along news? And Trent seen with his ex-wife again? That would be news.

It felt good to have Faith in the truck next to him again. The scent of her perfume tugged at memories and heartstrings at the same time, and he tried not to look over at her lest he betray what he was feeling.

"I'm surprised you offered to take me out to your uncle's farm," Faith said.

"Why?" he asked.

"Because I'm your ex-wife, and you didn't have to," she replied.

He shrugged. She made an excellent point. The truth was, he was rather surprised at himself, too, but he wasn't about to let Faith know that. He'd had no intention of even mentioning it, but then that phone call, and the look on her face—Faith looking uncertain, hopeful and kind of excited... It was like he was catapulted back to the time of their marriage where he might have messed up a lot of things, but he'd also been willing to do just about anything to see her excited like that. It had done the same thing to him that her perfume seemed to do—collapsed time in his head and left him at the mercy of that ache in his chest. He hadn't been able to stop himself.

"You needed to find more Amish antiques and my uncle was clearing out the attic," Trent said. "We might not be married anymore, but I still like being around you."

Faith cast him a rueful smile, and he knew it didn't actually make sense. He should just let her figure things out and carry on with his own life. That would be the smart thing right about now.

"I guess I also want to see you make a success of the antiques shop," he added. "I know I jumped the gun with leasing the space for your bookstore. I get it. I pushed you into something, and it failed. And I guess I feel like I owe you some support in your newest venture."

"That's kind..." she said.

"Don't sound surprised," he said. "It might not have worked between us, but that doesn't mean I don't have a heart. I do care."

Maybe he could make up for that mistake and leave her with slightly warmer feelings toward him. That was a selfish hope on his part. He knew that her feelings about him weren't in his control, and as her ex-husband, she was bound to feel some recrimination. But a guy could hope.

The drive out into the rural farm area where Uncle Albrecht and Aunt Mary lived wasn't terribly far. Apfelkuchen was a tiny town, and the next-biggest town was a half hour away. So most folks already assumed that Apfelkuchen was already just a dab in the middle of farmland. It was a bit bigger than that, but just outside the town limits they immediately hit pasture and crops.

"I'm wondering how Tyke did out there on the farm with no screens, no other kids to tangle with," Trent said.

"Are you worried?" she asked.

"He's just not used to that. He really cried when I drove away this morning. I almost turned around and went back for him." His chest felt tight, even remembering it. "But I guess it's a farm—what's not for a little guy to enjoy, right? Cows, horses, dirt."

Tyke really did love himself some good dirt to dig around in. He felt Faith's gaze on him and looked over to find a tender look in her eyes.

"You love him," she said.

"Someone has to."

Faith smiled faintly. "I wanted kids, you know."

"I know." They'd talked about that before they got married. They both wanted children. Eventually.

"Like...five or six of them," she murmured.

Trent looked over at her. "That many? You never told me that."

"Because you always said you didn't want to think about kids yet." She shrugged. "Look at the bullet you dodged."

Funny the things a guy could find out after the fact. But she was right—he hadn't wanted to think about kids yet. They had plans—his electrical business, and she had longed for that bookstore. He'd thought they'd start there.

He hadn't thought too much about raising smaller versions of himself. But now that he had Tyke, while Tyke wasn't biologically his, he sure thought about the ins and outs of raising a kid now. He'd also thought about having a partner in this...a woman by his side. But dating got a whole lot more complicated once there was a toddler's heart on the line, too.

"You could have told me," he said at last.

"Well, I told you I wanted a baby, didn't I?" she asked. "If you weren't ready for one baby, I'd be foolish to bring up more."

"I thought we needed more time," he said.

"I know." But there was a quiet sound in her voice that tugged at his heart. She sounded almost mournful.

"Had you wanted a baby that badly?" he asked.

"Yeah, I did," she replied. "But don't worry, Trent. You were right. We weren't ready. I'm not arguing that we were."

That little detail lodged in his heart, though, and he had an unbidden image rise in his mind of him and Faith with a baby. She'd really wanted a child, and he really hadn't—not yet, at least. What if she'd gotten pregnant without them planning it—would he have felt differently then? Probably, considering that Tyke turned everything around for him. But Faith wasn't the kind of woman to "accidentally" get pregnant. She was very straightforward in everything and she meant what she said. They'd have talked it through first. If he'd wanted to fulfill her wish and start their family, that would have been on him.

Albrecht's farm wasn't too far from town, and when Trent spotted their gravel road, he turned down it.

Tyke might be good and mad at him when Trent picked him up tonight. He was used to Abigail, and he liked her and the kids at the day home a lot.

"How long do two-year-olds hold grudges?" Trent asked.

"I don't know." She chuckled. "You'd know better than me, at this point. You really think he'll be mad at you?"

"He might be." Trent hoped he looked less anxious than he felt. Convincing Faith that everything was fine was almost as good as convincing himself. At least it used to be.

He turned down his aunt and uncle's, navigating around a familiar pothole.

"Albrecht and Mary might not be pleased to see me," Faith said. "I just thought of that now."

"Nah," he replied. "Remember what I told you about them not being able to deal with divorces? You get a taste of that today."

Faith smiled ruefully. "I think you're wrong."

"Do you?" He couldn't help but chuckle. "We'll see."

He was right, and he wasn't even going to protect her from it. If he had to deal with the pointed questions about "his wife," then she could deal with his aunt and uncle pretending the last two years hadn't happened, too.

Trent pulled up next to the buggy shed where his uncle's buggy sat, shining from a new wash and polish, and looked over toward the house. The side door was propped open, and there was a pile of stuff that looked like it was ready for the junk pile. His uncle had been busy.

"Ready?" he asked, meeting her gaze.

"As I'll ever be." She smiled, and suddenly it was like any other visit with his Amish family back when they were married, and his heart gave a squeeze. He missed that so much. But he didn't have time to entertain foolishness. She was his ex-wife now.

"You're back," his uncle said, coming around the side of the house as they climbed out of the truck.

Uncle Albrecht was a portly older Amish man with a full, gray Amish beard, which meant there was no mustache. He wore dark broadfall pants and suspenders, his white shirt rolled up to his elbows, and he mopped at his forehead with a blue handkerchief. His gaze moved from Trent to Faith, and then a slow smile spread over his features.

"So good to see you two," Albrecht said. "Faith, how have you been? We haven't seen you around here half-often enough. Mary is going to be so happy to get you in the kitchen with a cup of tea, I can tell you."

"Hi, Albrecht," Faith said, and she smiled. "I'm actually here for something business related."

"Business?" Albrecht pulled off his hat and mopped his head again. "What sort of business?"

"You know about me and my sisters inheriting the antiques shop in Apfelkuchen, right?" she asked.

She'd explain herself just fine, and Albrecht—in keeping with pretending all was well and no divorce had ever happened—would let her rummage through his pile of castoffs, Trent was sure.

"I'll let you two talk," Trent said, and he wasn't sure why he did it, but he reached out and touched Faith's elbow in farewell. The smile she flashed in his direction made his heart stumble in his chest.

Yeah, he had to stop that.

He sucked in a breath and headed toward the house. Aunt Mary appeared in the doorway, and he watched her gaze snap between him and Faith, too, and then a smile that matched her husband's appeared on her face.

"How'd Tyke do?" Trent asked before she could ask any questions of her own.

"He was just fine," Aunt Mary said, and she hooked a hand around his forearm and all but dragged him into the house. "Is your wife home again? This is wonderful! I knew if you just gave it some time—"

"Aunt Mary, it's not what it looks like. She's here looking for Amish antiques for her shop, and I'm here looking for Tyke." But he gave her a smile to soften the words.

Tyke was playing with a block set on the kitchen floor, and he jumped to his feet and came running pell-mell into Trent's legs. He was getting stronger and heavier, and one of these days he'd knock Trent over.

His cousin Sarah stood at the counter peeling apples. She and her mother both wore cape dresses—Mary in red and Sarah in blue. They had dark work aprons covering their dresses and white *kapps* covering their hair in the back.

"Hi, Trent!" Sarah said, looking up. Her fingers didn't slow down, though. "How was work today?"

"Pretty good," he replied. "I heard you met my apprentice, Eddie. He thought seeing an Amish farm was pretty neat."

Sarah's cheeks reddened. "*Yah*. He was nice."

Mary's gaze flickered toward her daughter.

"Be gentle with him, Sarah," Trent said, trying

to make a joke of it. "If you aren't careful, he might fall for you, and then you'd be forced to break his heart."

"He wouldn't fall for me," Sarah said. "He's just being nice. That's all. He's a new friend."

Good. Message sent—that should take care of it.

"Sarah is a smart girl," Mary said. "Of course she knows the difference, Trent."

Footsteps outside the door announced that Albrecht and Faith were coming inside. Albrecht was talking about furniture styles, and Faith's cheeks colored just a bit when she saw Mary and Sarah.

"Hi," she said, when Albrecht paused.

"Faith!" Mary said. "I'm so happy to see you! You're staying for dinner tonight, aren't you?"

There it was—the welcome Faith needed, and he was glad that his aunt was being so friendly. No one was angry with her here—in denial, sure, but not angry.

"No, no, I have to get back. My sister is making dinner tonight, and she's expecting me," Faith said.

"Are you sure?" Sarah pressed. "We haven't talked in so long, you and me."

Faith's eyes suddenly misted. "I've missed you, too, Sarah." Then she looked over at Mary. "All of you. It really is nice to see you again. But I can't stay this evening. We'll have to do it another time."

"Any time at all," Mary said. "You are always welcome here."

"Mary, I actually have a question for you about someone who made a quilt. My aunt noted her name as Rose Lapp, and said the year was 1948. I'm assuming that's when the quilt was stitched. Do you know anything about her?"

"Rose Lapp..." Mary frowned in thought. "What was the quilt like?"

"I can show you." Faith pulled out her phone and held up a photo of the quilt.

"Roselyn Lapp... I remember her quilts. She used the old style—wouldn't even brighten her quilting to sell it. She passed away a few years ago. She had what...fourteen children in total? Five with her first husband, and her second husband had five of his own from his first marriage, and then she had four more babies with her second husband."

"But her youngest passed when he was very small," Albrecht interjected. "I remember that funeral. It was heartbreaking."

"*Yah, yah*, that's right," Mary said. "But on a cheerier subject, she was a wonderful cook. I remember my mother saying that Roselyn's crust was impossible to match."

"What happened to her first husband?" Faith asked.

"Died in a grain silo," Albrecht supplied. "That story was being told when I was young, too. It was one of those cautionary tales. Very tragic. You've got to be careful around silos. If you fall in, you sink right down and drown in the grain. Terrible. She married within the year to another widower."

"That was quick," Faith said. "No time to grieve."

"He had those five little ones of his own that needed a *mamm*," Albrecht said.

"All those *kinner* needed love and full bellies," Mary added. "There isn't always time for grief."

Something flickered across Faith's face—a sadness that Trent's own heart echoed. It had been two years, and he wished he had finished grieving the loss of his marriage. At least having a little guy like Tyke need love and care forced him to keep moving.

"What year did he die?" Faith asked.

"That was a long time ago. In the seventies, I think."

"So the quilt I have was made during her first marriage," Faith said, nodding. "That's kind of nice to know. She sounds like she was a special lady."

Outside, the sound of a vehicle drew everyone's gaze. Sarah's face blazed red and she skipped over to the window.

"Oh, it's Eddie," she said, but by the slightly guilty tone to her voice, Trent doubted that this was any kind of surprise to her. "I wonder what he wants."

Trent looked over at Albrecht and the older man closed his eyes for a moment and shook his head.

"I suppose you'd best go find out," he said.

Sarah just about floated out of the kitchen, and she headed outside barefoot.

"Are you okay with that?" Trent asked his uncle.

"That Englisher boy?" Albrecht shook his head. "No, I am not."

"But if we forbid her, Albrecht..." Mary said gently.

"*Yah*, if we come down too hard, she'll just decide she loves him. Or so my wife assures me."

"The female heart is a complicated thing," Faith murmured.

Mary and Faith exchanged a knowing little look.

Tyke squirmed to be put down, and Trent complied. Tyke started to beeline for those blocks again, but then he stopped and looked soberly up at Faith.

"Hi, Tyke," Faith said, and she fluttered her fingers in a little wave at him.

Tyke lifted his arms. "Up?"

Faith bent down and scooped him up in her arms. She balanced him across her stomach and smiled at him.

"Hi, sweetie," she said softly. "How are you?"

Tyke stroked a pudgy hand down her hair, and bonked his forehead against her lips, and she kissed him.

"Kisses," Tyke said.

"Yeah, kisses." She pressed her lips against his head again. "You're a little heart-stealer, Tyke."

And watching his ex-wife kiss the toddler in his care, Trent had a strange feeling of the two halves of his heart hovering very close together. Faith was his past, and Tyke was his future, and while he knew that they were very separate, his heart seemed to be closing in around the scene in a very uncomfortable way.

"Well, anyway," Trent said, a little louder than

was probably necessary. "I hope my apprentice isn't causing any trouble around here."

Mary went to the window and she sighed heavily. "If that boy were Amish, it would be okay. But he's not."

Albrecht pressed his lips together into a thin line, but then his gaze landed on Faith.

"Oh, I was going to show you the old butter churn and the barrel chairs," Albrecht said.

"Yes, that's right!" Faith perked up, and she gave Tyke a little squeeze. Trent came forward to ease the toddler out of her arms. "Thank you, Albrecht. I appreciate it. Like I said, I'm prepared to pay a fair price."

"Nonsense," Albrecht said. "You're my nephew's wife. You're family. Come—you can take whatever you think you can sell. It's just using up space in the attic anyway."

Albrecht led the way up the stairs and Faith followed him, leaving Mary, Trent and Tyke alone.

"I feel it's only fair to warn you that Eddie's formed a pretty big crush on Sarah," Trent told his aunt once they were alone again.

"I don't blame him," Mary said. "She's delightful. Falling for her is only natural."

"You really don't mind that?" he asked.

"Well..." Mary turned thoughtful. "For a young woman, part of growing up is learning how to tell a man you aren't interested. It might be time for Sarah to learn that lesson. Once she's had to disappoint a good man, she'll be more careful about flirting in the future."

Aunt Mary had an interesting perspective, and Trent looked toward the window again. Eddie was leaning against his truck door, and Sarah was standing about a yard away from him, her hands behind her back. Very proper.

That poor sop was going to fall headlong in love with Sarah, wasn't he?

"If you'll take Tyke for a few more minutes, I'll help them carry down whatever Faith is taking," Trent said.

"Of course," Mary said, and she held out her hands to Tyke. "Come here, little one. Your *daet* needs to go help."

Daet...dad. He had no claim to that title. Trent was Tyke's guardian right now, and it felt like appropriating someone else's spot to claim to be more. He wasn't his father... But he loved him. And he wasn't Faith's husband anymore. But sometimes with Amish family, the fight wasn't worth it.

CHAPTER TWELVE

THE ATTIC WAS stuffy and overly warm, and a couple of cobwebs hung from the roof above her head. Albrecht brushed them down, muttering about not having gotten all the dust out yet. Faith could tell he was embarrassed at any sign of dirt up here—even where no one lived.

Faith crouched next to a crate, pulling out some old kitchen items. There was a rusted scale, an old recipe book, a wooden drawer for recipe cards, and when she pulled it out and opened the drawer, she found a couple of cards in the bottom—both written in German, so she didn't know what dishes they were for. There was a knife sharpener, and an iron skillet that desperately needed to be re-cured. That was all in this crate. But in the next crate beside it, she spotted some tin canisters, and almost hidden under some quilted pot holders was the aged, rubbed, blank face of an Amish doll.

"Albrecht, for some Englisher buyers, these items would be very exciting."

"For that old stuff?" Albrecht shook his head. "Englishers sure are odd..."

"It's like your respect for tradition," she said. "Englishers have a deep respect for the past. These items represent a simpler time. They spark imagination. They remind us of where we've come from, and of the values that we want to take with us."

Albrecht shrugged. "You can take whatever you like."

"Are you sure I can't pay you for these things?"

"No, no need to pay me. You're family, after all."

She winced. She was not family anymore, and she couldn't just take something for free.

"But—"

"Is there anything else here you could sell?" he asked. "I feel bad even offering because it feels like old junk to me. None of this even felt good enough to give to charity. But if it's of use to you, I'd rather see these items be used again than not."

"These recipe cards in the old card drawer—" She pulled one out. "Would you like them back?"

"My wife is a terrific cook," he said. "I promise you, she has all those recipes memorized."

"Full disclosure, Albrecht," she said. "People would love to buy this just for the cards written in Amish hand."

He gave her a funny look, and let the subject drop. There was plenty of curiosity about the Amish, but sometimes it was best to let the actual Amish people ignore it as best they could.

"Can I show you a picture of a dining room chair?" She pulled out her phone and held it up for

Albrecht to see. "Have you seen any chairs like this?"

Albrecht shook his head slowly. "I have, I just can't quite think of where. This is a pretty common chair design. Many men in my father's generation used this particular design, so...they'd be around."

"I have a buyer who wants three chairs of this design—old ones, not something made new."

"That's more complicated, then," Albrecht said.

Faith heard footsteps, and then the creak of weight on the drop-down stairs. Trent's head appeared in the opening as he joined them in the attic, and she found herself glad to see him. She'd wondered if he'd prefer to just wait down below. Had he missed her?

That was a question she shouldn't be entertaining!

"How's it going?" Trent asked.

"It sounds like your wife can sell a good number of these items," Albrecht said. "I'm offering to just give them to her."

Your wife. Yes, she could see what Trent had been talking about now. Those words were spoken gently, and they'd sounded just a little too sweet to her ear.

"Albrecht," Faith said. "You can't get Trent on your side for this. For example, I can sell this recipe box for twenty dollars, and I could sell the cards inside for five dollars apiece. And the doll could go for well over a hundred—depending on when it was made."

"Really?" Albrecht shook his head.

"Knowing what it's worth," Faith said, "you could sell these things yourself, or if you were still willing to part with them, I'll give you fifteen percent of what I can sell them for. That gives me some room to make a profit, as well. We've got bills, of course."

Albrecht shook his head. "Mary wouldn't be happy with me if I took a penny. Take what you want. Let's start with this crate here—take out what you don't want, and we'll fill it up with what you do. I'm sure Trent will carry it down for you."

Oh, this dear man. Faith felt her heart overflow for the generosity and kindness of Trent's uncle. She'd always loved his family, and having them treat her with the same kindness and gentleness as always was comforting in a way she didn't feel like she had a right to anymore.

"*Danke*, Albrecht," she said, using the Pennsylvania Dutch word to thank him. She put a hand over her heart. "Truly."

Some color touched the older man's cheeks and he shuffled his feet uncomfortably.

"We've got some old quilts, if you think those would sell. But they are very old. Made by my grandmother and worn almost to threads. We Amish tend to use things up, after all…"

As if that would ruin the beauty! Faith gratefully began to fill the crate.

"Albrecht, if there is anything I can do for you or your family, please let me know."

"Of course," Albrecht said. "We are not too proud for ask for help when we need it. But all is well for now. We are happy to contribute to your new business, Faith. May it prosper."

May it prosper, indeed. One year—they needed to survive and hopefully grow for one year. And then this bookstore in her heart could finally be her priority.

Maybe with a new bookstore and the soothing scent of paper and bindings surrounding her…in the city, far from her memories in Apfelkuchen, she would finally heal.

CHAPTER THIRTEEN

OUTSIDE IN THE YARD, the air was cooling as the shadows stretched long across the neatly mown lawn, and Faith watched as Trent hoisted three full crates up into the bed of his pickup truck. Loading up had interrupted Sarah and Eddie's little visit, and Albrecht seemed quite happy to have an excuse. He waved Eddie over to help lift the last of the items—a wooden high chair and a washtub filled with folded quilts—up into the truck.

Eddie gave Faith a sheepish smile.

"It's nice to see you, Eddie," Faith said. "You seem to like farm life."

"What's not to like?" Eddie said, and Sarah blushed, sensing that veiled compliment was for her.

Tyke was already buckled into his car seat, and when Trent banged shut the tailgate, Tyke twisted around to look, a smile breaking over his chubby face when he spotted Trent passing the window. Trent tapped on the glass for the toddler's benefit and pulled open the driver's side door.

Was Eddie planning on heading home anytime

soon? He didn't seem to have much sense of when to leave, but that wasn't her problem. Besides, Sarah was still looking at him with an adoring expression, twisting her apron in one hand.

"Thanks again," Faith said to Mary and Albrecht. Mary stood next to her husband, her cheeks flushed from the heat of her kitchen. Sarah stood on the other side of her father, and Eddie stood a little uncomfortably next to her. He was trying—Faith could give him that much.

"Come by anytime, Faith," Mary said, and she stepped forward to give her a hug that smelled like baking. Faith squeezed the older woman back, but she couldn't promise anything. This was Trent's family, and she didn't want to overstep, even if the Yoders made it tempting to do so. There was something so homey and comforting about this farm. She knew why Eddie was drawn to it.

"Be careful of that guy, Sarah!" Trent called to his cousin, his tone teasing. "He's a smooth talker!"

Now Sarah and Eddie were both blushing.

"I should be heading out," Eddie said. "Just wanted to say hi." He looked toward Albrecht. "Unless you wanted help with chores. I'm happy to pitch in."

He was certainly persistent. Faith didn't wait to hear Albrecht's reply. She got back into the truck and did up her seat belt before Trent backed up and then headed up the gravel drive. Faith looked in the side mirror, and saw Albrecht and Eddie in discussion.

"He's smitten, isn't he?" Faith said.

"Yup," Trent said. "And not too smart, either."

Faith chuckled. "I don't know. Sarah seems to like him a lot."

"Sarah can't marry him," Trent said. "And that's what it comes down to. She's baptized Amish, which means that she'd be shunned if she up and married an Englisher apprentice electrician."

That thought sent a chill through Faith's veins. She knew what shunning was, and how hard it was on both the one being shunned and the friends and family who had to turn their backs. She'd only seen it happen once—to a man who left the community just before his marriage. It was decent of him to do it before the wedding, because for Amish people there were no second chances there. His parents had been neighbors of Trent's parents, and Faith had seen a heartbreaking moment for the family when he'd come back for his mother's birthday. She'd refused to speak with him. He'd just stood there with a card in hand, and tears in his eyes...

Even now it made her choke up.

"I'm just saying—Eddie's getting some encouragement," Faith replied. "It's not all his fault. And sometimes people fall for each other...even when they shouldn't."

"Like us?" His gaze flickered toward her.

She smiled sadly. "Maybe."

But she couldn't say she regretted marrying Trent, exactly. She'd loved him so much that not marrying him would have probably hurt more than marrying him and having it not work out. At least she'd followed her heart.

"Your uncle and aunt were really generous," she added, wanting to change the subject. "I know Albrecht didn't want payment, but I feel like I should do something for them. Any ideas?"

"You never know. Someone might need a job in the future," Trent said. "This is more of a long game."

That was what she was afraid of. They were expecting her to be around for good, and she didn't want to leave town again without somehow repaying them for their kindness today.

"I guess I'll just have to wait and see," she said. "But I see what you mean about them refusing to acknowledge our divorce."

Trent barked out a laugh. "It's subtle, but they won't budge with it. Welcome to my unique torture."

Faith couldn't help but chuckle.

"Tent!" Tyke called from the back seat. "Tent!"

"Hey, buddy," Trent said. "Are you ready to go home?"

"Tuck?" Tyke asked.

"His truck," Trent translated. "We didn't bring it, buddy. It's at home. You'll see your truck soon, okay?"

Faith turned to look at the toddler, who had tears welling in his eyes.

"Oh, hey, Tyke," she said. "It's okay. Did you have fun at the farm?"

Tyke didn't look like he was ready to be mollified, and Trent used his phone to start up a preschool playlist, and "Baby Shark" started to play. Tyke's tears immediately dried and he perked up.

"'Baby Shark' for the win," she said. "That's impressive."

"The kid knows what he likes," Trent replied. "Hey, so how did dinner with your sisters go?"

Faith settled into the seat, the kids' music flowing through the cab.

"It was nice, actually. Elaine made pierogis."

"Oh!" He shot her a grin. "Elaine's pierogis were always really good. Those and her cabbage rolls."

"I know. It was nice to get some sister time again. And for once we weren't arguing about anything."

"How is Hope's husband?" he asked.

"That was almost an argument last night, but I managed to sidestep that," she replied. "The thing is, he works really hard. Hope knew that, but they got married so fast that I don't think she knew how much time she'd actually be on her own."

"Is she happy?" he asked.

"I don't think so. I mean, she loves him. But this is tougher on her than she realized it would be," Faith replied. "I'm determined to keep my nose out of it. No good can come from getting involved in someone else's marriage, but Elaine is a little snoopier."

"Right." He smiled ruefully, and she was actually glad she could talk about this with someone who knew her sisters so well. She didn't have to overexplain with Trent.

"She's just…younger than us," Faith said. "And she figures that if you're upset about something, you should just put it all out there, which isn't always the answer."

"I kind of wish you had," he said.

"What?"

"When we were married," Trent replied. "I wish you'd just slammed me with it when you were upset. You used to give me the silent treatment instead of actually telling me what I'd done."

"I shouldn't have done that." She regretted some of her behavior when she'd been really mad. "It didn't help. It wasn't very mature of me."

"Well, I wasn't exactly at my best in our marriage, either, but it meant that when you did finally blow and say exactly what you thought, it was… the end."

"We fought plenty," she said.

"And maybe it's on me that I didn't realize what it meant," he replied.

Faith fell silent. Had she not been clear with him when she'd been upset? But maybe there had just been too many things—constant head-butting between them. What had it all boiled down to? She wished she knew! Because she still wasn't sure. Maybe she could have expressed her dissatisfaction better if she could have put it into words for herself, too.

"All I'm saying is that maybe Elaine isn't completely wrong," Trent said. "Maybe Hope needs to talk to Peter and tell him how she feels. Men are dense. We don't pick up on hints. You've pretty much got to hit us with it between the eyes."

"I'm staying out of it," Faith said. "This is her life, and her marriage. No one could give me advice, either."

"No one?" His gaze flickered toward her.

"Nope."

"Hmm."

"Did you get advice?" she asked.

"Tons."

Had there been someone meddling on his end of things? She wasn't sure she liked that idea. She'd kept her problems pretty close to the vest, herself.

"What did they tell you to do?" she asked.

He shot her a grin. "Nothing that worked. Don't worry about it."

But now Faith was curious. Either his well-meaning family had dearly wanted them to stay together, or there had been someone who'd been against their marriage. Seeing as they broke up anyway, she shouldn't care, but she found that suddenly she wanted to know. What sort of advice had they given Trent? And had it really been as bighearted as Trent led her to believe?

CHAPTER FOURTEEN

TRENT TURNED ONTO the highway and headed back toward Apfelkuchen. Funny how driving with Faith could evaporate the last few years, and it just felt normal to be with her. Like it used to feel...like she was part of things.

"Come on, Trent," Faith said. "Satisfy my curiosity. What kind of advice did you get? And I'll tell you the advice I got."

Tempting, but Trent wanted to know something more important.

"First of all, answer me one question, and then I'll tell you all the piles of useless advice I got," he said.

"Fine. What's your question?" she asked.

"Why did you leave me?"

"Baby Shark" ended just then, and for a beat there was dead silence in the vehicle, and all he could hear was the thundering of his own heartbeat. Then the Elmo song started, and he risked a look over at his ex-wife. Tears had misted her eyes, and her chin trembled. Dang... His heart skipped a beat. His first instinct was to let her off the hook, take the question back... But he couldn't. He needed to know this.

"I've been wondering for the last two years," he said. "I signed the papers not knowing. I know we fought. I know I bugged you. I know we saw money differently, and... I've been going over it again and again. Because I know the accumulation of little things was a lot, but what was the root of it? What made you call it quits on us?"

"I've been asking myself that same question," she said softly.

"And?" he asked. "Have you come up with any grand answer?"

"Grand? Not really. All I know for certain was that I was lonely," Faith said. "We were married, but I never felt like you actually heard me, or knew me. We were just living our lives side by side, you and me. And I loved you—so much! But every time we argued, I could feel that we were constantly misunderstanding each other."

"That wasn't worth working on?" Trent asked.

Because they'd taken vows. He hadn't been cruel, or unfaithful. He had truly done his best. Wasn't *he* worth some work?

"When I lost my bookstore," she said, "you thought it was fine. Like I could just push it aside and carry on. But that had been my dream ever since I was a little girl. I used to set up all the books in our house to be my pretend bookstore in my bedroom. My mom used to come looking for the recipe book in my room when she needed it, and I made her pretend to buy it from me..."

He knew this story well. She'd always wanted a bookstore, and he'd tried to give it to her. He'd done everything he knew how, and it had never been right.

"When I lost the store," she said, "I lost more than a dream. I lost my sense of myself. And there you were, plowing ahead, not knowing that I was emotionally bleeding out behind you. You thought it was fine—I'd get over it. I'd tried and failed, and we could carry on. But... I couldn't."

"And you blamed me," he said.

"Yes... No! I mean, I did blame you. You'd pushed me into that lease too early and didn't give me any time to plan. I wasn't ready! But that wasn't why I left. I left because I realized that after three years of marriage you still didn't understand me. And I thought that I'd feel less lonely on my own than I did in our marriage."

"I loved you, though," he said.

"I mean, at that point, we were fighting a lot, and—"

"Hey." He reached over and caught her hand, and she fell silent. "Fighting or not, I loved you. More than you knew, obviously. But I did. You were unhappy and I knew it, and when I got that lease for you, it was my attempt at a grand gesture to try and give you something to fulfill you again. I wanted to be part of making your dreams come true."

Faith was silent, and then he felt her squeeze his hand back.

"I'm sorry I didn't see that."

He should pull his hand back, he knew, but he didn't. Her hand felt too good in his, and he was going to allow himself this little luxury.

"Okay..." he said slowly. "So you felt...disconnected?"

"Are you sure you want to hear all this?" she asked.

"Yes. It's like a battle debrief. A man learns from his mistakes."

"I'm not sure I like our marriage being referred to as a battle," she said. "I mean, maybe it was half the time, but...still."

"I meant the debrief part," he amended. "It helps me. I want to know where I went wrong so I don't go through life making the same mistakes."

She was silent, though, and he ran his thumb over her fingers. Dang, it was hard to focus on the road with her hand in his. What he wanted was to pull her closer. He wanted to tuck her right under his arm, but that wasn't going to happen. He'd have to make do with just her fingers. Not enough.

"It's okay, Trent," she said softly. "We've already done the hard part by divorcing. It's in the past. I'm not blaming you. I think we were just too different."

"I almost wish you would blame me," he admitted.

"No..." She sucked in a breath. "I'm tired of fighting. We don't have to do that anymore. We can just be amicable exes."

She released his hand, then, and his palm suddenly felt cold, and a little awkward as he pulled his hand back. He was so used to trying to fix things with Faith that it was hard to stop. But maybe she had a point. Regardless of what his Amish side of the family thought, they weren't married anymore. He didn't actually *have* to fix anything anymore. Was it okay to just…stop?

"Amicable exes? Is that what we are?" he asked.

"I hope so." She shot him a sweet little smile that made his heart stutter. "We don't have to resent each other or change each other. We can just appreciate each other as…as old friends."

An old friend. She was far from that, but he saw the point. He knew her too well to be just another pal, but maybe knowing her as well as he did didn't have to be painful, either. Could they really do this?

"For the record," he said, glancing over at her, "I'm sorry I wasn't enough for you. I really wanted to be."

Faith blinked at him, and for a moment, he thought she might answer, but then from the back seat, Trent smelled something familiar and rather odorous. He grimaced and lowered his window a few inches. Maybe it was better to just end the conversation there, anyway. He was being a little too honest.

"You might want to crack your window, too," Trent said. "We've got a diaper situation back there."

Tyke was chattering happily to himself in that toddler combination of baby babble and words he knew. He sounded like he was talking about a truck—the sounds it made, and then pointing to a passing vehicle and announcing a "tuck" on the way by. His diaper wasn't dampening his spirits at all.

"I'm not sure how you want to do this," Trent said. "I can change his diaper at your store before I unload your stuff, if you want."

"I can change him," Faith said.

"Are you sure? He's...a handful. I'm going to start potty training him pretty soon, but Abigail says that starting too early is pointless. She suggested starting when he's a bit closer to three."

"I'm not judging your potty training, Trent," she said, and she was silent for a moment, then blurted out, "And for the record on my end, you were enough. We just...maybe we were just too different."

Her big, brown eyes were filled with regret and sadness, and worse than all of that, he saw a spark of pity. That was the last thing Trent wanted from her. If he'd messed things up, he could face that. But he wasn't going to be the pathetic guy she crushed in the past. If he couldn't have her heart, he at least wanted her respect.

"You don't have to try to make me feel better, either," Trent said.

"Tuck!" Tyke hollered from the back seat, and a car passed them in oncoming traffic.

"Yeah, that's another one, isn't it, buddy?" Trent said absently.

He was still running over what she'd said. He'd been right there, and yet she'd felt lonesome. He hated that he hadn't been able to at least make her feel like she'd had a man in her corner. He'd done everything he could for her shop, knowing how much it meant to her! *Everything* he could.

A few minutes later, Trent pulled up to the curb by the antiques store. He got Tyke unbuckled, handed the kid a fruit leather to chew on and then passed him over to Faith with the diaper bag.

Faith unlocked the front door and disappeared inside. For a moment, Trent just stood there, listening to the quiet sound of traffic and smelling the sweet fragrant scent of baking from Marta's Bakery two blocks away. The stores were closed now, and there was no sign of either of Faith's sisters.

Trent pulled the first crate out of the back of the truck and carried it into the store. Faith had the changing pad on the floor and she knelt next to Tyke, looking pretty much in control of that situation. So he put the crate down and headed out to get the next one. He worked quickly, bringing in the next two crates, and when he came in through the door with the high chair, Tyke twisted out of Faith's grasp, bounded to his feet and made a run for it. Trent swiped him up into his arms as the toddler headed past him.

"Gotcha!" Trent said.

Tyke squealed in delight, and Faith came over, holding his pants.

"Can we get the pants back on between us?" Faith asked, then she smiled into Tyke's face. "Gimme a leg, Tyke."

Trent held Tyke, and Faith scooped him into his pants in one rather impressive movement.

"Done!" she said with a smile. "You're a good boy, Tyke. And now you're all clean, too."

Tyke held his arms out to Faith, and she accepted the toddler into her arms.

"I'll take care of the diaper," Trent said. It felt like the least he could do.

As Trent cleaned up the impromptu changing area on the floor, he glanced back to see Tyke looking thoughtfully up into Faith's warm eyes. Tyke had taken a shine to her, and he didn't blame the kid.

Trent came back over with the diaper bag slung on his shoulder, and Faith eased Tyke back into his arms.

"Thanks for helping out with the diaper," he said.

"No problem. Thanks for helping me get this stuff back. And for arranging it. This really will help the business. My sisters are going to be grateful, too."

"Hey, what are ex-husbands for?"

They stood there facing each other, and while he knew he should leave, he couldn't seem to make himself move.

"I'd better head out," he whispered.

"Yeah..." But still Faith didn't move, and he reached out and touched her chin. Her skin was soft under his calloused fingers, and for a moment, all he could think about was tipping her chin up and stealing a kiss. It would be the most natural thing in the world...and his gaze dropped down to her pink lips. And then Tyke drummed a hand on his shoulder, breaking the moment.

"See you, Trent." Her voice was softer than before, and he dropped his hand. He saw some complicated emotions swimming in her eyes before he turned away.

Yeah, this was complicated for him, too. He'd just found out tonight how phenomenally he'd let his ex-wife down during their marriage, and he needed to think that over. But more than that, he needed to get Tyke home and make some supper. A little boy's needs didn't take a rest because Trent was sorting through his feelings.

And maybe that was good. Like she'd said before, they were already divorced. He didn't *have* to fix this.

CHAPTER FIFTEEN

LATER THAT EVENING, once Tyke was in bed, Trent sank onto "his side" of the couch, some sitcom playing in the background.

He looked over at the empty space that used to be Faith's. She used to like to lie down and put her feet on his lap. He'd moved the couch since she'd left, though, to get a better view of the TV when he sat on it. She would have hated that, and there had been a little bit of satisfaction in the silent rebellion against her preferences. This was his place now—his place alone.

But he missed her still in quiet moments like this one... He missed that smell of her face cream that used to linger on her pillow. And the tinkle of her spoon against her coffee cup in the morning. He missed her smile, her laughter...even that irritated look she'd get on her face when he annoyed her somehow.

Faith used to be his reason for getting up early, and for making sure they never ran out of her hazelnut coffee creamer. She'd been his reason to come home after work, and while she did most of the cooking, he'd always been thinking ahead about getting the oil changed on her car, or bringing it through the car wash.

And for a whole year while she ran her bookstore, he'd been going around town telling everyone he knew about her shop, and how they should go buy a book. He was relentless. And he'd stayed mildly proud of that small accomplishment, because he'd had a hand in bringing people in—more than Faith ever knew. In the end, it hadn't been a problem with sales that had tanked her business. It had been a slew of other expenses that drained them dry.

Faith had been his reason for pretty much everything he did for those three years of marriage, and sitting here tonight, he missed her way more than he should.

His family had given him advice about how to keep his marriage. Everything from getting her flowers to marriage counseling. But it was Aunt Mary who'd suggested that they have a baby. He'd argued that babies were pretty high stress, and quite expensive from pregnancy through delivery, and that more pressure on them wasn't going to help things. But Aunt Mary had simply said, "But *kinner* give you a shared purpose. Think on it."

Was there wisdom there? He wasn't sure. The irony was, now that he had Tyke in his life, he couldn't just see how things went with a woman, especially not the woman who'd already left him once. Tyke had had too many hard goodbyes to risk another one. And he'd seen how the toddler had melted for Faith.

Trent rubbed his hands over his face and heaved a tired sigh. He should get to bed. He flicked off the TV. Tomorrow was another day, and even though it was really bad for him right now, he was looking forward to seeing Faith in the morning.

He wished his heart could just let go of her.

CHAPTER SIXTEEN

FAITH WOKE EARLY the next morning, and she lay in her bed, watching golden sunlight splash across the wall from the half-open curtain. She lay under a thick cotton sheet, a light quilt pushed off her to the side of the bed, and one foot stuck out into the warm pool of sunlight. She'd been awake ever since the first ray of sunlight sparkled past her curtain, and she'd been thinking about Trent.

He'd been thinking about kissing her... She knew he was. The way he'd touched her chin and his dark gaze had locked onto hers—she'd been married to the man, and she knew all the cues. And the part that had kept her awake last night was the realization that she would have let him.

He was still the same guy who could make goose bumps run up her arms, the same guy she'd fallen for all too young, and yet he'd definitely changed since their marriage. He seemed more cautious now, and maybe a little wiser. Maybe it was hard not to grow up a bit after a painful divorce. Because while he'd obviously been thinking about it, he hadn't kissed her.

The clock, ticking softly from the bedside table, told her it was seven, and Faith pushed back her sheet and sat up. The bedroom window was open, letting in a whisper of cool morning air and the scent of baking bread from Marta's Bakery down the street. Outside, the clop of hooves and rumble of a buggy's wheels moved down the road. Someone was out early—maybe heading to the bakery. The Amish were early risers.

She could hear the squeak of her sister's footsteps on the hallway floor.

"Hope?" she called.

The glass doorknob turned, and Hope peeked into her room.

"Good morning," Hope said. "How'd you sleep?"

"Terribly," Faith said. "How about you?"

"Pretty badly, too."

"We should have gotten up and watched TV or something," Faith said. "I didn't want to disturb you."

"What kept you awake?" Hope asked. She had a white cotton robe cinched around her waist, and her dark, glossy hair was pulled up in a high messy bun.

For a moment, Faith considered hiding the source of her own insomnia, but then her sister cast her a rueful little smile, and she crumbled.

"Trent," she said.

"Trent?" Hope came all the way into the bedroom and perched on the side of the bed. "What's going on with him? I thought you two were getting along."

"That's part of the problem," Faith replied. "I'm more comfortable being resentful than enjoying his company."

"So... You're enjoying him?" Hope's eyebrows went up.

"You make that sound more than it is." Faith shook her head. "It's just... There was a reason we fell for each other to begin with, right? I mean, we weren't a good couple. We didn't understand each other well, and both of us felt lonely in our marriage. Obviously something was missing. But..."

"It's the tool belt," Hope said.

"What?"

"It's Trent in a tool belt," Hope insisted. "That's the problem. You think he's cute."

"Trent has always been a good-looking man," Faith countered. "I know that. I don't think that's it."

"I was giving an easy out there," Hope said with a sympathetic smile. "The other option is you just really miss him."

Faith rubbed her hands over her face. She'd had to stop herself from texting him three times last night in those dark, melancholy hours. There was something about Trent that would always make him feel like he was hers...and she had to stop that.

"We weren't happy together," Faith said. "Not ultimately."

"I know."

"And he drove me up the wall. He didn't understand me. Although yesterday he did tell me that he'd truly loved me."

"He told you that?"

She nodded. "And did you know that I'd wanted a baby?"

Hope stilled. "What? No. You never told me that."

"Well, I did." Faith tried to push back the sadness. "And you'll say I was just trying to fill a void in my marriage, and maybe I was a little bit, but I did want to be a mom. I really did—"

Faith's voice broke and she cleared her throat. She hadn't expected to say that out loud, or to have all those old longings come surging back up again. Because even now, she was thinking about Tyke's sweet little toddler ways.

"Did Trent want a baby, too?" Hope asked.

"That's the thing. He kept saying we needed to wait until we could afford a baby better. He was just starting out with his electrical company, and I wanted to start a bookstore..."

"Oh, sweetie..." Hope reached out and took her hand. "And now he's got Tyke."

Faith nodded. "Now, not only does he have Tyke, but he's so deeply happy and satisfied as a dad. He just didn't want to become a dad with me, I guess."

"He didn't have much choice with Tyke, though," Hope said.

"Sure he did. He was a divorced guy running his own business. He could have said no."

Hope nodded.

"And he's happy now," Faith said. "I mean, I can see a much deeper satisfaction in him. He's so much more settled. And the way he looks at Tyke…" She smiled faintly. "I'm happy for him."

"Are you?" Hope asked.

"I'm trying to be," Faith replied with a faint smile. "That's got to count for something."

Hope laughed and shook her head. "That's more honest. And I can tell that you are happy for him. But he broke your heart, too, so… There's that."

Faith went to the window and looked out onto the street. The buggy was on its way back again, the horse clopping along cheerily, metal horseshoes ringing against the pavement. An Amish man sat in the front of the open buggy, a couple of bakery boxes on the seat next to him. So her guess had been right about where the buggy had been headed. She'd missed this town.

"So what kept you up last night?" Faith asked, turning back to her sister.

"Do you think I made a mistake?" Hope asked quietly.

"A mistake in what?" Faith asked, though she had a feeling she knew about what.

"In marrying Peter," she replied. "When I was planning the wedding, was there any point where you thought I was making a phenomenal mistake?"

Faith froze. "That's not really a fair question. We hardly knew him, and you two were getting married so fast! So of course I was caught off guard, and maybe I wasn't as generous about your happiness as I should have been at first—"

"I'm not trying to catch you out in something," Hope said. "I'm serious. Because I'm wondering if maybe I got married too quickly."

"But you love him," Faith said softly.

"I really do!" Hope's lips trembled. "But I hardly see him! He took three weeks with me after the wedding, and then he was gone for work again three weeks at a time. He's home for a few days, and then gone again. I've never been more lonely, and I'm a newlywed!"

Loneliness in marriage seemed to be a family theme here. Except Faith had crawled into bed next to her husband for three years and still managed to feel utterly lonely.

"He calls you," Faith said. "He texts you."

As if on cue, Hope's pocket pinged. She pulled out her cell phone and held it up. He'd texted her an emoji heart and said, "Good morning, baby."

Hope's expression softened, and Faith felt a sad tug at her own heart.

"I do love him," Hope said quietly. "Am I overly emotional lately?"

"I don't know," Faith replied. "I hate that when we women are upset about something, it's always dismissed as us being emotional. Some things are worth being emotional about."

Husbands, marriages, feeling loved and appreciated—those things merited some emotion, in Faith's humble opinion.

Hope typed something into her phone, and then it rang.

"It's him," Hope said.

"Go talk to your husband," Faith said with a smile, and her sister picked up the call, fluttered her fingers at Faith, and slipped out of the room again.

Faith exhaled a soft sigh. Whatever troubles that Hope was having with Peter, Faith didn't want to see those two split up. Hope was frustrated and lonely... But divorce could be lonelier still. Faith would never wish a divorce on anyone.

She might as well have her own shower and get ready for the day. She stifled a yawn. Trent would be here in a couple of hours, and in spite of her tumultuous feelings around her ex-husband, she felt a little cheerier at the prospect of seeing him again, too.

She *really* had to stop that!

CHAPTER SEVENTEEN

Trent surveyed the store, checking his clipboard and ticking off each outlet and light fixture that they'd completed rewiring. Thinking about the electrical grid was less complicated right now than his feelings. Yesterday had gotten out of control. He wasn't sure exactly when it had happened, but something had changed between him and Faith, and if Tyke hadn't distracted them, Trent would have kissed her...

The worst part? He kind of wished he'd tried! But that was dumb, because she probably wouldn't have let him. But getting her mad would have at least set him straight, because having Faith be all sweet and understanding wasn't helping matters. There had always been a powerful draw between them, and that had never been enough.

Work-wise, it had been a busy morning, and lunchtime was looming. He was getting hungry, and he had a particularly good sandwich waiting for him. Maybe that could settle him into a better headspace.

After this, he and Eddie were moving upstairs to rewire the apartment. He glanced upward.

He remembered her bottles of shampoo and various skincare products that had been stored in a basket beside the tub when they'd been married. He used to like the way they made the bathroom smell when it was all steamy still from her shower, and she'd come out in a thick terry cloth robe and a towel wrapped around her head... And there was the way she always left the kitchen washcloth hanging over the tap. Silly details to remember. Sillier still to miss, he realized, and he tried to push them back.

Faith stood in front of a quilt, her arms crossed and a thoughtful look on her face.

"It's nice to know who Rose Lapp was. It gives the quilt a little extra something, doesn't it?" she said thoughtfully.

"What's that?" Elaine looked up from a display of old tins. Trent recognized the tins from lard, from motor oil, from canned tomatoes, coffee, tobacco... He'd noticed one large, brightly painted tin that had survived quite well that had been used for cigars. Back before anyone worried about what they'd do with all those accumulated metal containers over the decades.

"It's kind of neat to know the story behind Rose Lapp," Faith repeated.

"I like how the Amish make sure everyone is taken care of," Elaine replied. "When tragedy strikes, they take care of each other. The community would have gotten behind that second marriage and helped them set up a new home."

"What if she wasn't done grieving, though?" Hope put in. "The answer isn't always another marriage."

Trent glanced over at the sisters. It did feel a bit odd to be in the middle of this dynamic again. He'd missed it, truth be told. He'd enjoyed Faith's family. Her sisters had started to feel like his own.

"With five kids to feed, it would have been practical, though," Faith was saying. "But that did occur to me, too. I mean, you love a man with everything you've got, lose him to a tragic accident, and then have to simply move on to keep the kids fed..."

Love him with everything you've got... Did Faith know what that felt like? Had she ever loved him that much?

"I'd say it was a harsher time, but I think it still works like that with the Amish," Elaine said. "When someone dies, the surviving spouse and kids need support."

"The community helps out financially and with childcare or help doing farmwork," Faith said. "But how long can they keep doing that? There is a practical side to it."

"Still—marriage is deeply intimate," Hope said, some emotion entering her tone. "I can't imagine marrying a man just for some physical provision. That's a little cold."

"It's easy enough for you to say that," Elaine replied. "You're very well provided for in your marriage."

"Except I didn't marry him for that!" Hope shot back. "Sure, he makes good money, and I live very comfortably as a result, but I married him because I love him. And I'd be willing to live in a cardboard box just to be with him."

"A cardboard box?" Elaine rolled her eyes. "Let's say you'd be willing to live in a two-bedroom apartment. You know, so you'd have an office space, and maybe an extra bathroom."

The air just about sparked with the glare that Hope shot in her younger sister's direction. Trent purposefully turned his back on the conversation, trying to focus on his work.

"What do you know what I'm willing to do?" Hope snapped. "I did not marry Peter for comfort. I married him because I love him!"

"All I'm saying is, there's romance, and then there's just being stupid," Elaine retorted. "You said you'd live in a cardboard box with him. And I'm saying that you wouldn't. Come on. A cardboard box? You're standing by that?"

"Yes!"

"A cardboard box... That's not the slightest exaggeration?"

Trent refused to turn around. He knew they'd all be glaring at each other, and he was not about to be pulled into this.

"What do you think, Trent?" Faith asked, her voice just a little louder than it needed to be.

He cleared his throat and looked over his shoulder innocently. "What?"

"What do you think?" Faith asked.

"About...cardboard boxes?" he asked feebly.

All three women turned their attention to him, and that was not a safe position to be in.

"I don't know," Trent said. "I think that it depends on whether the guy is doing his best or not. I mean, if he's got ample opportunity to work, but he's choosing the box, then choosing him and the box would be foolish, right?"

"My point exactly," Elaine said. "Thank you."

Faith looked disgruntled, but he wasn't even sure why. This whole conversation was about a hypothetical situation! But you know what—maybe he could identify with a guy who could only offer a quality cardboard box right now. He sure felt that way these days. He hadn't been enough. He hadn't had enough. Whatever it was, his wife had chosen to leave.

"But then, let's say something happened that was entirely out of his control," Trent went on, turning to face them and crossing his arms over his chest. "Let's say he'd done his best and life just kicked his legs out from under him. That does happen, you know. A man might start in a box and end up in a mansion. But even if he didn't, that would be loyalty for his woman to stand by him."

Faith froze and slowly turned toward him again. Men didn't have it easy, either. They were supposed to provide, support, be romantic and give a woman a life she could be proud of. That was an awful lot for one man to do—heaven knew he'd tried.

"Unless the problem wasn't the cardboard box at all," Faith countered, and her voice shook slightly. "Maybe it was something else entirely. Women aren't so shallow as to walk away based on money. Not a good woman, at least."

"So why is she walking away, then?" he asked, spreading his hands.

"Maybe it was their relationship," Faith said. "Maybe she didn't feel seen or heard."

She'd said that before, but he *had* been listening! And he had cared. Was this what she told people about him—that he was some unfeeling lout who hadn't even listened to her?

"Maybe he'd done his absolute best to give her everything he could possibly give her," he retorted. "Maybe he'd worked his tail off, built up his own business, bought her the wedding ring set she really wanted even though it cost twice what he could afford. Maybe he'd even tried to make sure she was able to reach her own personal ambitions—"

"Maybe she didn't need his help with that!" Faith snapped, her voice rising. "And maybe all she'd ever wanted was his heart." Tears welled up and Faith irritably looked away from him.

Hope and Elaine were both silent. From downstairs, Trent could hear Eddie's boots on the steps as he headed up to the main floor.

This had really gotten out of control. He and Faith were staring at each other, his heart thudding in his own ears. Eddie appeared in the doorway, and he glanced around the silent shop.

"Did I hear someone talking about cardboard boxes?" Eddie asked hesitantly. "Because if you've got some extras, my cousin is moving and needs some."

All eyes swung toward Eddie, and the younger man took a physical step backward.

"Not exactly what we were talking about," Trent muttered, and he stalked over toward the front door. He didn't actually need anything from his truck, but he could use a breath of fresh air, and maybe two minutes to get his temper back under control.

"What was that?" Trent heard Hope ask as he let the door swing shut behind him, closing off whatever answer Faith would give.

He headed over to the truck and leaned back against the tailgate, breathing deeply. The sound of hooves ringing against the asphalt behind him was soothing, but he didn't look up until the buggy pulled up by the curb right in front of him.

"Hi, Trent."

He startled and looked up to see his cousin Sarah pulling her buggy up next to the sidewalk ahead of his truck. She wore the same pink dress he'd seen her in that morning when he'd dropped off Tyke, except she'd added a crisp white apron to her ensemble. She'd taken the courting buggy—that was the little open-top two-seater. He pushed back his bad mood and squinted into the sunlight. Had there been an accident or something?

"What's going on?" he asked. "Is Tyke okay?"

"*Yah*, Tyke's fine," Sarah said, hopping down and heading around to tie up the horse at one of the regular hitching posts along the side of the street. "He's with Mamm. I just came to town for lunch."

"Oh, okay," he said with a short laugh. "Sorry, I just automatically jumped to the worst-case scenario there, didn't I?"

The front door to the store opened then with the soft tinkle of the overhead bell and Faith same outside. She shaded her eyes with one hand.

"Hi, Sarah," she said. "What brings you by?"

"Lunch," Sarah said, and she reached up into the buggy and pulled down a covered basket. "Is Eddie inside?"

"Yeah, he's...in there," Faith said, gesturing vaguely behind her.

"Danke," she said with a smile. "Do you mind if I go in and find him?"

"No problem, go on in," Faith replied.

Sarah shot Trent a sweet smile and headed into the shop, the picnic basket at her side. As the door swung shut again after her, Faith shot him a questioning look.

"I have no idea," he said with a shrug. "You know as much as I do."

"Huh..." Faith headed over to tailgate and leaned against it next to him. "I came out to apologize."

"Forget it," he replied.

"Thanks, but I really am sorry," she said. "I don't know where that came from. I really did think I'd sorted out my feelings around our divorce. I didn't mean to get into it with you."

"Neither did I," he said.

Faith dropped her gaze, her arms crossed over her chest, and for a moment they just stood there in the warm sunlight in silence.

"I didn't leave because I thought you weren't providing well enough."

"Okay," he said. He wasn't sure he even wanted to talk about this.

"I mean it. You were a good provider. You did your best."

"Why am I feeling like you're patting me on the head?" he asked.

Faith rolled her eyes. "I don't know. That's on you."

"I know you wanted more," he said. "We'd talked about having kids, and—"

"And you were adamant that we couldn't afford it," she said.

"I mean, could we?" he asked. "I'd just started my business, we were paying off debt, you had dreams of a bookstore—"

"And when you didn't want a baby with me?" Her gaze flickered up toward him uncertainly, and then she looked quickly away.

"We would have had to fight over custody, too," he pointed out.

"Did you know we'd end up divorced back then?" she asked. "Did you see it coming?"

Trent shook his head. "No, but I was afraid that

a baby would only make things harder between us. I figured if we had a baby, we'd end up split up."

And irony was, they'd split up anyway. So maybe it was for the best he hadn't given in to her request to start their family. It would be a whole lot worse right now if they were arguing over custody time and child support payments.

Faith didn't answer, but she looked grim.

"I've learned something with Tyke, though," Trent went on. "You're never actually ready for a kid—not financially or emotionally. I didn't take him in because I was ready, but I did figure it out."

The shop door opened and Eddie and Sarah came outside, that basket now in Eddie's hand, swinging between them.

"Just taking lunch, boss," Eddie said.

"Yeah, sure," Trent replied.

Sarah looked a little shy, and Eddie looked rather proud of himself as they ambled down the sidewalk together. There was a little park about a block up the road, and Trent was willing to bet they'd end up there on a bench.

Faith watched them walk away with a sad look on her face.

"If someone had warned you that it would never work between us, would you have listened?" she asked quietly.

Would he have? His family had all adored Faith from the start. There'd been no warnings at all. But what if they had seen all this pain coming?

"Nah," he said. "I was head over heels about you. I would have taken my chances."

And when he looked down at her, he caught her gaze locked on him, her eyes wide. He'd surprised her, had he? What was the point in lying to her? He'd always told her the truth, and he had no intention of stopping now.

"I loved you, Faith," he said. "I loved you so much it hurt. Did you really not know that?"

She licked her lips and dropped her gaze. For a moment, she didn't move. Then she pushed herself off the back of the truck.

"Well, that was a long time ago," she said.

But it hadn't been that long ago, and while he'd done his best to stop loving her, he wasn't sure he'd succeeded.

Faith headed toward the store, and Trent's gaze followed Sarah and Eddie's retreating forms. When young people were in love, there was no warning them. It was a fact of life.

CHAPTER EIGHTEEN

As FAITH HEADED back into the shop, Elaine looked out the window in the direction Sarah and Eddie had gone.

"Everything okay?" Elaine asked.

"Yeah, it's fine," Faith said.

But was it fine? He'd loved her so much it hurt… That's what he'd said. Her heart fluttered in her chest. Did he know what words like that did to a woman? But he'd always been rather smooth when she least expected it, and that annoying tendency of his was throwing her off-balance.

"So what's up with Eddie and the Amish girl?" Elaine asked.

"That's Trent's cousin," Faith replied. "And her parents are going to hate it."

"I'll bet," Hope murmured. "Well, good luck to them."

"I don't think even luck will make that work out," Faith replied. "Sarah has already joined the Amish faith, so if she dates—or heaven forbid marries—an Englisher guy, she'll be shunned."

Hope and Elaine sobered, and Hope sighed and reached for her purse.

"Are you going to break for lunch, too?" Hope asked.

Faith shook her head. "Nope. I'm not hungry."

"I'm starving," Hope said. "I was thinking of getting the soup and bread deal at the Amish bakery."

That did sound good, but Faith didn't have the strength to make small talk with her sisters right now, and she didn't want to talk about these swirling, unfair emotions that she couldn't quite get a handle on, either. Trent was in her past. He was her ex. Whatever seemed to be stewing up afresh was not real. They'd already chosen to part ways, for crying out loud!

"You two go ahead," Faith said. "I'll make myself a sandwich upstairs later."

"Suit yourself," Elaine said.

Faith's sisters headed outside, leaving her in solitude. If anything, Faith should learn from Sarah and Eddie. She could see that there was absolutely no hope for them, yet the two of them seemed determined to ignore the fact. Would it save them in the end? Of course not. They'd both be crushed and heartbroken, and it could all have been avoided if they'd just been rational from the start.

But who was rational when they were in love?

The rotary phone beneath the counter started to ring and Faith picked it up.

"Amish Antiques, Faith speaking," she said.

"Hi, Faith, it's Mary."

It took Faith a moment to place the name, but then she recognized Mary Yoder's voice.

"Mary! How are you?"

"I'm good," Mary said. "I came out to the phone shanty to call you. We have a few more items we dug out of the basement that Albrecht thinks might interest you."

"That would be great," she said.

"Um..." Mary sounded a little hesitant. "There was one other thing I wanted to ask you about, and since Sarah is in town running some errands, this is my chance to talk to you alone."

Running errands? Was that what Sarah had told her mother?

"Of course," Faith replied. "What's going on?"

"Albrecht and I have been talking about it, and it looks like Sarah is feeling much more for this Eddie boy than is entirely safe. I know this might sound offensive to you, but she can't just marry someone outside of our faith. It's not just our preference, it's not done. She'd be shunned, and that would be truly awful." Mary's voice shook.

"I understand that," Faith said. "Don't worry about hurting my feelings."

"There are times when a young woman just won't listen to her mother," Mary said. "She has to make her own decisions, but I don't think she appreciates the heartbreak in store for her if she keeps this up. And I was hoping you might talk to her."

"About what, specifically?" Faith asked. She

wasn't the one to talk to a young woman about the pain of an Amish shunning.

"About divorce."

Faith froze. "So you're going to admit that I'm divorced now?" Faith asked quietly. "I thought you were all pretending it hadn't happened?"

"Faith, we know that you and Trent have split up." Mary's voice was just as quiet. "We hate it. We hope you find your way back together. That's all very true. But you understand how badly it hurts when a marriage falls apart. In our community, there is no divorce. There is a very different kind of pain when a woman chooses badly in marriage, because there is no escape. It's a vow for life. But if my daughter married an Englisher, and if their differences were too great, she could very well find herself divorced. And if she was divorced, she could never come back and remarry here. Remarriage is not allowed with Amish unless your spouse is dead."

"I can see how much she stands to lose," Faith said. "But what makes you think she'd listen to me?"

"She always looked up to you. All I'm asking is that you explain to her what it's like to go through a divorce," Mary said. "Sarah deserves to have all the information, and in this situation, we can't tell her everything she needs to know."

Faith had been wondering how she could pay this family back for all they'd done for her, and this was her opportunity.

"I'll do my best," Faith said. "The next time I see her—"

"Could you come for dinner tonight?" Mary asked hopefully. "Bring Trent with you. He has to come pick up Tyke anyway, and I'm making a pot roast."

The front door to the store opened and Trent came back inside with an opened can of Coke in one hand.

"I can ask him," Faith replied. "And sure, I'll come by for dinner, then. I can't promise it'll work, but I can talk to her."

"*Danke*, Faith," Mary said. "I'd better get back. Albrecht is feeding Tyke, and sometimes a woman needs to supervise that."

Faith chuckled. "Understood. I'll see you all later."

She hung up the phone and Trent glanced over at her. She could see the curiosity on his face, but he was trying to hide it.

"That was your aunt Mary," Faith said. "She's invited us for dinner tonight."

"Us?" His eyebrows went up, then he sighed. "Don't feel in any way obliged to play along with this. I know how they are, but—"

"She wants me to talk to Sarah about how hard it is to get divorced," Faith said.

"Oh…" Trent exhaled a long breath. "So they're accepting that we're divorced now?"

"Well, for Sarah's sake, they want her to see how

tough it is," Faith replied. "But she said they still want us to get back together."

Trent stayed sober and shook his head. "You don't have to do this, Faith."

"I know, but I owe them," she replied, her gaze moving toward the window again, and her mind following after the young couple. "Besides, if we can spare those two a little bit of heartbreak, shouldn't we try?"

"We?" Trent asked, and when she didn't take his bait, he shrugged. "I doubt they'd listen."

"Your aunt pointed out that there isn't anyone in the community who can tell Sarah how tough it is to break up," Faith said. "No one can explain how much that hurts."

That was a bitter truth. The Amish simply didn't break up after marriage. They might struggle with typical marital problems, but divorce was simply not the answer. They found solutions, and it was starting to make Faith wonder if maybe she should have looked harder for solutions herself in those lonesome days instead of giving up. But even allowing the thought to enter her mind tore at fresh, tender scars, and she pushed the thought back.

It was too late now, anyway.

"So we're to be the example of pain, are we?" Trent asked.

"It might be a step in the right direction for them accepting our divorce," she said softly.

Although she'd grudgingly enjoyed visiting a place where the clock seemed to have reversed, both in how they lived, and that they still treated her and Trent like a married couple. That had been oddly sweet... And while she knew it wasn't healthy, being Trent's "wife" again had soothed a place deep in her heart that had ached for the last two years straight.

"Okay, fine." Trent's gaze warmed in a way that made her stomach flip. "Dinner at my aunt and uncle's place. What could go wrong?"

CHAPTER NINETEEN

EDDIE RETURNED TO the antiques shop after lunch with a goofy grin on his face and a faraway look in his eye that didn't bode well. Not only was this awkward for Trent, but it shouldn't be his business! Eddie was his apprentice, and Sarah was his cousin. He was mildly annoyed that Eddie couldn't find a woman to moon over who wasn't related to his boss.

"We'll need to start on the apartment next," Trent said, and he glanced toward Faith, who was arranging some linens on display on a quilt rack. "Is that okay?"

"Um... Yes. Of course," Faith said. "Let me just check on things really quickly?"

Trent smiled. "Sure."

Faith was a generally tidy person, but he understood the vulnerability of letting someone into her personal space. Especially him. She disappeared up the side stairs.

"How was lunch?" Trent asked Eddie.

"Good." Eddie met his gaze a tad defiantly. "*Really* good."

"How's my cousin?" he asked.

"Sarah's doing well," Eddie said, cracking just a bit. "She brought lunch for us. Have you had that peanut butter spread they make?"

"Yeah, Amish peanut butter is really good," Trent replied. "It's a bit sweet for me, though. Makes my teeth hurt."

"It's delicious," Eddie said. "It was really nice of her to come by like that."

"You didn't ask her to?" Trent asked, surprised.

"Well, I mentioned that she could come by any time to say hi," Eddie said. "I didn't expect her to bring food!"

"Amish people will feed you," Trent said, but a nagging worry had set in. Sarah was definitely interested in Eddie as more than just an Englisher friend. Amish girls didn't bring picnics for guys who had been friend-zoned. Aunt Mary might have a right to be worried.

"If I were to bring her family a gift of some sort," Eddie asked, "what would they appreciate?"

"You don't need to—"

"Hey, if I were to," Eddie interrupted. "I know I don't have to. I know they don't like the idea of me and Sarah dating. I understand all that. I'm not an idiot. But if I were to try and win them over, how would I do that?"

"You can't," Trent said quietly. "They're Amish. You're not. There is no middle ground there when it comes to Sarah's heart."

"Okay..." Eddie frowned. "But I'm thinking Sarah wouldn't waste her own time on me if she weren't enjoying my company. And she wouldn't just toy with me if she didn't think there was some hope. So maybe Amish people typically don't encourage this, but I'm just looking at Sarah, here. And I think there's a chance."

Trent sighed and rubbed a hand over his face. "Okay... I get that. But Sarah's dad is going to have his own ideas about this."

"With all due respect, I'm not trying to date her dad. I'm trying to date her."

Trent smiled at the humor there, but Eddie really didn't understand the culture he was trying to infiltrate.

"If you wanted to bring something they'd like, maybe food—Amish people love pizza and burgers. They don't eat out a lot, so that's a treat."

Eddie nodded. "Okay. Thanks. I appreciate it."

For whatever it was worth. Because while Eddie was definitely falling for Sarah, she came with a whole family—a whole community—who wouldn't support the match. But maybe Eddie was going to have to get his heart shredded to see the light.

Faith came back down the stairs and gestured to the staircase. She met his gaze for a split second, then stepped back. "Be my guest."

"Did you want to come with us?" Trent asked.

"No, no, it's fine," Faith said. "I have work to do down here. I trust your professionalism."

"All right," Trent said. "Eddie, let's get the electrical map and I'll get you to grab the 14-2 and the 12-2 spools of cable and meet me up there."

Trent headed up first, and he let himself into the apartment. He'd been up here before her aunt had died, so he knew the layout and had a map of the outlets, but it felt different now. He could smell the faint scent of her perfume—she hadn't changed it. And he spotted a couple of her items—a quilt that had been made to look like a bookshelf with different-colored book spines visible thrown over the back of the couch. That had been a birthday gift from her mother one year. But the furniture was all her great-aunt's. And when he glanced in the kitchen, he saw the dishcloth hanging over the tap...

That was like a punch in the chest.

"Cut it out," he muttered to himself. Eddie wasn't the only one letting his heart play around where it shouldn't.

Eddie came into the apartment and dropped the spools of electrical cable onto the wooden floor with a thunk.

"Let's start with the kitchen today," Trent said. It was the least personal place in the apartment.

He headed into the room—the window over the sink overlooking the parking lot in the back of the store. It wasn't much of a view back there, but the window did let in ample sunlight.

On the counter were a couple of dishes—some water glasses, and a mug he recognized. It was the mug Faith had used every morning for her coffee—it sported a Jane Austen quote: "The person, be it gentleman or lady, who has not pleasure in a good novel, must be intolerably stupid."

He reached out and touched the handle. Dang. Why did every little item she brought with her have to come with so many memories?

"That's funny," Eddie said, gesturing to the mug.

"Yeah." Trent put the mug into the sink and pulled out his screwdriver to take the outlet plate off the wall.

"How long were you two married?" Eddie asked.

"Three years."

"That's it?"

Trent winced. "Yeah, well... It didn't work out."

"Who broke up with who?" Eddie asked.

"It was mutual."

"So she broke up with you," Eddie said. "That's what 'it's mutual' means. It's never mutual."

"How would you know?" Trent asked. "You're a kid."

"I'm twenty-two."

"Like I said, a kid." Trent shot him a rueful smile. He was not taking any gentle ribbing from anyone about his divorce.

"Divorces are complicated," Trent went on, focusing on the outlet. "It's different after vows. I know you probably won't believe that, but getting married and promising before your friends, family and the American government that you'll love and take care of that woman for the rest of your life really changes how breakups work."

"Sarah was telling me how the Amish don't divorce," he said. "It's beautiful."

"It's idealistic," Trent retorted.

"It's a fact," Eddie countered. "They don't."

"And maybe they don't get the kind of love that they want, either," Trent said. "Being stuck with one person isn't the same as choosing to stay with one person."

Eddie was silent.

"I'm not bashing the Amish ways. Half my family is Amish," Trent added. "I know how beautiful it all looks from the outside. I'm just saying that marriage is more complicated. I didn't want Faith staying with me because she had no other choice. I wanted her there because she wanted to live her life with me."

Eddie glanced over at him. "Yeah, I get that. So what happened?"

"We were too different," Trent said. "Not that this is your business, but it might help you to know how this works. Sometimes, you and a woman you love a whole lot are so different that you can't make it work."

Eddie settled down in front of another outlet and started to unscrew the plate.

"I think when she's the right one, though, it just works," the younger man said.

Trent pressed his lips together. No, it didn't just work. And what made a woman the right one? Faith had been the only woman to make his heart soar, the only woman he'd ever even considered committing to, and when he'd married her, he'd meant it with every atom of his being. Sometimes it didn't "just work."

"Don't you think?" Eddie asked.

"You don't want to know what I think about that."

"Because you're all bitter now that you're divorced?" Eddie asked, leaning back. "I'm asking. Hit me with it."

"Look, Eddie, I can tell you've really fallen for my cousin," Trent said. "You're right—I am bitter and divorced. I don't want to dampen your enthusiasm or your belief in romance. That's a beautiful thing. But when you're from different worlds, it doesn't matter how much you love a girl."

"What if she loves me?"

"Does she?" Trent asked.

Eddie didn't answer, and Trent sincerely hoped it hadn't gone that far. But again, this wasn't supposed to be his business. Let Eddie learn the hard way, if he insisted upon it. Besides, Sarah's parents were already working in the background to make sure Sarah opened her eyes to reality.

One of them would have to face it...

And Trent wasn't heartless. He sympathized with Eddie's situation. He knew what it felt like to fall in love head over heels. But he also knew what it felt like when that ended. And that was the pain he was trying to spare him.

But it might already be too late for that.

CHAPTER TWENTY

When it was time to head out to the Yoder farm for dinner, Faith went upstairs and got changed into a tea-length floral dress. She'd always liked it, and it was cut conservatively, which was kind of a must when visiting an Amish family. They'd never be so rude as to comment on a woman's clothing, but when you were around a dinner table with everyone else in Amish dress, the neckline mattered.

Faith pulled her hair up into a twist as Hope and Elaine watched her from the doorway.

"What are you two doing tonight?" Faith asked her sisters.

"We're going to a movie," Elaine replied. "We've got to keep that old theater in business."

"That sounds fun." Faith reached for a simple gold chain and did up the clasp behind her neck. Her gaze moved toward a tool bag that Trent had left in the hallway. It felt strange having some masculine reminder of him in this apartment... And it stung a little, too.

"This is a date, you know," Elaine said.

"It is not," Faith replied. "I'm going there to eat

dinner and to tell Sarah exactly how much it hurts when a marriage ends. That's not a date."

"You're going with your ex-husband," Elaine said. "Dinner...with Trent."

"He's part of the lesson," she countered. "Besides, he has to pick up Tyke."

"She's cute when she decides to be blind," Elaine said, casting a rueful smile in Hope's direction.

"Tell me about it," Hope replied with a low laugh. "Faith, have you not noticed how he looks at you?"

"How he looks at you *still*," Elaine amended.

"You know why he's here! He's rewiring the place," Faith said. "You aren't being fair."

"We know why he's here between the hours of nine and five," Elaine replied. "But there seems to be a whole lot of extracurricular time spent together. That's what you can't explain away so easily. And tonight, you're doing yourself up like you're getting ready for a date."

Faith froze with her lipstick held aloft in front of her face. "I'm making myself presentable."

"This is very Amish-appropriate—the lipstick, the jewelry."

"This is the highest neckline I own!" Faith snapped.

Hope and Elaine both broke into laughter, and Faith irritably finished applying her makeup. There was nothing wrong with looking nice. There was nothing wrong with letting her ex-husband eat his heart out, either. Faith pressed her lips together and recapped her lipstick.

"I don't have to dress like an Amish woman to have dinner with an Amish family," Faith said. "And as for Trent and I, we have history. Nothing is going to erase that, and yes, we probably do have to find a new balance between us. I'm back in Apfelkuchen for at least as much time as it takes for us to run this store together, and Trent and I can't just sullenly avoid each other. So… We're doing our best. I'm sorry if it isn't as graceful as you might like, but it is what it is."

"We're just teasing," Hope said, softening her tone.

"Speak for yourself. I'm making a solid point," Elaine said.

"We're *teasing*!" Hope said more firmly. "But maybe you should know that Trent does look at you like you're the whole world. And dressed like this tonight, it's not going to help matters. You look amazing."

"I'll take that as a compliment," Faith replied. "Thanks."

She glanced at her perfume. If she were alone in this room, she'd put on a spritz, but with her sisters watching, she felt like she'd only make their point. So she grabbed her purse and slipped past her sisters, and headed out of the bedroom.

"I'm not dating my ex-husband," Faith said.

"Is it nice to see him again?" Elaine asked. The teasing had left her tone.

It was more than nice. It was filling up a place

in her heart that she'd banished to emptiness. And that was dangerous.

"It is," Faith admitted. "But that's where it stops. I'll see you two later."

Faith headed out the front door and pulled it shut behind her. The narrow staircase led toward the daylight-illuminated foyer below. Her sandals tapped against the wooden stairs as she started down.

Her sisters knew her too well, and she wasn't keen on discussing all these confusing emotions right now. She was on her way to explain to a young woman that divorce was a deep wound. Maybe she could use the reminder, too, just to keep herself moving forward.

CHAPTER TWENTY-ONE

As Faith hopped up into the passenger side of Trent's truck, Trent's eyebrows went up and he gave her a once-over. Then he put the truck into gear and leaned forward to look over his shoulder before he pulled onto the road.

"I always did like that dress," he said.

Faith looked down at the dress—peach colored with a summery floral pattern. It was an older one... She was surprised he remembered it.

"It's the highest neckline I own," she said, feeling like a broken record.

"It's also really pretty," he said. "Didn't you get that for my brother's wedding?"

"Oh, that's right," she said, surprised. She'd forgotten that. It had been a beautiful summer backyard wedding, and she and Trent had sat side by side, watching the couple say their vows...

She glanced at him, but his attention was on the road as he pulled up to a four-way stop with an Amish buggy waiting.

"I feel like a bum," he said. "I'm not dressed for dinner."

"That's okay," she said. "You worked hard all day. Your uncle and aunt will appreciate that."

"Yeah..." He pulled onto the narrow highway and settled back into his seat. "It's nice having you around again."

"I thought I'd be cramping your style," she said.

"I don't have much style to cramp these days," he replied with a low laugh. "And I missed you."

"You missed me?" she asked, and she felt her middle warm.

Trent's hands tightened on the steering wheel, and he grimaced. "I didn't mean to say that."

Somehow, she didn't think about him missing her. She thought about him being angry, perhaps, or his moving on. Not the loneliness. That had felt like her burden alone.

When she didn't respond, he murmured, "Of course I missed you."

"Well, I missed you, too," she said.

Trent glanced toward her and he smiled faintly. "Good."

She laughed at that and turned her attention out the window. They'd left town behind, and they'd moved into farmland now—this stretch of fields being a young, green wheat crop. Wind ruffled over the waving grasses, rippling like water. Leave it to Trent to get the last word in. He was always good at that. But she had missed him—even though she tried so very hard not to.

"I missed the way you hung your dishcloth in the kitchen," he said.

She tore her gaze from the farmland. "What?"

"You had this way of hanging it up so that it would dry faster, but it would droop over the front of the tap."

"You hated that," she countered.

They used to bicker over that stupid dishcloth. He'd liked to fold it once and drape it over the side of the sink. She'd liked it hung over the tap. She thought it dried better that way, he thought it was gross having a moist dishcloth hanging down like that when he wanted to get a glass of water. They'd both dug their heels in over it. It was ridiculous—she could see that now. But it had been a button.

"I know I hated it. I still missed it."

She shook her head. "You could always hang your own dishcloth over the tap, you know. You don't need me do it."

"I could," he said, and he shot her a rueful smile. "But it's gross."

"That is what drove me up the wall!" she said, half laughing. "You don't make sense."

"I guess it just reminded me of you," he said. "And once you'd moved out, there were little reminders of you everywhere."

"Yeah... I know that feeling." She exhaled a sad breath. "For me, it was your shaver that you always left out. I hated that, but when I had a bathroom to myself to arrange just how I wanted it, I missed those little masculine things that take up space and clutter up the counter."

"But you got used to all that space and tidiness, I'm sure." His tone was lighter again.

"Of course," she said with a forced laugh, and her mind went back to that tool bag in her hallway. It was in the way. One of them was bound to trip over it, but it was still strangely comforting.

In fact, she'd been telling herself that this divorce was what she needed, what she wanted. That the next man she committed to would have to be a bit cleaner, to boot. And then she'd go and stare at that clean counter and she'd get that swell of melancholy. She'd been hoping time would heal that wound, but it hadn't yet.

"I'm actually glad to have you along for dinner tonight," he said. "My family can't give me the third degree with you there."

"To be fair, Mary invited me. You're the one along for the ride tonight."

He belted out a laugh. "All the same, I'm getting a little bit tired of being invited over for dinner at various family members' homes and having them either ask about you, ask when I last talked to you and hint wildly that I might want to try and fix things…or be set up with someone's work friend."

"Do they try and set you up?" She tried to keep her tone neutral, but she did feel a little prick of jealousy. Not that she had a right to it.

"Of course. Well, the non-Amish side of the family does. I'm single. They have to fix me. Don't you get that, too?"

Not as much as she would have liked. No one was too bent on finding her a new man.

"My sisters miss having you around," she said instead. "You're hard to replace, it would seem."

A slow smile spread across his face.

"Oh, cut that out," she laughed. "I will replace you, Trent."

And she did intend to. She wasn't going to sit around being lonely and sad for too much longer. Her heart had been broken, and she'd been nursing that, but she wasn't about to waste the rest of her life with a broken heart, either. This hurt too much to linger in any longer than she had to.

"I'm sure you will." But a smile twitched at his lips anyway.

The wheat field stopped at a barbed wire fence and turned into pasture dotted with black-and-white cattle. This was Yoder land now, and she recognized their drive up ahead.

"Are you ready to set Sarah straight on all the pitfalls of marrying the wrong guy?" Trent looked over at her, and this time, despite the joking tone, she saw a glimmer of sadness in those brown eyes that brought a lump to her throat.

"I guess I'll have to be," she said.

This was why she had been invited over, after all. But somehow it felt like a betrayal to the time she'd spent married to Trent, all the same. It wasn't all bad. It wasn't all frustration and argument. There had been good times, too.

"It's possible to love a guy with all your heart

and still have it not work out, Trent," she said. "I did love you."

Oh, how she'd loved him. And maybe it was because she'd loved him that much that she'd needed more from him. She'd needed his whole heart. She had to be more than a romantic roommate. And she didn't know what she even meant by that—just that she'd felt the lack, and that lack had constantly hurt.

Trent reached over and caught her hand in his calloused grip. The gesture was so familiar that her heart squeezed almost painfully. His hand was warm and strong, and she had to resist the urge to twine her fingers through his like they used to do in the early days…

And then he let go, slowed and made the turn onto the Yoder driveway.

Time to be a morality tale for an Amish woman who needed the warning.

CHAPTER TWENTY-TWO

Trent hadn't meant to take Faith's hand, but his fingers still tingled from when he'd touched her. He'd always felt this way about Faith—she was like a magnet for him. Even when he could feel things falling apart and he didn't know how to fix them. Even when he could feel her heart slipping through his fingers.

He risked a glance over at her and saw that her cheeks had pinked. Yeah, she'd felt it, too. He'd missed her an awful lot, and she'd admitted to missing him right back. He wasn't sure what any of that meant, but at least he wasn't the only one feeling conflicted. There was mild comfort in that.

Trent pulled to a stop beside the house in a patch of dappled shade. Beyond was the corral with three horses inside, and past that was green lawn and a big vegetable garden. Mary and Sarah spent a lot of time out there weeding, watering and tending to the plants. That crop would end up in glass canning jars in their basement that fall and would feed the family through winter. His aunt's dill pickles were to die for.

Trent turned off the engine and looked over at Faith. He wasn't sure what he wanted to say, but he didn't want to leave things like this.

"Tent?" Tyke's little voice called from the direction of the house.

A smile touched Faith's lips. "He spotted you."

Tyke was in the doorway, standing there in only a diaper and a shirt, his plastic truck under one arm. Maybe this interruption was better—it saved Trent from trying to explain himself when he didn't think he could.

"Tent!" Tyke yelled. "Tent!"

That little guy with his excited holler just warmed his heart, and he pushed open his door and got out. Faith did the same from the passenger side.

Aunt Mary materialized behind the toddler and opened the screen door to let him out. A cat slipped past Tyke, making a run into the garden, and Tyke went for the stairs.

"Turn around, Tyke," Mary said. "Put down your toy."

Tyke did as she told him, putting his truck on the step and turning around and going down backward. That was new! And useful. If he could get Tyke to navigate stairs more safely, that would make a lot of things easier. The toddler grabbed his toy again and came running across the scrubby grass toward them, and Trent caught Tyke up in his arms.

"Hi, buddy," he said. "Did you have a good day?"

"I got my tuck," Tyke said, and he smacked the truck against Trent's shoulder. He winced.

"Ouch. I see that. Did you have fun with your truck today?"

In response, Tyke started to make some wet truck noises, then accidentally dropped his truck, and it fell with a clatter behind him.

"I've got it," Faith said, picking it up as she followed Trent toward the house.

Teamwork. It felt good to be doing something together with Faith again, and he shouldn't be letting himself feel that, but it couldn't really be helped.

"Hello, how are you?" Mary greeted them. "Come on in, the food is almost ready."

Albrecht stood at a side sink, his hands covered in soapsuds as he washed up. His iron-gray hair looked mussed and sweaty, and there was a hat line around his forehead, but he shot them a welcoming smile.

"Good to see you both," Albrecht said. "Welcome, welcome."

Sarah was setting the table with plates and cutlery and she shot them a smile.

"Hi, Trent! Hi, Faith!" Sarah said. His cousin's gaze trailed behind them, and her smile faded slightly. She'd been hoping to see Eddie, no doubt.

The food already on the table smelled wonderful. There was pot roast, mashed potatoes, bowls of pickled carrots and cauliflower, a big pan of brown buttered noodles and another dish of sliced sausage and vegetables fried up together. His stomach rumbled.

There was a newer-made version of the high

chair that Albrecht had given to Faith set up at the table, and Trent brought Tyke over and attempted to put him into it.

"No!" Tyke hollered giving a kick that almost sent the high chair over.

"What's wrong, Tyke?" Trent asked. "We're eating supper here tonight. I'm going to sit next to you."

He attempted to put him into the chair again, and Tyke arched his back and kicked again.

"Hey, buddy—" Trent said more firmly this time. "That's not okay."

"He's tired," Mary said. "And this has been different than he's used to for two days in a row."

"That's true," Trent said. Tyke didn't deal well with change, considering that a year ago everything in his small life had been turned upside down when Kylie died.

Sarah pulled the high chair away from the table, and Trent took a seat and balanced the toddler on his knee. Maybe this would work better.

"And you can sit here," Sarah said to Faith, tapping the chair next to him.

Sarah gave Trent a coy little smile. She probably thought she was helping the family cause by treating them like a couple still. And maybe she was... Amish family could have two angles going at once. While Sarah was Faith's project tonight, it was possible that Faith and Trent were Sarah's project.

Faith slipped into the seat next to him, and the rest of the family took their places around the table. Albrecht sat at the head, and once everyone was seated, he bowed his head. After a moment of silence, he cleared his throat, and all heads popped back up and they started dishing themselves up.

"Brown buttered noodles, Faith?" Mary asked, passing the dish to her.

"Thanks." Faith dished herself a spoonful, and then without so much as a glance at him to see what he wanted, she added a spoonful to Trent's plate, too. The dish was passed on to Albrecht, and the pot roast came to Faith next.

She did the same—took a piece for herself, then put two pieces onto Trent's—and at that moment seemed to realize what she was doing, because she froze. She looked hesitantly toward him, and Trent tried to smother his grin but wasn't sure he managed it.

"It's fine," he said. "Thanks."

"It's just that your hands are full," she said, nodding to Tyke.

"Yeah, I know. It's appreciated."

The rest of the meal passed in front of him the same way, and he grabbed a dinner roll for Tyke to start eating. Once their plates were filled, Trent tried to give Tyke a bite of noodles, but Tyke made a face and started squirming.

"Come on, Tyke, aren't you hungry?" Trent asked. He took a bite of the noodles, himself, and they were delicious. Then he offered Tyke another bite.

Tyke pushed himself against Trent's arm and flailed in Faith's direction. Tyke was normally a lot easier to please than this, and he had no idea what had gotten into the kid.

"Tyke, this is our meal," Trent said, keeping his voice low. "Leave Faith's food alone."

Faith shot him a grin and took a bite of beef.

"I don't mind," she said.

Well, Trent did. Tyke needed to behave himself, and it looked like he was bent on acting up tonight.

"What did you do when the kids were like this?" he asked his uncle. As the words came out, he realized that the answer might be some sort of discipline, and he wasn't sure how he felt about that.

"Oh, at that age, the *kinner* would eat with me or with Mary—it didn't matter who they ate with," Albrecht said with a shrug. "So long as food went into them. Right, Mary?"

"*Yah*, that's the truth!" Mary said with a light laugh. "It was a team effort to get them fed when they were little. That's why it takes two parents."

And that was all fine and good, except Faith wasn't Tyke's mom or his guardian or any part of the parenting team.

"Hey, Tyke, do you want a carrot?" Sarah asked brightly.

Tyke set up a howl then, and arched his back again, drumming his heels against Trent's leg. Normally Trent had quite a bit of patience with Tyke, but he could feel his own irritation spiking now, too.

"Tyke," he said, keeping his voice low. "Enough!"

But Tyke didn't seem to much care if Trent had

reached his limit or not. And no one else at the table appeared the least bit fazed by the tantrum. Mary passed a dish of pickled cauliflower to her daughter, and Albrecht passed the basket of dinner rolls right over Tyke's head toward Faith, who accepted them with a smile.

Trent smothered his instinct to snap and instead laid Tyke on the ground next to the table to let him howl it out. Tyke started howling even louder then, spinning himself around on the floor in an absolute rage. Trent kept an eye on him, but took a big bite of dinner at the same time. He'd better get food into himself while he could, because it looked like this was going to be a long evening.

Tyke's crying became quieter then, and he rolled over into a little ball, sobbing softly.

"Come sit with me, buddy," Trent said, and when he leaned down to try to touch him, Tyke started to yell again. Tantrum not over, it seemed.

"Tyke?" Faith said.

Tyke opened his eyes mid-holler, and looked at Faith hesitantly.

"Come here, baby," she said, holding out her arms to him, and Tyke boosted himself back up and went hiccupping over to Faith's embrace.

"Do you mind?" Faith asked.

"No, it's fine," Trent replied. But he did mind. He was supposed to be this boy's comfort, and he had been up until Tyke had taken a shine to Faith.

Faith scooped the toddler up into her lap, cuddled him close and offered him a bite of noodles.

Tyke didn't want it, but he did lean his head against her shoulder. She smoothed a hand over his damp curls. Her movements were so easy, so loving, and Tyke seemed to attach himself to something in her feminine touch, settling down into a tired little heap in her arms.

"There you are," Mary said with a smile at Faith. "Sometimes it takes a woman's touch, doesn't it?"

"I'm not sure," Faith said. "I'm not usually the one kids choose, so I guess I'll take the cuddles where I can get them."

"Oh, toddler cuddles are healing," Mary said. "I miss those days, but I get to relive them with my grand*kinner*."

"So, how was your day, Trent?" Albrecht asked.

"Uh—" Trent looked over at Faith once more. "It was good. I'm working on the upstairs now at Faith's shop, so we're a little over halfway done. It was a productive day."

Sarah's cheeks had reddened. She was looking very pointedly at the food on her plate. So she hadn't told her parents about her visit to Eddie, it would seem. Wow, Sarah had a sly side, didn't she? He smiled faintly.

"And your apprentice—Eddie—helps you with all that?" Albrecht asked.

"Yeah, he's really good," Trent replied. He wouldn't lie about his apprentice's skill. "He works hard. I can't complain about him at all."

"And he helps you here at the farm, too, right, Daet?" Sarah added.

"*Yah*, he's pitched in a few times," Albrecht agreed. "He's a hard worker. But he's English, all right."

"Can't be helped. Some of us were born that way," Trent joked.

Albrecht laughed in good humor. "True enough. Can't help the life you were born to. And there is nothing more English than an electrician!"

That was a joke, since the Amish didn't use electricity. Everyone around the table had settled into comfortable companionship. When Faith drained her juice glass, Trent refilled it for her. She gave him a smile of thanks and continued eating one-handed. She managed to get a few bites into Tyke, too.

This would be great—beautiful, even—if he and Faith were together. But this was his challenge, and he didn't want to be leaning on anyone, not even Faith. Maybe especially not Faith.

So what really happened was that Tyke had pitched a fit, and someone on the outside had had to step in and deal with it for him. And while Trent was grateful to Faith for helping him out, this wasn't a long-term solution.

Tyke needed to know that Trent was his answer, and that hadn't happened tonight. So he was happy enough to let it go without saying anything in front of his aunt and uncle, but deep down he felt like he'd failed.

Of course, everyone thought he needed a woman to help him with Tyke, but the truth was, he didn't.

He could do this on his own. He'd accepted a challenge, and he wasn't backing down.

He just hoped that Tyke would grow up to appreciate it.

CHAPTER TWENTY-THREE

HALFWAY THROUGH THE MEAL, Tyke roused himself and slid off Faith's lap. She let him go, and he dropped down into the space between her chair and Trent's and tugged on Trent's arm. Trent scooped him up one-handed, and offered him a bite of beef, which Tyke accepted. Faith shot Trent a smile.

He was good in this role. If their relationship had lasted, he would have made a good father. Not that it mattered now. She dropped her gaze.

"Trent, I wonder if Tyke would like to see some kittens in the barn," Albrecht said, pushing back from the table. He wadded up his cloth napkin and tossed it into a hamper beside the basement stairs.

Trent glanced over at Faith, and she recognized the cue. This was a ploy to get the men out of the house so that Faith could talk with Sarah.

"You go ahead," Faith said. "I can help with dishes."

"Oh, don't worry about that," Sarah said.

"It's no problem," Faith assured her.

Sarah looked nervously toward her mother. Did Sarah think Faith would rat her out?

"Why don't you start on dishes, Sarah, and I'll go out and pick a few strawberries. We can have them later on this evening," Mary said. "It won't take me too long."

"Sure," Sarah replied, and she sounded relieved.

Faith watched as Trent with Tyke balanced on one arm and Albrecht headed outside first, and then Mary followed behind with a big metal bowl, the screen door bouncing shut after her. Faith watched them trudging together past the window, and Trent looked up as he passed, a rueful little smile on his face.

"Let me help clear the table," Faith said, and she started to stack plates.

"*Danke* for not mentioning my visit with Eddie today," Sarah said, her voice low. "I don't think my parents would understand."

"That's what I thought," Faith said. She was relieved that Sarah had brought the subject up. That would make it easier. "How is it going with Eddie?"

"He's very kind," Sarah said with a wistful smile. "And he listens to me as if everything I say is the most important thing he's ever heard."

Ah, the first flush of love. Faith remembered those days rather well. They carried the dishes to the counter, and Sarah started putting the leftovers into Tupperware containers to go into the icebox. They didn't have electricity in the kitchen, but they did have a deep freeze that had the cord removed. It was well insulated, and the Amish bought ice from the iceman who delivered it weekly so they could keep their freezers refrigerator cold. The leftovers would be chilled until they heated them up again on the big woodstove.

"How did you meet Trent?" Sarah asked suddenly.

"What?" Faith asked, surprised by the change of topic.

"Trent—how did you meet him?" Sarah asked.

"Sweetie, you know we're divorced, right?"

"*Yah*, I know. It's just... The only way we have to meet men here is at youth group," Sarah said. "And I'm twenty now, so I'm getting a little old for that. The girls are mostly all younger than me. My friends I grew up with are married now."

"Trent and I were friends ever since high school," Faith replied. "And we started dating shortly after."

"How do you meet men...now that you're single again?" Sarah asked.

"I don't know. There's online dating sites—but you have to make sure you find a local guy and after meeting online, move it to a coffee shop. Or there are book clubs, or dinner groups, or classes at the gym... Why?"

"Maybe it's easier for you than it is for me," Sarah said.

Faith thought about the spinning class she'd taken, the volunteering at the SPCA, the online dates she'd met... All of that, and she'd only met a couple of guys who were eligible. And those dates hadn't gone anywhere.

Maybe she just wasn't ready to date yet, because stick her in an old pickup truck with Trent, and she was getting goose bumps. Trent was still in her system, and maybe it wasn't fair to try to start something up with someone new, knowing she felt this way still.

"It's not easier." Faith sighed. "It's tough out there. I get it."

"Well, meeting a man like Eddie who came to our farm to see how it ran, and walked right into my life—that doesn't happen every day."

"I can appreciate that," Faith agreed. "But he's English."

"So are you."

"Nice deflection, but you know what I mean. You aren't English."

Suddenly Faith saw a different possibility. She'd been assuming all this time that Sarah was simply not thinking about their differences—not considering what commitment would look like. But maybe she had.

"Are you considering leaving the Amish life for him?" Faith asked softly.

Sarah went to the sink and started the water. Her head was down, the strings from her white *kapp* hanging down her back. From this vantage point, Sarah looked younger than her twenty years.

"Are you?" Faith pressed.

Sarah's shoulders sank, and she glanced back. "I might be. Please don't tell my parents that. I'm just thinking. I have to weigh my options. I don't have too many marriage prospects out here. Not that I even want them! I don't know…"

"Are you…in love with Eddie?" Faith asked.

Sarah nodded. "I know it's fast, but I've never felt this way before. I don't want another man. No one could measure up to him!"

"But, Sarah, if you married him, you'd be shunned," Faith said.

Sarah sighed. "What if you had to choose between having the man you love and having to start over alone, or staying with everyone you know and love and staying single the rest of your life?"

"That's no kind of choice," Faith agreed. "But shunning… That's incredibly painful."

Everyone Sarah knew would be forced to turn their backs on her, to stop speaking to her, to not even look at her. She'd be left utterly alone unless she came back… But how could she return with an Englisher husband? She would have sacrificed every person she knew and loved for one man. What woman should be asked to do that?

"It is painful. Horribly. But so is giving up the man you love." Sarah's chin rose. "Besides, you and Trent wouldn't shun me."

Tears misted Faith's eyes. "Of course not."

This was much more serious than Mary and Albrecht suspected, and Faith felt a flutter of anxiety rising up inside her.

"But there are a few things you aren't considering," Faith added.

"Like what?"

And here it was—the point where she was supposed to warn Sarah off Eddie. Was she doing the right thing here? Because she recognized something in Sarah's eyes. Sarah wasn't a girl anymore, and she was in love. That didn't come along every day. It didn't even come along every lifetime.

"Look, you have a right to choose the life you want. I know the life your parents want for you. And I know what your community wants. But you have the right to choose something different, if you want to."

"Danke," Sarah said. "I appreciate that."

Sarah plunged a dishcloth into the sudsy water and started to wash the dishes. Faith took a tea towel off a hook on the side of the cupboard and joined her at the sink.

"But you both come from very different cultures," Faith said. "And that can be really hard on a relationship. What does marriage mean to you? What does it mean to him? What do you expect in order to feel loved? What does he?"

"We'd talk about all of that."

"So did Trent and I."

A flicker of worry crossed Sarah's face. "You did?"

Sarah rinsed a plate and put it into the dish rack.

"Of course!" Faith said. "No one gets married thinking it'll end."

"But I wouldn't divorce him," Sarah said. "We Amish don't get divorced."

"You wouldn't be Amish anymore," Faith reminded her. "Look, I'm not trying to say that this will happen. It might not. All I'm saying is that it's a possibility, even if it's a remote one. If you married an Amish man, you'd have your whole community surrounding you, holding you together. You're fighting? Well, every man your husband knows is going to tell him to go make up with you because that's how things work. Every single man. If you're struggling with something, every woman you know is going to tell you that these things happen and to go talk it out. Right?"

Sarah nodded.

"And even between the two of you, divorce would just not be an option. I mean, it wouldn't even be virtue on your part! It just wouldn't be possible, and stay Amish."

"True."

"Don't take that for granted. Out here, there are other options," Faith said. "People don't have to stay together. They aren't forced to figure it out when it gets really hard. Trent and I had our problems, and we split up. But it wasn't because I didn't love him, Sarah."

"Then why?" Sarah asked softly.

"Because he felt so distant, and nothing I did brought him closer. I felt cut off from his feelings, and my heart was in tatters, and he just seemed so oblivious. At the time, it felt absolutely earth-shattering. And once we started talking about divorce, and he didn't look horrified by the idea, it just started rolling. We were both so tired of trying all the time. Marriage was hard for us. I suppose the fact that we were able to go through with the divorce means something."

Sarah pressed her lips together, and she looked like she was holding back tears.

"Like I said, there is no saying that will happen," Faith said softly. "But you have to at least think about what would happen if it did. If you and Eddie loved each other desperately but things changed, what would your life look like then?"

"I'd come home," she said.

"And they'd welcome you with their whole hearts," Faith said. "But with a living husband, you wouldn't be able to marry a nice Amish guy then. That would have been your kick at the can. No more chances. You could come home, but you'd be single for life."

Sarah's washing slowed. "That's true."

"Now, let's say it does work out. You and Eddie are great together and completely united and strong. You'd never be able to speak to your parents again, or your friends, or your aunts and uncles. No one. They wouldn't be there for your first baby. They wouldn't be part of your life—birthdays, anniversaries, good times and bad. No advice from your mom. No encouragement from your dad. Nothing. You have the right to choose an English life, but don't make that decision lightly. Know what you're choosing," Faith said. "You owe that much to yourself."

Sarah nodded. "It's something to think on."

"That's all I ask."

Outside, they heard the bowl of berries deposited on the wooden steps. Mary was getting ready to come inside.

"Please don't tell my mother I've been visiting Eddie," Sarah said softly.

"That's your business," Faith said. "I wouldn't dream of telling your secrets."

"*Danke*, Faith."

This was all Faith could do in all good conscience. And she'd never speak on the subject again. Sarah could make her choice now, and whatever she chose, Faith would wholeheartedly support.

Albrecht's voice and Trent's deep bass sounded faintly from outside. They were on their way back. Then Mary called out a greeting.

"Are you men interested in some strawberries and cream?" Mary asked.

Faith couldn't make out the words of their replies, but their tones were enthusiastically positive. This private conversation in the kitchen was over, but as Faith looked out the window and spotted Trent and Tyke walking along next to the older Amish man, her heart gave a painful squeeze.

When a marriage ended, it wasn't just the complication of cultural differences or the possibility of remarriage. It was a heart that kept on aching, that wouldn't forget the one man who'd been her everything for a few short years. Some people bounced back. And some people, try as they might to do the rational thing and get over the pain, didn't.

Faith had thought she'd be able to pull her heart back together again—she really had! But two years later, it still hurt. Heartbreak was never so simple.

CHAPTER TWENTY-FOUR

THE STRAWBERRIES AND cream were delicious, of course, but Trent noticed that his cousin was rather reserved for the rest of their visit. The sparkle had gone out of Sarah, and when she thought no one was looking, she'd gaze wistfully out the window, looking like she might cry.

He could guess what had happened. Faith had gotten through to her where her parents hadn't been able to, and while he was pretty sure that was for the best, it did snag at his heart. Eddie was smitten with Sarah, and she seemed to return the feelings. He hated to be part of breaking up two people who really cared about each other.

Trent pushed his empty dish aside and Tyke squirmed up onto his lap, his eyelids looking heavy.

"Are you tired, buddy?" Trent asked.

Tyke whined a little and rubbed at his eyes with one pudgy fist. Trent looked over at Faith and she gave him a nod.

"We should get going," Trent said. "Thank you for dinner, Aunt Mary. It was delicious as always. Thank you, Sarah. It was a great meal."

"You are ever so welcome," Mary said. "*Danke* for coming. Will you bring Tyke back tomorrow?"

"Actually, I just got a text from Abigail that the day home is open again, and Abigail can take him," Trent said. "But I really appreciate you helping me out for a couple of days. I don't know what I would have done without you."

"We're family, Trent," Mary said, and she patted his arm. "This is what family is for. If you need us, we're here."

"It goes both ways," he said with a grateful smile.

Faith said goodbye to Mary and Albrecht. She waved across the kitchen to Sarah.

"See you later, Sarah?" he asked.

Sarah nodded. "I'm sure. Take care."

So why did Trent feel a little guilty? Faith shouldered the diaper bag, and they headed out to the truck. Tyke didn't fight going into the car seat tonight, which was a nice change. Maybe he was tired out from his day.

Trent buckled him in as Faith got into the passenger side seat.

"There's your truck," Trent said, putting Tyke's favorite plastic toy into his hands. Tyke held on to it and thankfully didn't pitch it across the seat.

"So what happened with Sarah?" Trent asked, feeling somehow relieved to be getting back on the road.

"She's seriously considering leaving the Amish life," Faith replied.

Trent shot her a shocked look. "Seriously?"

"Yeah. She loves Eddie, and she thinks that if she stays Amish she might not find a guy she loves like that. And she might be right."

"Wow…" Trent shook his head. "I never thought she'd consider leaving it all. I mean—she'd be shunned."

"We talked about that," Faith said quietly. "She knows what she has to lose, but I filled her in on Englisher marriage. As in…the possibility of divorce. There is no communal support holding a couple together no matter what."

Sometimes Trent wished they had had some social pressure of their own to keep them working on their marriage through that last difficult stretch. He didn't blame anyone for their divorce. Maybe even a bunch of well-meaning family wouldn't have been able to change their course, but he wondered if things could have been different, all the same.

"That doesn't mean they'd split up," he countered.

"True. And I told her that really clearly," Faith replied. "It doesn't mean that they won't survive, but it might be something they should talk about before she sacrifices everything she knows for him. He might see divorce differently."

Trent nodded. "Sounds like you gave her some good advice."

"So why do I feel so bad about it?" she asked.

"Do you?"

"Yeah, I kind of do."

Trent pulled onto the road and stepped on the

gas. Out here in Amish country, everything seemed to move more slowly. There were times that he enjoyed the slower pace, but tonight he wanted to feel speed and a growling engine. He wanted distance between himself and the familial pain they'd just left behind.

"I know it's their way of life," Faith said, "but it's cruel. If she doesn't choose the path they want, they cut her off completely."

"It's a bit more complicated," he replied. "If she hadn't already made her choice to join the Amish way of life, they wouldn't. She could leave and still come back to visit, like my *mammi* did. Because she already made her vow to live by Amish rules that changes her situation. Vows matter—and I'm not saying they don't matter for us—but we love to idealize the Amish for maintaining their distinct way of life. But we really hate the discipline that it takes to do so."

"Do you really think if they gave people the freedom to marry who they love they'd lose everything?" Faith asked.

"Probably." Trent shrugged. "Look, you know I agree with you. The choice seems cruel to us—her family or the man she loves. That's heartbreak either way. But the fact that the Amish take their promises this seriously is why we respect them so much. You can take them at their word. They'll stand by it. And it's why their marriages last like they do—they don't just stand back and let things take their course. They put their noses in other people's business and keep them together. And if someone goes back on that vow, there are communitywide consequences."

"We'd be shunned if we were Amish," she said.

He considered that, then cast her a sad smile. "Nah. We'd only be shunned if we turned our backs on our community in order to get divorced. Honestly? I think if we were Amish, we'd still be married."

Faith was silent, and he looked hesitantly over at her to see tears standing in her eyes.

"Hey..." He reached over and grabbed her hand. "I'm sorry. I didn't mean to sound like I was joking, or anything."

Her fingers tightened on his hand, and his heart gave a squeeze. He had to let go of her hand as they came up to the highway so he could turn, and it left him feeling strangely bereft. Whatever they were now to each other, they were far from strangers, and his heart was still entangled with his ex-wife. Maybe it always would be. Maybe the Amish didn't enforce vows so much as understand them, because his wedding vow had changed something inside him rather permanently. Even post-divorce.

He pulled onto the highway and sped up. The sun was low, glowing golden across the fields to the west as he headed toward town. The cows grazed on, and their shadows stretched long across the scrub grass and summer weeds they fed upon.

The town of Apfelkuchen wasn't far now, and soon enough they were driving through town toward the central core of shops. A few stores were still open, and a couple of buggies were rattling down the road, but mostly there were cars and people walking down the sidewalk. One Amish couple caught Trent's eye—they were pushing a baby in a stroller, and each had an ice cream cone.

That was the kind of family unity he was afraid to long for right now. He was too busy holding things together for Tyke to let himself waste any extra energy hoping.

"What do you think Sarah should do?" Faith asked.

Trent pulled to a stop in front of the antiques shop. The front door was shut, and a sign in the window with an old Coca-Cola logo read "Closed." He turned off the engine and glanced into the back seat. Tyke was sound asleep in his car seat. If he slept too long now, he'd be up until midnight, but he was momentarily glad for the time alone with Faith.

"I don't know..." he admitted.

"Come on," she said. "I just had a really personal talk with your cousin for your aunt and uncle. You owe me this much. What do you think?"

Trent smiled faintly. "Yesterday, I would have said she should dump Eddie. No question. But today? I don't know... I think she should follow her heart. If she loves him, marry him."

"That's brave," she said.

"Not really," he replied. "It's better than going a lifetime wondering what would have happened if you took the leap. If she loves him like I loved you, then I say do it—marry him. At least there will be no risks untaken."

"Don't you ever wish you hadn't married me?" she asked. "Could have saved yourself some heartbreak."

"Nope," he replied. "It would have been a different kind of heartbreak. I would have had to watch you marry some other guy, and that would have hurt a lot, too. I did what I did. I stand by it."

"You are a strange man," she said, but she was smiling again, and that was a victory.

"Why, do you ever wish you hadn't married me?" he asked.

There was a beat of silence, and then Faith sucked in a breath. "That's a hard question. I do wish that I could have avoided this pain. Nothing hurt so badly as our divorce, Trent. Nothing. It was agony."

"So do you wish you hadn't married me?" he pressed, unable to help himself.

"No," she said quietly. "But I do wish we were two or three more years into the future so I could be over you."

Her words took a moment to land, and when they did, he found himself reaching for her hand again. He caught her fingers—bare of rings now. Not too long ago he used to be proud of that engagement and wedding ring set on her pretty fingers. They'd been expensive, but she'd been worth it.

"You're not over me?" he asked.

She dropped her gaze. "Not entirely."

"I'm not over you, either."

Faith's gaze flickered up to meet his, and she seemed to hold her breath. He could see the flutter of her pulse at the base of her neck, and he swallowed.

"We should work on that," she whispered.

"Getting over each other?" he asked. His voice sounded like gravel in his own ears.

She nodded. "It's not good for us to go on like this. We know why we didn't work out. We should accept that."

Right—this was the rational, fully in-control version of his ex-wife. She had a plan for everything—even grief, it would seem.

"I'm trying to," he said.

"So am I…" A tear glistened in her eye. "I'm trying really hard."

Faith was still the most beautiful woman he'd ever known. He'd memorized her face years ago, and he could see some extra lines around her eyes now, and little more depth and sadness in her gaze. Was he responsible for that?

Trent leaned closer, and there was something so familiar about this moment. How many times had they sat in this very truck together? He reached over and took a tendril of her glossy hair and twisted it around his finger. Her lips parted slightly, and he leaned closer. She smelled of strawberries and cream, and all he could feel was the thundering of his own heart in his chest. He didn't know how to sit with her in a moment like this one and not kiss her. She was like a magnet for him when her defenses were down and her heart shone in her eyes like that.

"Trent..."

He leaned closer, the truck seat creaking with the movement, and just for a second he thought she'd pull back, but then she leaned forward and her lips touched his. He exhaled a relieved sigh and slipped a hand behind her neck, pulling her in closer. He'd missed this so much.

From the back seat, Tyke made that fussy, whining sound he made when he was waking up. Trent broke off the kiss and dropped his hand. They both looked back, and Tyke blinked his eyes open.

Right... There was Tyke to consider in all of this. He slowly unwound her hair from his finger, tucked it behind her ear and dropped his hand.

"I'd better get inside," she said softly.

He nodded.

"Tuck? Where's my tuck?" Tyke asked.

"Here—" Faith reached back and picked up the fallen toy and handed to Tyke. "Bye, Tyke. I'll see you later, alligator."

Tyke smiled for that, and Faith pushed open the door and hopped out. It was like she took half the oxygen with her, and even the colors seemed to fade with her gone. She slammed the door and headed toward the front door. He watched her fiddle with the keys and then disappear inside. She looked over her shoulder once, and then she was gone.

Trent wasn't over her. Not one bit. And now he'd kissed her, and it had awoken all sorts of muscle memory for him. He knew how to be with her… And balancing on a line between loving her and walking away was getting harder and harder to do.

He put the truck into gear and pulled back onto the street.

"Let's get home, Tyke," Trent said, trying to sound like this was just a normal drive.

Home was now the safe little place he shared with Tyke. Except that house was starting to feel almost haunted with memories of his marriage. He could move a couch, but he couldn't sweep out the memories. And Trent couldn't let his own emotional upheaval affect this little boy.

"You want 'Baby Shark'?" he asked with exaggerated enthusiasm. "Let's put it on…"

Sometimes it was easier to let a soundtrack take over when his mind was sailing elsewhere. Like back to Faith, and why he couldn't stop thinking about her lips, and the depth in her eyes, and that soft little flutter at the base of her neck that had made him wonder if her heart had been racing, too.

CHAPTER TWENTY-FIVE

FAITH HEADED UP the side staircase, her sandals tapping against the hard wood. It smelled like old wood polish on these stairs, and the polish flaked away in some places. Another thing to add to the list of repairs to be done when they could afford it.

She stopped at the top of the stairs, her heart pattering.

He kissed me...

And she hadn't stopped him. In fact, she'd kissed him back. There had been one second where she'd known she should stop him, but it would have meant pushing him away, and she just couldn't bring herself to.

She shouldn't be doing this! She'd spent the last two years doing her best to get over Trent, only to let herself slide right back to the start again? She couldn't do that! It wasn't fair to herself. She needed to heal, get him out of her system and find the courage to get out there and start dating again. That was what she needed to do!

But here she was, remembering what his hand felt like wrapped around hers, and the soft tug of him twining her hair around his finger... It wasn't fair to miss a man this much. If only her determination to get over him could match her ability to do so.

Faith unlocked the apartment door and dropped her purse on the little table just inside. The door swung shut and she leaned against it with a sigh. Home... The lamps were on inside, filling the apartment with a soft glow that matched the hue of the sky outside the living room window.

Faith went over to the couch and sank into it. She was half tempted to call her mother and unload this onto her, but Mom would read too much into it. She'd think that they were getting back together to start with, and that would only complicate matters. The problem with a divorce was that the family were already invested in Trent, and if she admitted to conflicted feelings, they'd only get their hopes up.

The bathroom door opened and Hope came out. She was dressed in a pair of jeans and floral peasant top that was particularly cute on her. She looked a little pale, though.

"Hi, Hope," Faith said. "How was your evening?"

There was something in Hope's hand, and she slowly raised it. It was white, and at first glance looked like a pen, but then Faith froze.

"Is that..."

"Yep." Hope looked down at it. "It's a pregnancy test."

"And?" Faith leaned forward. "What does it say?"

"It says I'm pregnant."

Faith jumped to her feet and flung her arms around her sister's neck.

"Congratulations! Oh my goodness! I'm going to be an aunt!"

Faith pulled back to look at her sister's face. A smile tickled her lips, but there were tears in her eyes.

"Sweetie, what's the matter?" Faith asked. "You're having a baby! This is wonderful news!"

"I know. It is!" Hope wiped at a tear that slipped down her cheek. "And I'm happy. I am! But this is not part of the plan."

"What plan?" Faith asked.

"My plan! I've been married for four months, and my husband is constantly working. How am I supposed to go spend time with him on his work trips now? I can't do that with a baby! I'll be stuck at home with an infant, and I'll never see him!"

Hope was obviously panicking, and Faith led her over to the couch, then sat down next to her.

"You two wanted a baby at some point, right?" Faith asked.

Hope nodded.

"Look, some women really want a baby, and for whatever reason, can't have one." Faith had an inkling of what that felt like. "So the fact that this happened so quickly could be seen as a blessing. No struggling for you."

No trying to talk her husband into it, either.

"I know I'm supposed to be grateful for all of

this," Hope said. "I'm supposed to be grateful that I'm married, and grateful that he makes good money. I'm supposed to be grateful that I don't have to work, and now grateful than I'm pregnant. And I get it! I don't have the same worries as other women. But maybe I'm tired of the gratitude, because I'm not grateful that I never see the man I married. I don't feel welcome to go see him when he's traveling for work, and trust me—I've wondered why that is. I'm not grateful that every time I try to talk to Peter about it, I get brushed off because this is how he makes the money that keeps me so secure, and I'm not supposed to want anything else!"

Hope's voice was rising both in volume and in pitch.

"Okay, okay..." Faith said. "You're mad."

"Yes, I'm mad! Everyone tells me to be thankful—Mom, Dad, you, Elaine! Even Peter! Everyone thinks I should be so ever-loving thankful that my actual worries are brushed aside!"

"I was just trying to be supportive of your marriage," Faith said. "I didn't realize you were worried. I was trying not to cause you worry. I'm really sorry, Hope."

Hope leaned her head back against the couch. "It's okay. It's not your fault."

"So what do you need to feel better?"

Hope was silent, and Faith let her think about that. This was a big adjustment, and while Faith was ready to jump into baby mode with her sister, it looked like it would take Hope a little more time.

"I need my husband to work closer to home," Hope said finally.

"Okay, that's good to know," Faith said. "So talk to Peter about it."

But Hope didn't look in any way comforted.

"What else do you need?" Faith asked quietly.

Tears spilled down Hope's cheeks. "I'm so embarrassed to say it, but I need him to choose me. *Me*, not the baby. Not the job. Not the money. I need him to choose me."

"And then you'd feel like everything will be okay?" Faith asked.

"Yeah, I think so." Hope sucked in a shuddering breath. "I know we love each other, but I'm realizing now how little we know each other, and how much more I need than what I've been getting."

"That's good to know," Faith said. "So, talk to Peter."

"He's a busy man," Hope said, and she pressed her lips together.

"I'm sure he won't be too busy to hear that he's going to be a father," Faith said.

Hope slowly shook her head. "That's the thing. I want him to come home because he misses me, and because I asked him to, not because I tell him I'm pregnant. I'm his wife first, and then I'll be the mother of his child second. He has to choose me."

This didn't sound like a good idea to Faith, though. Her sister wanted Peter to prove he loved her, but he also deserved to know that they were having a baby. He might be deeply hurt later if he found out that she had been holding back that information.

"Oh..." Faith breathed. "Hope, I've been married before—"

"Stop there," Hope said. "I'm not looking for marriage advice."

"Okay," Faith said. "That's fair. So all I'll say is talk to him."

Hope pushed herself up from the sofa and pulled her cell phone out of her pocket. She slipped into her bedroom for more privacy, but Faith could hear her voice clearly enough to make out the words through the wall.

Faith was tempted to go downstairs to the shop, or something, just to give Hope the privacy she needed, but something stopped her.

"I miss you, Peter," Hope said. There was a pause. "Me, too. Why don't you come see me for a couple of days...? I know, I know. You're always on the verge of a sale. Make the buyer sweat. Come home for one night, and then go back... Because I miss you... I know, I know. You only get paid when you get the commission. I get it, but we're newly married! What about time together...? Video chats are not the same thing, Peter..."

Faith slipped out the door and shut it softly behind her. Faith could see Hope's point now. Peter was definitely taking his new bride for granted, and he seemed to think that the money he brought in was more important than his personal presence.

But then, the man worked in luxury sales. It

could be feast and famine, depending on the economy. And he was trying to provide. There were two sides to every marriage.

Downstairs in the dim shop front, Faith stopped in front of a box she'd brought back from the Yoders' place. There was the recipe box inside, a scale, some quilted pot holders and some tin canisters. She opened the recipe box, and she pulled out the handful of faded recipe cards inside. The top one was dated in the bottom right-hand corner—1923. Albrecht hadn't seemed to think they mattered much, but she'd have to at least try to return those to Mary—they might be precious to her, and Faith would hate to strip her of her own family heritage for a sale.

And underneath those cards was a small piece of paper. Written in pen with spidery writing were the words *Ich vermisse dich. Es tut mir so leid*. Faith knew enough rudimentary German to know that the first part said *I miss you*. But she wasn't sure about the second part.

Even the Amish had their hidden dramas behind the scenes. For all of those enforced marriage vows, there were hearts behind them. There were women who kept little scraps of notes...from a husband, maybe? From their time of courtship, perhaps?

Or from a boy she'd never married? A memory from an earlier love?

If there was one thing that Faith was convinced of, it was that women were the same, regardless of language or culture. Love looked the same, and so did longing.

Faith sighed. Marriage was not easy, was it? Neither was love.

She heard Hope's footsteps on the stairs and she looked over to see her sister appear in the doorway.

"Well?" Faith asked.

"He's awfully busy. He'll come back in three weeks like planned." Hope sighed.

"So go down there and surprise him," Faith said.

"I'm not sure I want to do that." Hope dropped her gaze. "Not yet."

"Did you tell him about your pregnancy?"

Hope shook her head. "That's a conversation to have in person. And if he chooses to wait to come home, then he's choosing to wait to find out about the baby."

Hope and Peter were both digging in. Faith recognized that, but Hope didn't want marriage advice.

"I found this in the Yoders' recipe box," Faith said, and she passed the note over to her sister. Hope had done some traveling in Germany, and she'd taken some German-language classes. So she had a better chance of understanding the note than Faith did.

Hope frowned. "Wow. What was going on?"

"What does it say?" Faith asked. "I can't make out the second part."

"It says, *I miss you. I'm so sorry.*"

Faith met her sister's gaze. "And the woman kept it…"

What had happened in the quiet life of that Amish woman who had kept this scrap of a note? Who had written this note to her? It wasn't explicitly a romantic note, but there was something about the words and the fact that the woman had kept it secreted away in a place that would have belonged just to her that suggested it was. And what had it meant to her? Was it from the same time as those recipe cards? Faith's mind was spinning ahead.

Even with their enforced wedding vows, the Amish had hearts to break, too.

CHAPTER TWENTY-SIX

TRENT DROPPED TYKE off at the day home the next morning, and Abigail gave Tyke a big hug, telling him how happy she was to see him. A little girl a bit older than Tyke stood in the doorway, joyfully hollering to Tyke, and he bounced inside without a backward glance.

"Thanks, Abigail," Trent called, and she gave him a wave.

Tyke would be fine, but Trent couldn't quite get the image out of his head of Faith holding out her arms to him and Tyke crawling up into her lap as if it were the most natural thing in the world.

Come here, baby...

Even the memory of her gentle words brought goose bumps up on his arms. Cuddling Tyke had seemed utterly natural for her, too. It would be nice to have someone to raise Tyke with, someone who could love him like he did, and not feel threatened. And somehow, whenever he imagined a woman in that role, she looked a whole lot like his ex-wife. And that wasn't going to work! Faith had left him once when the going got tough, and if Tyke hadn't taken to her quite so readily, maybe it wouldn't worry him.

But Tyke had lost his mother, and there might be a place in his little toddler heart where he was going to try to replace her. If Tyke got too attached to Faith, it could do more damage than anyone imagined. Tyke was a sturdy little boy in most ways, but he had a fragile heart.

The day was a busy one—pulling electrical cables, dealing with some tangled cables in the walls and doing his best not to have to cut any holes in the drywall. Faith was there like usual, and they bantered a little too cheerily. They were both avoiding talking about this kiss, but it felt so good to be near her, and he didn't want to mess with that.

Eddie worked hard, too, and he didn't mention Sarah at all, although he did seem to be waiting around lunchtime to see if she'd show up, and she didn't.

The next morning when Trent arrived at the store, Eddie wasn't there yet. So Trent headed upstairs to get back to work.

Trent was working on the electrical outlets in Faith's bedroom today. Her room was neat, the bedding smooth, and the air smelled ever so faintly of her perfume. He couldn't help but remember when their bedroom together used to smell this way. He'd come in after work, stripping off dirty work clothes, and their dresser would be covered with little bottles of serums and creams, and there would be this delicate fragrance that permeated the space... He'd liked that smell. When she left, it had taken a few weeks to dissipate fully.

He could still remember the day he came back home and the smell was gone, and his chest constricted at the memory. That was the kind of thing he couldn't let happen to Tyke. Faith was too easy to love.

Eddie was an hour late, and when Trent heard the front door open and Eddie's boots on the floorboards, Trent pushed himself to his feet and headed out into the living room. Eddie looked pale and he was scruffy as if he hadn't shaved. There were shadows under his eyes betraying a lack of sleep. If he didn't know Eddie so well, he'd think he was hungover, but Eddie didn't drink.

"Are you okay?" Trent asked.

"Fine," Eddie replied tersely.

So they were going to play it that way, were they? Eddie nodded to the clipboard. "What outlets are we wiring today?"

Trent put the clipboard under his arm, out of Eddie's line of sight. "You're fine?"

"I said so, didn't I," Eddie grumbled.

"If there's no problem, then I'm going to point out that showing up an hour late is unprofessional," Trent said. "But you don't look fine to me."

Eddie put down his tool belt. "Sarah called me from the phone shanty last night."

"Oh?" Trent had a feeling he knew where this

was going by the look on Eddie's face. Sarah had done her thinking and she'd come to a decision.

"She broke up with me," Eddie said.

"I'm sorry," Trent said. And he truly was. It wasn't like he agreed with the Amish stance on allowing someone to leave the community after they'd made their decision to join the faith. But they had their ways, and they took those vows very seriously. Still, Trent would have rather seen Sarah get the man she loved and keep her family, too. It just wasn't possible.

Eddie rubbed a hand over his stubbled jaw. "She didn't even explain. She said she wouldn't see me anymore, asked me to stop coming by the house, too. She said we were too different, then she burst into tears and hung up."

It sounded like a painful conversation, but a whole lot less painful now than later. Eddie might not believe that in the moment, and it was certainly not something to tell a heartbroken guy the morning after his heart was handed to him, but it was true. Have that conversation after three years of marriage, and see how much deeper it could stab.

"I really don't get it," Eddie said. "I just don't..."

Trent sighed. Yeah, he'd had this conversation with some family members when he and Faith had split up. How had they gotten there? The heart was the last part to recover after a blow like that.

"Sometimes a woman changes her mind," Trent said quietly. "And you have to respect that. Even if it doesn't make a lot of sense right now. You can't go charging over there and upsetting her more. She contacted you and said her piece."

Eddie shot him an irritated look. "You sound like you knew this was coming."

"I didn't know it was coming," Trent replied. "But I can understand it. Look, Eddie. If she chose you, she'd be shunned. That means totally cut off from her friends, her family and her whole community. This is the only life she's ever known. She'd have to walk away from them completely. That's a big request of a young woman—and I dare say it's *too big* of a request."

"I'm not asking her to do that!"

"Yes, you are!" Trent said. "Come on, I explained this to you before!"

"She said she loved me," Eddie said. "She said she'd never felt like this about any man before, and she said she couldn't wait to see me again. That was two days ago. What changed?"

"I can't speak for her…" Trent said. "But let's say she chose you. Let's say she let her entire community shun her, and she never saw her parents again. Never saw her friends, her cousins, her aunts and uncles…no one. And all she had was a spattering of Englisher cousins, my grandmother who is her great-aunt, and you."

"I'd love her."

"I know you would, but loving a woman isn't always enough. The point is, a woman needs more than a husband. She needs her siblings, her parents, her girlfriends, her extended family. She needs a community, and a place in it. You can't be everything to her. You can be the man who loves her, but she needs more than you. What about your kids? They'd be cut off from that side of the family, too. Your choice would affect generations."

Eddie was silent.

"Faith needed more than me, too, man," Trent went on. "She needed her dreams fulfilled, and something to chase down and achieve. I tried to hand it to her—to be her hero and make it happen. I can tell you, that doesn't work, and it only ruined what was left of our relationship. I know that TV and movies make it look like love is all you need, but that just isn't true. You need more than love in your life, and so does she. It's just a plain, painful fact. So it's better this way."

Eddie sighed. "I would have tried to be enough."

"And it wouldn't have been your fault when you failed at it," Trent said, putting a hand on Eddie's shoulder. "You can't be father and mother, or her brother or sister. You just can't fill those roles! I'm sorry that the Amish push the point, but she'd have to choose between you and absolutely everyone else."

"Would you have supported us if she chose me?" Eddie asked.

"I would have tried," Trent said after a moment of thought. "But I'd still have warned you. This isn't a fairy tale where the prince gets the princess and that's all they need to be happy ever after. Take it from me, marriage can be really complicated when you can't figure out how to make her happy…when you aren't what she needs to feel fulfilled."

"I don't think I'll ever find another woman like her," Eddie said.

"You won't," Trent agreed. "But she can be a beautiful memory."

"Is that what Faith is to you?" Eddie asked, his tone barbed. "A beautiful memory?"

Eddie was goading him now, lashing out a bit in his pain.

"No, she's more than that. She's stuck in my heart and I can't dig her out," Trent retorted. "I am still trying to stop loving that woman! So you're right—it's not so simple. Heartbreak doesn't just fade away, not when it's someone you love that much. I'm not trying to downplay your pain. But do yourself a favor and start trying to heal now instead of waiting until it'll take you years to get over her. Sometimes your heart leads, but right now you need to let your head take over. That's my advice—if you'd like to avoid ending up like me."

Eddie didn't answer, and Trent rubbed a hand through his hair. He wasn't sure if he was any help at all.

"Do you want the day off?" Trent asked after a moment.

"No, thanks," Eddie replied. "I'd rather work."

"Okay, well…" Trent sighed. "For what it's worth, I'm really sorry you're going through this, Eddie. You're a good guy."

"Thanks." Eddie swallowed. "Can I see the map now?"

Trent handed the clipboard over. He understood. Sometimes work was a better solace than rest. By himself, Eddie would be left with his questions and his heartbreak. At least with work he had something else to focus on.

If only Eddie had listened to him before, because he could never say that Trent hadn't warned him. Still… He couldn't help but feel guilty, like he'd helped end a really good couple. Those two could have been so happy together if things were different.

Sometimes life just wasn't fair.

CHAPTER TWENTY-SEVEN

THE DAY PLODDED ON, and Trent found that he and Eddie got a lot more done than he thought they would. With Eddie depressed and trying to avoid his pain, he worked with unbreakable focus.

So when they finished up the day's work early, Trent sent the younger man home.

"I can keep working," Eddie said.

"Nope," Trent said firmly. "Call up some friends. Go out for wings and get some moral support."

"Yeah, I guess I could do that," Eddie agreed. "Thanks, Trent. I'll see you in the morning. I'll be on time."

Eddie headed down the stairs, his work boots thunking solidly on each step, and Trent followed him down. Eddie headed out the front door, and Trent watched him go.

Faith was working alone in the shop, and she had her phone pressed up against her ear.

"So, just like the dining room chairs that the woman was asking about?" Faith said into her phone. There was a pause. "And how much? That's all? Hold on…"

Faith pulled the phone away from her face and she turned toward Trent. He knew that look on her face—she needed a favor.

"Trent?" she said hesitantly. "I know this is a lot to ask, but I don't have a big enough vehicle of my own…"

"You found those antique chairs in the right style?" he asked.

"Sure did. This is Elaine on the phone. It's a long story, but she found them at an estate sale, and if she buys them, we need to pick them up today. Is there any way you'd be willing to drive me out to Lancaster this afternoon?"

"Sure," he said.

"I mean, I know you're on a schedule with the wiring and—"

"It's fine," he interrupted. "We're a bit ahead of schedule, so I can do it."

She put the phone to her ear again. "Elaine, buy them—all six. Trent says he'll give me a ride and we'll be out there to pick them up in…" She looked over at Trent, eyebrows raised questioningly.

"About an hour," Trent said.

"In about an hour," she repeated into the phone. "Thanks, Elaine. See you soon."

She ended the call and shot him a smile. "We found those chairs! I'll send a picture to the customer who was asking about them after we've purchased them. I'm sure she'll be thrilled!" Her gaze moved toward the door again. "You sure this won't upset your schedule?"

"Nah, we got a lot done today. In fact, I just sent Eddie home."

Faith frowned. "He doesn't look good."

"She broke up with him."

"So soon?"

"I guess your talk with her was effective," he said.

She sighed. "I knew it was inevitable, but it's still sad."

Trent knew what she meant. He knew what heartbreak felt like, and seeing someone else go through it wasn't fun. He pulled his keys out of his pocket.

"Should we head out?" he asked.

Faith nodded. "Thank you, Trent."

That soft sound in her voice—the sincere gratitude—had always melted his heart with her. Funny how the more time he spent with her, the more of their good times he kept remembering.

"How is Eddie holding up?" Faith asked as they stepped outside onto the sun-warmed sidewalk. Faith locked the door behind her and dropped the key into her purse.

"Not great," Trent admitted. "He didn't see it coming. The last time they'd talked, she was looking forward to seeing him again, and they'd been confessing their feelings for each other."

They both hopped into his truck. "Where are we headed?"

She passed him a scrap of paper where she'd jotted down the address, and he typed it into his GPS. The driving time showed forty-five minutes, which wasn't bad.

They headed out of town and onto the highway. He couldn't help but remember that the last time he'd been in this truck with her, he'd kissed her.

"You're having fun with this antiques business," he said as they pulled onto the highway heading toward Lancaster.

"I guess I am," she agreed. "If I can make this store make money, I'll feel better about…everything."

About her shop that failed. That was what she meant.

"Sometimes things just go wrong," Trent said. "And it isn't your fault."

"I don't agree," she replied. "It takes planning and preparation. Then your chances of failure are significantly reduced."

"Okay, so let's say you planned, you prepared, and then something much bigger than you came along and demolished everything. Would you still feel like you'd failed?"

She was silent for a moment. "Probably."

Trent chuckled. "Faith, you're good at business. You care about your customers, and you think outside the box."

"I hope it's enough," she replied.

"That's the difference between how you see yourself and how I see you," he replied. "You see someone who might be good enough…you're not sure. I see a woman who is smart, capable and talented. I see a sure bet when I look at you."

"You always did."

"It's part of why I leased that shop for you," he said. "You were so hesitant, and I believed you could do it."

"I proved you wrong," she replied.

"It was just life coming at us," he replied, and he looked over at her hopefully. "Look, now that I've got my own business off the ground, I get the importance of cash flow. And I can understand why you wanted to plan a little more before you jumped in. But these things happen even in the face of the best planning. I mean look at other people's stories! Look at the stories behind antique items. People's lives are riddled with challenges and blocks. They just carry on."

"Isn't that what we're trying to do?" she asked.

Yeah, maybe they were.

"I'm not giving up, for the record," Faith said. "I've applied for a bursary in the city. They're giving local residents with small business plans a grant to start a business and access to a loan to keep it running."

Trent was impressed. "Good! I'm glad to hear that." He paused, his enthusiasm waning a little. "So, if you get it, you're going back to the city?"

"I'll have to keep a thumb in this pie for the year, but yes," she replied. "I'd start up my used bookstore and give it another proper try."

"Good luck, then," he said, and he did mean it. This was what she'd wanted, wasn't it?

"Thanks, Trent." She cast him a smile, and his heart squeezed just a little bit. It would be nice to keep her around town, but it was only a matter of time before she slid away again. But this was the personal satisfaction she needed to feel complete—this was the part he couldn't give her, and that didn't come in Apfelkuchen.

The estate sale was occurring at a large property outside Lancaster. The house was gorgeous—three stories of red brick with a generous patio that surrounded one side. The garage looked like it used to be a carriage house, and it was now converted into a four-car garage separate from the house. Behind it, Trent could make out stables and pasture with about fifteen fine-looking horses out there grazing.

There was a good amount of parking out on a stretch of grass and there were a few buggies parked amid the cars and trucks, so news of the estate auction had traveled. And Elaine and Hope were waiting for them in the parking area.

"There they are," Faith said, pointing.

Suddenly it was like the years had evaporated out from under them again, and he was just the devoted guy making things happen for the woman who filled his days. It hit him like a punch to the chest… This was what they could be like still if they hadn't split up. This was what he'd been unfairly hoping for if she stuck around town. He really was a fool, wasn't he?

But he steered in the direction of Faith's smiling sisters and lowered the window.

"Where do we pick up the chairs?" he called.

"Around the side of the house under the portico,"

Hope said, pointing to the covered side entrance of the house, big enough for guests to park under and be dropped off.

"I can't believe you found them!" Faith called, leaning closer to Trent's open window, and closer to him as a result. She propped herself up with a hand on his leg, her attention on her sisters outside. Faith was petite next to him. It was her personality that made her seem to take up more space than she actually did, and there was something about the way she leaned on him that made him feel stronger than he really was, too.

"I know!" Elaine came up to the window. "Hi, Trent. Nice of you to help us get these chairs back to the shop."

"No problem," he replied.

"The owner of this place passed away and they're holding the sale to liquidate," Elaine went on, her attention back on Faith. They talked about a couple of details that Trent didn't even remember, his focus being on her hand on his leg, and then Faith leaned back and Trent put the truck into gear. She didn't seem to notice how close she'd been to him, or that she'd rested against him in the same way she used to. Her scent lingered.

They loaded up the chairs, and then Trent circled the truck back around toward the road. He moved slowly and carefully, and nodded to a couple of Amish men who were walking down the drive toward the house.

"I really don't know what I would have done without your help, Trent," Faith said.

"Yeah, no problem," he said, but he did warm at her words all the same. He'd always liked being her hero...maybe a little too much.

His phone rang, and it was connected to the truck dash, so he punched the button on the dashboard to pick up the call.

"Hi, Trent, it's Abigail."

In the background, he could hear Tyke's crying. He could recognize Tyke's wail anywhere.

"Is he okay?" Trent asked.

"He's got a fever," Abigail said. "So he's feeling pretty crummy. I need you to come pick him up, if you can."

Trent looked over at Faith next to him—and she just nodded quickly. She'd heard enough of the call to know what was going on.

"I'm on my way now," he said. "Thanks, Abigail. I'll be about forty-five minutes."

He punched the button to hang up as he pulled back onto the main road. It would take longer than that—

"Poor little guy," Faith said. "He sounded pretty miserable."

"Yeah. This isn't his first fever, but he's pretty clingy when he's sick. He needs extra attention. I should have told Abigail it would be closer to an hour," he said. "I've got to drop you and your chairs off at the store—"

She shook her head. "You just went out of your

way and burned your own gas to help me get these chairs. Do you want a hand with Tyke?"

"Really?"

It was a generous offer, and he was tempted. A sick toddler could be a lot to handle on his own, especially when Tyke wanted to be on him every minute.

"If you don't mind," he said.

"I'd be happy to," she said. "I owe you one, right?"

But her smile said she wasn't serious about keeping score. She was just offering to give him a hand, and he appreciated the offer more than she knew. He was responsible for Tyke, but that didn't mean that doing this alone wasn't overwhelming. Having someone... Having Faith specifically by his side this afternoon was comforting. She wasn't his anymore, but she still built his confidence.

"Thank you," he said. "Tell you what. Let's drop the chairs off at the store and just put them inside the door. It'll take five minutes. Then we'll go grab Tyke."

It was a plan, and he felt better already.

CHAPTER TWENTY-EIGHT

Faith wasn't entirely sure why she'd offered to help Trent with Tyke. There was something about that little guy that had pierced through her armor. Those big eyes, and the way he'd snuggled up into her arms, had made her heart melt in her chest, and hearing him cry in the background had pricked at some elemental urge inside her to help.

But he's not mine...

That was the part she had to remember. She and Trent were not doing this together, and Tyke wasn't hers to love, any more than Trent was. He was a sweet little guy who needed love and care, but she wasn't part of this.

Was it just her biological clock ticking—a longing for a baby of her own? Or was she emotionally raw still from all the changes around here, and she hadn't been able to stop herself from feeling protective over a sweet little toddler? She hoped it was the latter, because she wasn't ready to look at her longing for a family of her own right now. She had other things to deal with first.

When they got back to the shop, Faith unlocked

the front door and swung it open, holding it in place with a heavy metal iron used in Amish homes for ironing clothing. She looked inside at the now-familiar layout. This shop was starting to feel like home—familiar, warm, safe.

Behind her, the tailgate dropped with a clang, and Trent hoisted down the first chair. They were solid hardwood and heavy. He undid another strap holding the chairs in place and pulled down a second chair, lowering it to the asphalt. Faith picked up one of the chairs and carried it inside. It was heavy and a little awkward, but she handled it just fine. Trent followed her with two more chairs, one in each hand, his biceps bulging.

"I've got the rest of the chairs," he said. "It'll just take a minute."

"I can carry chairs," she said.

"Hey—" He caught her eye and raised an eyebrow. "What am I here for, then?"

Faith stood back as Trent pulled down the last three chairs and carried them in two trips into the store, leaving them in a neat row of polished old wood in front of the cash register.

When they were married, he used to carry all the heavy groceries himself, and she'd take the bag that had the bread and eggs. She'd forgotten what it felt like to have a strong man carry the load for her.

"Thanks," she said.

"When I'm around, I do the heavy lifting," he said. "Remember?"

"I didn't think that rule applied post-divorce," she admitted.

"Well, it does," he said gruffly. "Let's go."

Trent marched past her and back toward the truck, and she had to smother a smile. Fine, then—she'd accept a hand if he was offering like that. There was something from their marriage that had remained in spite of it all, and she tucked that warm feeling away to think over later.

She locked the shop up and they drove the few blocks to the day home.

"Sit tight, I'll go get him," Trent said.

"Sure."

Trent got out of the truck and headed up to the front door. She watched as Abigail ushered him inside. When Faith was alone with Trent, when they were driving together or he was working on the rewiring, it felt incredibly familiar, but sitting out in the truck waiting on him to pick up his toddler, nothing could feel more different. And she'd been the one who'd wanted a baby when they were together. Trent had been the one unready for parenthood. Now he was in the thick of it, and she was the one on the outside... Maybe that was a familiar feeling, after all, feeling disconnected to the things that mattered most to him.

The door opened again and Trent came out with Tyke in one arm and the diaper bag held in the other. Tyke leaned his face into Trent's neck, his little body shuddering with tears. Faith hopped out of the truck to open the back door for Trent, and Tyke squirmed and snuffled against Trent's neck. He'd need a tissue for that, she realized ruefully. Did she even have one on her? Faith wasn't a mom—she didn't have wipes and snacks, tissues and Band-Aids.

Trent put Tyke into the car seat, and Tyke started to cry louder.

"Come on, buddy," Trent said. "We'll get you home, okay?"

It took him a little longer to get the buckles done up, and when he handed Tyke his plastic truck, Tyke flung it across the cab immediately.

"He's really feeling sick," Faith said.

"Yeah, I think so." Trent straightened. "Maybe we can stop for some baby Tylenol at the drugstore on our way back. I don't have any at home."

"Sure," Faith said. "I can run in for it, and you can stay in the truck with Tyke."

"That would work," Trent said, and he sounded a little less stressed now with a plan.

The drugstore was on First Avenue, and they were arriving early enough in the day that it was still open. There was angle parking along the wide street in front of the shops, and Trent chose a spot right in front of the pharmacy.

Trent kept the truck running and started playing the kid's music, and Faith hopped out and headed into the drugstore. She'd never bought baby Tylenol before, she realized. She'd never had reason to, but she knew that it existed. She headed down the cold and flu aisle, scanning the boxes.

"Can I help you find anything?" the pharmacist asked. He was an older man with silver hair. She'd never known him personally, but she'd seen him around town.

"Yes, I'm looking for some Tylenol for a two-year-old with a fever," she said.

"Just a fever?" he asked. "Does he have an upset stomach? Diarrhea?"

"His stomach is fine, from what the day home lady told us, but he has a snuffly nose. We just picked him up, though, so we haven't been watching him for too long. He's really not feeling well. Lots of crying and fussing."

"There are a lot of colds going around," he said with a nod. "Make sure he stays hydrated—juice might be the easiest thing to get into him when he's feeling sick—and give him this once every four to six hours as needed."

He handed her a box of baby Tylenol and showed her the right dosage to use. Then Faith followed him to the counter to pay.

"It's tough when they're sick at this age," the pharmacist said. "I remember when our kids were little. They'd get sick and they'd pass it on to my wife and me, and the whole family would be down with whatever bug the kids picked up. Hopefully you'll skip it."

He was assuming she was the mom, she realized. "I sure hope so," she agreed, handing over the cash. "I don't want this cold next."

That was true, but she wasn't the one who'd be

with Tyke overnight. She wouldn't be getting up with him while he fussed, not feeling well or doing the mental math about when he was due his next dose of Tylenol. That would all be Trent.

"I hope your little fella is feeling better soon," the pharmacist called as she headed out the door, and there was something so wholesome and sweet about that farewell that her chest ached. This was the life she'd wanted—even the tough parts, like sick kids.

He's not mine, she reminded herself. She was just helping out her ex-husband. But this life that included a little person to love and care for was an awfully tempting one. This was the life she'd imagined for her and Trent before it had all fallen apart. And here they were playing the parts. Was she foolhardy to be putting herself into this situation tonight with a man she still had feelings for?

Faith headed out into the sunshine. An uncovered Amish buggy passed, horse clopping along at a steady rhythm. A man and a woman sat side by side—young and newly married by the look of his sparse beard. A planter filled with geraniums sent a sweet, pleasant scent into the late afternoon air. From the truck, she could hear the strains of an Elmo song.

Faith opened the door to the full blast of the music and hopped up into the passenger side seat. She lifted up the paper bag as evidence.

"This was what the pharmacist recommended," she said.

"Perfect." Trent turned around to look behind him and backed out of the spot, then pulled onto the road again. He was silent for a moment as he drove, the playlist filling the cab with music. Then he glanced in her direction, his brown eyes warm. "I'm glad you're here today."

And in spite of all her own misgivings, in spite of her own unmet longings that she'd rather bury right now than face, so was she.

CHAPTER TWENTY-NINE

TRENT OPENED THE front door, and held it for Faith as she came into the foyer. This was his home now, but once upon a time it had been theirs together. He watched as her gaze slid around the little entryway and stopped on the living room. She was still for a moment, and he couldn't read her expression. He could feel the irony of the moment. He was welcoming Faith as a guest into the house that used to be theirs.

"Does it look the same?" he asked, dropping the diaper bag onto a bench by the door and switching Tyke to his other arm.

"Yeah, it does..." she said softly. "Well, except you've got a new couch, and you've moved things around."

There was also the half-emptied toy box on one side of the room and wooden train tracks strewn around. They'd been a gift from friends whose kids had outgrown them, and Trent spent many evenings constructing long tracks that circled around and connected in on themselves again so that Tyke could pull the wooden train along the tracks, happily saying "chugga chugga" under his breath. The end of the game was always when Tyke tore the whole track apart in one glorious, destructive burst.

"Excuse the mess," he said. "I wasn't expecting company."

Although even if he was expecting company, he wasn't sure he could present a much cleaner home. Tyke was always busy, and keeping up with cleaning up behind him was next to impossible.

Trent bent and put Tyke down. Tyke rubbed at his eyes again and headed over to Faith. He held his arms up and Faith bent down and picked him up. Tyke gazed into her face and for a moment, they both just looked at each other.

"Hi, sweetie," she crooned.

Tyke whined again and tipped his head onto her shoulder. Tyke was really taken with Faith. He'd just leaned into her from the start—he wasn't quite this cozy even with Abigail, and she looked after him five days a week. But if Faith would hold Tyke, Trent could get a few things done.

"Do you want to sit down? I'll get his Tylenol," Trent said.

Faith went over to the couch that was angled in front of the television, and she sank into it. This was a new couch, but she chose the same side she'd always sat on—the far left. Tyke squirmed to get more comfortable in her arms, and she brushed his hair off his forehead. She was gentle and tender with him—just what a kid needed when he wasn't feeling well.

Trent opened the bottle of medication and used

the little syringe included to suck up the proper dose, then he went over to where Faith and Tyke sat and gave Tyke a taste first, then squeezed the rest into his mouth.

"That'll help, buddy," Trent said.

Tyke put his head back down on Faith's shoulder, and Trent felt Tyke's forehead. He did feel pretty warm, but he had medication now, and he'd get over this cold like he'd gotten over others. It seemed day cares spread colds and germs faster than anything else.

He left them sitting together and headed into the kitchen.

"I'm going to make some dinner," he called into the other room. "Are you hungry?"

"I could eat," she called back.

Like she'd said a hundred times in their short marriage... It all felt so normal, all of a sudden, maybe too comfortingly so. But she was here tonight, and he needed the help. He'd sort through his confusing feelings on the matter later.

"How about some pasta?" he asked, poking his head around the corner.

"That sounds great." She smiled. "Thanks. I always did like your pasta."

That was why he'd suggested it. His chicken Alfredo pasta was great.

Trent pulled some chicken out of the fridge and the frying pan out from the bottom of the stove and set to work. About half an hour later, the meal was done and Faith sat on the couch with a now-sleeping toddler stretched across her chest. Tyke was audibly snoring, and Faith shot him a helpless look.

"That smells wonderful," she said softly. "I'm going to need help getting Tyke onto the couch, though. I don't have mom muscles."

"Mom muscles?" he asked.

"Moms build their strength as their child grows. Moms of toddlers are surprisingly strong! I wouldn't tangle with one if I were you."

Trent chuckled at her joke. If she stuck around much longer, she might start building up some of that muscle, but he didn't want to think about that too deeply. There was a part of him that yearned toward it too eagerly for it to be entirely safe.

Trent eased his arms underneath Tyke's sleeping form, which meant he slid his arm across Faith's midriff, and he tried to ignore that. He lifted Tyke and laid him on the couch so he could continue sleeping, and Faith rose to her feet.

"He's really taken to you," Trent said.

"I wonder why." Faith looked down at Tyke fondly, then followed Trent into the kitchen.

Trent took two plates from the cupboard and Faith opened the cutlery drawer and grabbed them some forks. It was just a casual thing, but she wasn't quite a guest here, was she? She was something more.

"I think it's because he misses his mom," Trent said.

Faith froze, then her gaze flickered up to meet his. "He has you, though."

"She died when he was a year old, so he had a year with her before he came to me. So… I think he remembers a woman's touch, a woman's love. And he misses it. In her will she said she didn't want him raised Amish, so that took a lot of really good homes for him out of consideration."

"And you think they'd do better than you are?" she asked.

"Undoubtedly."

"I don't know about that," she replied. "I've been watching you with him. You're a good dad."

"I'm not his dad, though—"

"You should probably get used to it, because if you're going to raise this child to adulthood, that's exactly what you are."

Except Tyke didn't call him Dad. He called him "Tent." It was cute, and special. Trent was Tyke's protector, and his best buddy, and his biggest fan. But he hadn't started out on this journey considering himself a father, so it was hard to switch. Trent used some tongs to put some food onto Faith's plate, then dished up his own.

"Whatever you want to call me, I'm not going to be able to give him the same kind of childhood that Albrecht and Mary could, for example."

"True." Faith took a bite and then raised her eyebrows in appreciation of the food. "But you can give him a high school education…send him to college, or get him started on a trade… You can give him a regular American life where he can compete on an even playing field. It sounds like that mattered to his mom."

Trent nodded. "I can't imagine handing him over to anyone else."

"I think that's the part that matters." She paused, then shot Trent a small smile. "My sister Hope is pregnant."

"Really?" Trent's eyebrows went up. "Did she just find out?"

"Yeah." Faith swirled up a bite of pasta and put it into her mouth. She spoke past the food. "It's a big secret. I shouldn't have told you."

"It's okay, I'm still safe with your secrets."

Faith swallowed. Her cheeks had pinked. Embarrassment?

"I really shouldn't have told you that. I don't know why I did. It's Hope's news, not mine. So, please don't tell anyone."

"I meant it. You can tell me stuff, Faith. I won't tell anyone else. Besides, you obviously are feeling something about this, too."

She poked at a piece of chicken with her fork.

"I know it's tough for her, and she's struggling with an unplanned pregnancy, but I would have been ecstatic if I'd found out I was pregnant. I wanted exactly what she has… Okay, maybe with a more present husband, but to be pregnant? Expecting a baby of my own?" Her gaze turned wistful.

"I didn't know the longing was that deep for you," he said. "I really didn't."

"I guess I've been thinking about it more since

I've been on my own," she replied. "I want to be a mom. Maybe I should just face the reality that I'm single and do something like you are—be a single mother to a child who needs love."

"Are you okay, Faith?" he asked.

She took another bite of pasta, then shrugged. "Mostly. I'll be fine."

Here he was wanting to be her solution again—he had to stop that! It hadn't worked when they were married, and it wasn't going to work now.

Tyke's feet sounded on the floor and Trent looked over to see the toddler coming into the kitchen. His cheeks were flushed, and he rubbed at his eyes and snuffled.

"Hey, Tyke," Trent said, holding his hands out to the little guy. And Tyke almost went into Trent's embrace, but then he swerved and headed for Faith again.

"Up," Tyke said plaintively.

Tyke hardly knew Faith, and he was choosing her already. Trent was the one who worried about him, and played with him, carted him around and made sure he got his naps and his proper bedtime. Trent was the one who organized his day home schedule and worked to provide for him. Trent was the one who loved him like a rock, and given the choice, Tyke wanted Faith.

Faith shot Trent a questioning look, and Trent shrugged.

"He wants you," Trent said. "That's okay."

Faith gathered Tyke into her arms and he snuggled in, his eyes heavy and nose runny.

Tyke was getting attached. This was more than a woman being sweet with a toddler. This was a toddler wrapping his heart around a woman who wasn't staying.

"Actually, it's pretty close to Tyke's bedtime," Trent said.

"Oh, of course." Faith straightened. "You've got to go to Trent, buddy. It's time for bed."

Then a thought occurred to him. "You need to get home at some point, too," Trent said. "Maybe I'd better get him into the car seat first so we can take you. But you need to eat your dinner."

"Nonsense," Faith replied. "I'm a grown woman, Trent. I can call an Uber or one of my sisters."

Not too long ago, he would have been her solution, but those times were past. Her ride home felt like his responsibility, but maybe it wasn't anymore. His responsibility was here, in need of his pajamas and a good sleep.

"I'm sorry," he said. "I mean—if I'm not driving you, you could stay for a while. I just need to get Tyke to bed first."

Faith eased Tyke into Trent's arms and gave Tyke a smile. Trent put the toddler up on his shoulder and patted his back the way the little guy liked it. He could feel Tyke melting into his embrace. Trent was the one who'd last—the one who'd be here day in and day out.

She pulled out her phone, typed in a text, waited a moment, then shot him a smile.

"Done," she said. "Hope is on her way to get me."

"I'm not chasing you away, Faith," he said.

"I know. But I don't dare stay, either." Her smile dropped. "I can't be sitting with you in a quiet living room, remembering what it was like when we were married, and…" Her cheeks grew pink again.

"I could promise not to kiss you," he said, giving her a roguish smile.

"I don't think you could," she replied, and she stroked a hand over Tyke's curls. "I know what happens when I cozy up with you on a couch, and I've promised myself there will be no snuggling and kisses tonight."

"Deal." He looked down at the boy in his arms tenderly and sighed. "You're easy to love, Faith."

That had come out a little too honestly. Faith blinked at him.

"I'm not just talking about me." He winced. "We should probably be careful with Tyke, too. I want to limit his difficult goodbyes. That's all."

He knew what losing Faith felt like, and as a grown man it had cut him off at the knees. What would it do to a little boy who was trying to find a mommy to love him? It could mess him up for the rest of his life, and Trent couldn't let that happen.

"It's okay," she said soberly. "I understand. I hadn't thought of that."

Trent spotted a white Lexus coupe pulling up through the living room window. This was terrible timing. He had a feeling he'd messed things up tonight, and he could use a few more minutes to explain himself, to minimize the damage here.

"That's Hope," Faith said, and she forced a smile. "Thanks for everything today, Trent. Truly."

She picked up her purse and headed for the front door. Trent followed her and stopped at the open door as she headed outside.

"Good night," she called, but she sounded strained.

He knew that sound in her voice. He'd hurt her feelings, hadn't he? He hadn't meant to, but he had to be careful with Tyke's little heart, too. Trent might be willing to shoulder a whole lot to spare Faith some pain, but he couldn't ask that of Tyke.

CHAPTER THIRTY

Faith hopped into the passenger side seat of her sister's car. Hope had the air conditioner on, and Faith shivered.

Through the window, Trent met her gaze, gave her a nod. For a moment, he didn't move, and her breath caught. He'd said that she was easy to love, and well... So was he. She'd fallen for him so very easily, and if she wasn't careful, she was going to slide down that slippery slope all over again.

Trent gave her a half smile, and shut the front door, and she released her breath from that catch in her throat. He'd be taking Tyke to bed...right where the little guy needed to be.

"That didn't take you long," Faith said. "Thanks for coming to get me."

"It's not that far to drive," Hope said with a low laugh. "So how are things with Trent?"

Hope put the vehicle into Reverse and backed out of the driveway.

"I'm getting in the way," Faith replied.

"How?" Hope asked as she turned onto the road and started forward again.

"With Tyke. The little guy wants a woman's touch, I suppose. He was really wanting me tonight, and Trent got a bit territorial."

Hope shook her head. "That seems like Trent's going too far. Is he feeling insecure?"

"No..." Faith sighed. "He's being a good dad."

"Okay, first things first," Hope said. "Are you hungry?"

"I just had pasta," she replied.

"Do you want ice cream?" Hope stopped at a stop sign. "Because I do."

Hope was eating for two now, after all. She looked over at her sister. Hope looked a little sad, too. Maybe they both needed a pick-me-up.

"Sure," Faith said.

Hope signaled a turn and headed downtown. The sun was hanging low in the sky, and Faith watched an Amish couple file into a pizza joint, the gray-bearded father holding the door as the wife and seven children passed into the restaurant in front of him. A family night out. That was going to be expensive! But it was a nice problem to have—one that some might not appreciate. Faith never worried about the cost of a restaurant...or about a child with a fever, or about buying more running shoes for a kid that just kept growing. Women who had those problems were lucky.

"Have you told Elaine yet about your pregnancy?" Faith asked.

"Yeah, I told her. She squealed a lot."

Faith chuckled. "What can I say? We aunts are excited."

They drove in silence for a couple of minutes.

"So what's going on between you and Trent?" Hope asked.

"Nothing," Faith replied.

"Come on, Faith. You can tell me it's none of my business, but don't lie to me."

"I don't know what's happening between us," Faith admitted. "Trent has always been my weakness, and here he is being all sweet and helpful and doing the wiring on our shop and agreeing to pick up chairs and... It's more emotionally complicated than it should be."

"Do you love him still?" Hope asked.

Faith shot her sister an annoyed look, but maybe the question wasn't completely out of the blue. She'd been spending a lot of time with Trent since her return, and she'd been trying to fend off whatever feelings were creeping in between them.

"I shouldn't," Faith said.

"But do you?"

Did she? Had she actually slipped down that emotional slide again with this man? Or was she simply working through her feelings still?

"I might. I'm working on that." Faith leaned her head back against the headrest.

Hope signaled another turn and pulled into the Beiler Dairy Ice Cream Shop's parking lot. There was a stable behind the shop, and two buggies were parked back there, horses in the stalls. Beiler Dairy was owned and operated by the Amish Beiler family, and while they sometimes hired an Englisher teenager to work the front till, normally customers were served by the Beilers.

"And Tyke... Are you falling for him, too?" Hope asked.

Faith looked over at her sister. "He's a great little guy. I mean—"

She hadn't actually considered what she was feeling there. Of course, she adored him. He was an adorable toddler. Who wouldn't love him?

"He's very sweet," Faith said. "And lately I've been reminded of the family I longed for with Trent when he wasn't ready yet."

Hope nodded. "Seems rather unfair he's ready now."

"A little." Faith sighed. "But the fact remains, he didn't want to have a child with me."

"It might be more complicated than that," Hope replied.

"I know. And Tyke is a special little guy who just thinks I'm the best," Faith said.

"Do you ever wonder what it would be like to be a little family—you and Trent and Tyke?" Hope asked.

"That's a little bit cruel," Faith said, and she blinked back a mist of tears. "Yes, I have. But that's not going to happen. When Trent and I were together, he felt so far away. I told him then how much I wanted a baby, and it didn't mean the same thing to him. So now he has Tyke, and he's a really good dad. And I haven't been part of any of it! So maybe I understand how you feel about Peter right now. I needed Trent to choose me a long time ago. He didn't."

Hope nodded. "I talked to Peter today, and I told him I missed him so much, and I just couldn't keep doing this. It's not going to work for me to be at home on my own for weeks on end."

"And?" Faith asked.

"And he said he'll be home in two weeks, and we can talk about it more then. Maybe he can scale back his traveling."

"That sounds reasonable," Faith said.

"I know. Rationally, it does. But on a heart level..."

"Divorce hurts a whole lot. It doesn't just go away. It's not like breaking it off with a boyfriend. Divorce is a whole different beast. I know you're upset, I know you need something from him that he's not figuring out right now, but don't give up. Trust me—it hurts more to give up."

Hope reached over and squeezed Faith's hand. "I don't want to leave him."

"Then don't toy with these feelings, either," Faith replied. "There are some points of no return. You love him. He loves you. You're having a baby! Is he reacting perfectly right now? No, but from where I'm sitting, he's still a really good guy. He's trying to provide."

Hope nodded. "Yeah, you're right."

"So let's go inside and eat ice cream," Faith said. "We're eating for three."

Inside the Beiler Dairy Ice Cream Shop, Faith scanned the menu board. There were some delicious options—soft-serve cones, whoopee pie sundaes, banana splits, Amish peanut butter parfaits...

"Hi, Faith."

Faith looked around and spotted Sarah behind the counter. She wore a Beiler Dairy apron over her dress, and there was something about the young woman that looked rather vulnerable. Maybe it was the heartbreak shining through.

"Sarah! I didn't know you worked here." Faith went up to the counter with a smile.

"Today is my third day," Sarah replied. "I applied for work when I thought—"

She stopped there. Right. When she thought she was going to pursue more with Eddie and she'd probably need more ready money of her own.

"I think it's great that you've got a job," Faith said.

"Thanks." She sucked in a breath.

"This is my sister Hope."

"Of course. Hi, Hope. It's nice to see you again."

There was a little bit of polite chitchat between Hope and Sarah, and Faith remembered the recipe cards she'd tucked into her purse for safekeeping until she could return them to the Yoders.

"Sarah, I have something you might find neat," Faith said, and she opened her purse and pulled out the cards. The little slip of paper with the note from long ago was there, too. "These were inside a wooden recipe box your parents donated to the shop, and I thought you might want them back."

She passed the cards over and Sarah squinted at the faint, spidery handwriting.

"1923... That would be my great-grandmother's recipes, maybe?" Sarah's gaze lit up. "Wow. That's really special." She looked closer. "Is this a recipe for scrapple? I think so. It starts with a whole hog's head."

"This was in there, too," Faith said, handing over the other note. Sarah accepted it and took a closer look. Her lips moved as she read the words. "What is it?"

"I thought you might know," Faith replied. "I know it isn't really my business, but I was curious."

"Is it from my great-grandmother, as well?" Sarah asked.

"I don't know," Faith replied. "It looks like there might be a story behind it."

"If there is, I never heard it," Sarah replied. "I'll ask my *mamm* tonight after my shift."

Maybe they'd find out...maybe they wouldn't. But Faith was curious all the same. The prim-and-proper Amish community could hide a lot more drama than people guessed.

"Can I get you some ice cream?" Sarah asked.

"I'll take the whoopee pie sundae," Hope said.

"A vanilla cone for me," Faith said.

They'd have their treat, they'd talk and they'd remind themselves that everything they were going through now had been endured before by generations of women. There had been marital difficulties. There had been heartbreak. There had been family trials, and surprise pregnancies, and women who'd longed for babies. None of this was brand-new. And there was some comfort in that.

CHAPTER THIRTY-ONE

THE NEXT MORNING, Trent woke up to the sound of Tyke sniffles from the baby monitor. It sounded like he was awake, and like he had a cold. At least the fever had lessened last night, and Trent had slept better knowing that.

"Tent?" Tyke called, but then his little voice lowered to something more conversational, chattering about his plastic truck, and then his toy robot that he called a "bot-bot." Maybe it was just because he was a little boy, but all of Tyke's favorite toys had hard edges to them.

Trent tossed back his covers and sat up. He'd changed the bedroom completely since the divorce. He'd had to. She'd taken the old bedroom furniture, and he got rid of his half of the old sheets and blankets, and he'd started from scratch. He'd marched into the only furniture store in town and bought a gray fabric headboard and a chest of drawers in the same charcoal gray color, and had ordered some black bedding online. The result wasn't exactly more attractive, but it had purged Faith from the room. She wasn't so easy to purge from his memories, though.

And this morning, he found himself missing that scent of face cream and perfume, and makeup—that feminine combination that had lodged itself deep in the back of his mind so that he remembered the scent so strongly sometimes that he almost thought he could smell it.

Having Faith back in town wasn't helping with that, because this morning he almost thought he could smell that faint, feminine scent again...

Trent rubbed his hands over his face.

Last night, he'd said too much. But then, she'd always had that effect on him. He couldn't help but say what he was feeling with her around. He picked up his phone off his bedside table and spotted a text. He hadn't noticed when it came in.

It was a picture of the recipe cards and a little note written with pen on a slip of paper.

Sarah thinks these might be from her great-grandmother. Any relation to you?

So she'd been thinking of him. He smiled faintly. It was possible it was some great-aunt, and it was neat that she might have left some part of herself to be discovered by later generations, but Sarah would feel a closer connection to all of that.

He typed back: I'm not too sure, but it's neat. I don't read Pennsylvania Dutch, so I don't know what they are even recipes for.

He pressed Send.

Good morning, by the way, he added.

It felt good to have this little connection to Faith again—a text to wake up to. She was comforting, sweet, interesting... And he found himself falling into the old trap of wanting to help her get whatever it was she wanted out of life.

"Not my job..." he muttered. Maybe it never had been, because it hadn't worked anyway.

"Tent?" Tyke called, a little more insistently now.

"I'm up, buddy!" Trent called back and he slipped his feet into his slippers and shuffled out of the room and into Tyke's. His family had all pulled together to sort out Tyke's bedroom last year. There was a giraffe growth chart on one wall, and two mismatching toy boxes that were packed with toys. A play carpet was on the floor with roads depicted on it. There was also a solid crib that could be taken apart and turned into a toddler bed when he was ready, but Trent wasn't ready yet. Keeping Tyke corralled at night still just seemed smart. Maybe in a few months.

Trent picked up Tyke—his diaper heavy and drooping—and carried him over to the changing table. He felt his head. He was still a bit warm, but not too bad. Tylenol would take the last of the fever away for a few hours.

"Let's get you freshened up, kiddo," Trent said. "You're staying home today so you don't give all your friends this cold."

Although he'd probably gotten it from one of the

kids, but Abigail had firm rules about sick kids—they didn't come to day home if they were sick enough to require medication. Trent felt Tyke's head again. Yeah, there was still a fever. Trent was far enough ahead with the wiring that he could afford the day with Tyke.

Trent changed the diaper and then deposited Tyke on his feet on the carpet.

"You know what, buddy?" Trent said. "I'm going to introduce you to that potty today."

Tyke looked up at him, eyes round.

"You'll like it," Trent said. "No more wet diapers once you figure it out."

"I got a tuck!" Tyke said, holding up his plastic truck.

"You do," Trent replied. "Come on. Let's get breakfast first. I have to let everyone know I'm not coming in today."

"Toast?" Tyke asked hopefully.

"Yeah, buddy. I'll make toast. You want jam on your toast, too?"

"Yeah!" Tyke said.

Trent headed toward the kitchen, Tyke padding along behind him. His phone pinged, and he looked down at a text from Faith.

Good morning, Trent.

He couldn't help but smile at that. He could almost hear her voice. She was up, and he was willing to bet he'd gotten her first text. Well, she'd gotten his.

You free to talk? he texted back.

In response, his phone rang with her number, and he picked it up.

"Hey," he said. "How are you?"

"Not too bad," she said. "One of the recipes is for scrapple, by the way. Sarah says it calls for a whole hog's head."

"Scrapple is like sausage," he said with a low laugh. "It's delicious, but you should never ask what's inside."

She laughed, too.

"How's Tyke?"

"Still a bit feverish. I'll have to keep him at home today," he replied. "So I won't be coming in today. But we only have one more solid day of work to do. I'll get it done before the deadline."

"Thank you..." Her voice was quiet.

"It feels good to talk to you again," he said. "I missed this."

"Me, too."

He warmed at that thought.

"So what are you up to today?" he asked, and pulled out a loaf of bread and popped two pieces into the toaster.

"The customer looking for the chairs is coming in today. We settled on a fair price that still makes a profit for the store," she said.

"Congratulations. Your first sale?"

"My first sale. The first of many once we open up on Monday, I hope."

"I think you'll do great," he said.

"Yeah?"

"You will." He fished out the baby Tylenol and checked the label for the right dosage again. He didn't want to mess that up. Then he used the syringe to measure and held it down for Tyke. Tyke ran up and opened his mouth for his medicine. It must taste pretty good. He put a drop on his own finger and put it into his mouth. It was kind of like candy—that explained it.

Trent checked the time on his phone, and then set a timer. Four to six hours before Tyke could have more.

"Tent?" Tyke asked plaintively.

"Yeah, buddy?" He bent down.

"More?" Tyke pointed at the Tylenol bottle.

"No! That's medicine, not breakfast," he chuckled. "Come here. Let's put you in your chair, and we'll get ready for toast, okay?"

Trent picked up the toddler and deposited him in the high chair. He touched his head again, and it was cooler already.

"I'm thinking of including little stories about some items in the shop. It might make some good social media content to get the word out about our store," Faith said.

"Are you doing that thing Elaine suggested—telling your own story?"

"Me?" She laughed breathily. "No, it's stories about the items."

"You should introduce yourselves, too."

The toast popped up and he buttered both slices, cut one up into strips and brought the strips over to Tyke. He hungrily dug into the toast. Oh, right. Jam.

He went over to the fridge.

"Why so quiet?" he asked.

"I'm thinking about that."

"Can I tell your story?" he asked. He was tempted to tease her with something—make up a story about a very serious woman, or something. But he wouldn't do that.

"Fine, what would you say about me?" Faith asked.

"Once there was a woman who loved books," he said. "And not just bestselling, current books. She loved books that had been forgotten, tucked away somewhere, that had hardly sold any copies at all, but still had some magic in the pages. She loved beautiful bindings, and inscriptions in the front page. She loved books that had been previously loved by others long ago, and when she touched the pages or inhaled that vanilla scent of bookbinding glue that was deteriorating over time, she felt connected to the ghosts of those who came before her."

There was silence on the other end—not quite silence. He could hear her breathing, but she didn't say anything. "Faith?"

"How do you know me that well?" she breathed.

Because she'd been lodged in his heart for years... for years longer than she should have been, too. Because while he didn't communicate it very well, he had understood her. Or he'd learned to. Maybe these last two years away from her when all he could do was go over what she'd said, and what she'd done, had been the most educational for him.

"I always did," he said, and emotion choked off his voice.

It just hadn't been enough. He'd always given her the best he knew how. But she'd been unhappy.

He grabbed the jam from the fridge and added a bit to one of Tyke's strips of toast.

"Yum!" Tyke said.

"Yum." He tried to smile, but he felt that old ache in his chest again.

Loving her was the most painful thing he'd ever done, and it still hurt.

"I'd better get going," Faith said. "I have to get dressed and get ready for my sisters to arrive."

"Sure," he replied. "I'll see you tomorrow."

"Looking forward to it," she said, and while he knew it was probably just a habit to reply that way, he was looking forward to it—more than he should.

"Me, too," he said. "See you then."

He looked thoughtfully at Tyke.

"Daddy," Tyke said softly.

His throat choked closed. "What was that?"

"Daddy," Tyke repeated.

Where had he gotten that? Maybe from a book Abigail read him, or a TV show... But those big brown eyes looking up at him needed some reassurance. He'd been "Tent" up until now. He hadn't been sure that Tyke would ever want to call him anything else. That had been okay. He didn't think of himself as a father, so much as the brick wall between a small boy and a big world. But yeah… maybe "dad" fit after all.

"I am your daddy," he said, and he swallowed hard. "And you're my buddy, right?"

Tyke grinned.

Life had moved on. Faith wasn't his anymore, but Tyke was. And together, he and this little boy were going to make a future. He just needed to get his heart to catch up.

CHAPTER THIRTY-TWO

Faith stood back, looking at the shop as they'd arranged it so far. There was one section of furniture—although she used the surfaces to display other items. There was the section of quilts, linens and old items of clothing. Women back then seemed to be slimmer—or at least those were the clothes that had survived to be sold now. Tiny waists, petite sizes...kitten-heeled shoes in size 5. There was a little pillbox cap with a short bridal veil attached, ladies' white gloves that had yellowed with age, some fur stoles from the days of fur as both a fashion choice and a warm necessity. They didn't only have Amish items here. Aunt Josephine had insisted that the store reflect her own family—Amish and English together.

And then the shelves of classic kitchenware—hand-cranked egg beaters, vintage Pyrex mixing bowl sets nested together, measuring cups, an array of teacups and saucers. The cast-iron skillets were worth a good deal to the right cook—cured over the better part of a century! But it was the far side of the store, nestled in the back, that tugged at Faith the most.

It was the book corner. There were archaic hardcover grade-school readers gracing those shelves that school-aged children used to read a hundred years ago. There were heirloom Amish hymnals, too—some inscribed inside with names of the previous owners. There were some *Farmer's Almanacs* and classic comic books that they'd dug up from the basement. Apparently, those retro comics hadn't interested Aunt Josephine, but these days they were very popular for collectors. A row of Nancy Drews in their classic yellow hardcovers warmed Faith's heart particularly, and there were a few hardcover classics published nearly a hundred years ago, which would sell for a good price. But Trent had been right—her favorite books in the little collection were the old novels that hadn't been appreciated by the critics—the gothic romances, the spy thrillers from the sixties, the Westerns featuring hard-riding cowboys. Those were books that had entertained countless people—tugged them through lonely evenings or provided an escape during long, winter nights. Those were the books that felt more connected to generations past than the books they "ought to have read."

Monday was their soft reopening when their rewiring would be complete, and they could start making some sales…hopefully.

And yet, Trent's description of her love of these

kinds of books lingered. There had been something so tender in his voice, as he'd described her to a tee.

There was a tap on the front door and Faith turned to see a middle-aged woman standing there, a hopeful smile on her face. She had short, curly hair and wore a pin-striped shirt dress, belted at the waist. It was in the same color of gray that highlighted her hair, and it was a pretty look. Faith opened the door.

"Hi, I'm Susan," the woman said. "I'm here about the chairs."

"Right! It's nice to meet you, Susan. Come on in," Faith said, stepping back with a smile.

This was their very first sale since taking over—the very first sale that they'd orchestrated and worked on together as a team of sisters.

"You aren't open yet, I see?" Susan asked.

"No, not yet. We're just getting some electrical work finished on the building, and then our grand opening is on Monday."

"Well, it looks great in here," Susan said with a smile. "Very inviting."

"I've got the chairs waiting for you here by the till," Faith said. "Did you want to come take a look?"

Susan followed her over to the till, and squatted down next to the chairs. She ran a hand over the hardwood lines.

"These are spectacular," she said. "I can't believe you found them!"

"My sister did," Faith said, and she retold the story of how Elaine had stumbled across them. "I was pretty excited, too. Now, like I said, we have six chairs in total. You are welcome to all six, if you want them. If not, I'm sure I'll find other buyers."

"I promised my husband I was only getting three..." Susan winced. "But when will I get a chance like this again?"

Faith didn't answer—this wasn't her battle, it was Susan's.

"I'd better call him and discuss it," Susan said. "Do you mind if I just browse while I talk to him?"

"Of course! Feel free," Faith said.

Susan popped in an earbud and made her call. Then she started perusing the store as she talked quietly to her husband on the other line. Faith heard her describe the chairs excitedly, then explain how rare it would be to find more in the future if they ever decided they wanted to enlarge their dining room seating.

Just a married couple discussing a purchase, but there was an obvious shared excitement about the antique chairs, and they discussed whom they normally had over for holidays, Susan counting people off on her fingers.

It was sweet—that looked like a happy marriage. She wondered if they had a secret to staying united. What created a lasting bond like that? What made a couple pull together instead of drift apart? Because she'd spent the last two years looking back at her relationship with Trent, wondering if there was some early sign that they wouldn't last, and she couldn't find one. There had been no red flag.

There had been no character flaw in her husband. They'd just…butted heads a lot.

So maybe instead of looking for red flags, she should be looking for the signs that showed a couple would make it.

The bell above the door tinkled, and Hope and Elaine came into the shop. Hope was on her cell phone, and Faith heard her say, "I have news, Peter…" Then she turned away so that her words were private.

"Hi, Faith," Elaine said, and she cast a curious look toward Susan, who was also on her phone.

"This is the customer for the chairs," Faith said.

"Right!" Elaine smiled. "Excellent. We're hitting the ground running."

"What's going on there?" Faith asked, glancing toward Hope, who was preoccupied with her own phone call.

"I think she's telling Peter about the baby," Elaine said. "Apparently, you gave her something to think about last night, and she says she just wants to share this pregnancy with her husband."

"Good," Faith said. "I'm glad. I know it's tough right now, but once the tension is past, I'm sure they'll be fine."

"How many chairs is the customer taking?" Elaine asked.

"She's discussing that with her husband right now," Faith replied.

But her gaze slid past their customer toward Hope. Hope was also talking to her husband, and

Faith could see her sister's profile. She was smiling now, nodding.

"Okay... I'll see you soon, honey," Hope said, and she hung up the call, looking down at the screen with a little smile on her face.

Susan hung up her call just then, too.

"We're taking all six!" Susan announced with a smile.

"He's coming home!" Hope said, at nearly the same time, and both women looked at each other in mild surprise.

Faith's gaze whipped between her customer and her sister.

"Let me just ring up these chairs, and then I want the update," Faith said.

It didn't take long, and then the three sisters helped to carry the chairs out to Susan's van. When they got the last chair in, they said their goodbyes and turned back toward the store.

"He's coming home, Hope?" Faith asked.

"Yeah. I told him about the baby, and he understood why I was feeling rather emotional, and he said he was really sorry that he hadn't listened to me sooner. He's taking the next flight tomorrow morning, around ten."

"Just like that?" Faith asked.

"I guess so!" Hope smiled. "Thank you for talking me down last night. It's not easy, is it?"

"What part?" Faith asked. "Marriage or pregnancy?"

"I guess both." Hope shrugged. "Peter and I will

figure something out. I'm just glad he's coming back. I've really missed him. He'll come meet me here and then we can drive back to the city together."

And it was fixed... Hope had talked things out with Peter, Peter had seen exactly why Hope needed him at home right now, and he was doing the right thing.

"How long is he coming back for?" Elaine asked.

"He says he can probably make it back for three days, but then he has to go back to finalize some sales, and I'll come back here. But I understand. The commission on those sales is going to go toward baby preparation, no doubt."

Her phone pinged, and Faith looked down at her device to see an incoming email. The preview made her heart hammer in her chest. Elaine and Hope moved on to discussing strollers. Apparently, Elaine had a friend who'd bought the newest jogging stroller and just loathed it, so there were some things to consider. So Faith headed over to the book corner and tapped on the email to open it.

Dear Ms. Fairchild,
We are pleased to offer you a bursary for your used bookstore proposal for the city of Philadelphia...

There were the details about how much money was offered, when the bookstore would need to be opened by and how much of a loan they were offering on the side for other business expenses.

But this was it—her bookstore would truly be a reality!

In Philadelphia.

She looked around the Amish Antiques Shop, from her sisters who were now looking up different jogging strollers on their phones, to the arrangement of vintage finds for their future customers. She ran a finger over the cracked leather cover of an old Amish hymnal, and she let the information settle into her mind.

She'd have a generous bursary—money to get her off the ground, at least—and access to a decent loan, too. She already had a stash of used books she'd been adding to boxes in a storage locker, and she finally felt ready. She'd been planning this, researching it, and with that bursary, she'd be okay. There would be a cushion for unexpected emergencies.

"Faith?" Elaine called. "How come you look stunned?"

"I got the bursary!"

It took a couple of minutes to catch her sisters up to speed, but she filled them in on the details.

"But what about the antiques shop?" Hope asked. "We have to run it together if we're going to inherit it in a year."

"I'll split my time between Philadelphia and Apfelkuchen," Faith said. "We can make this work, can't we?"

Elaine had her kindergarten class. Hope was having a baby. This bookstore would be Faith's dream come true, and they'd all have the very things they'd dreamed of.

Almost everything... Life wasn't perfect, was it?

"Of course we can make it work," Elaine said. "We'll figure it out, Faith. We know how much you want this."

But somehow, in the midst of all this news and these plans, Faith knew it wouldn't feel real until she did one thing...

"I'm going to be back in an hour or so," Faith said. "Is that okay with you?"

"Where's Trent?" Hope asked, glancing around.

"Tyke is sick. He's at home with him."

"Oh... Oh!" Hope's eyebrows went up. "Are you off to tell him about it?"

"Yeah," she admitted. "I think he needs to know."

Faith could try to hide it, but her sisters would see through her feints anyway. But she needed to talk to Trent. Because starting up a store in Philadelphia would mean a whole lot less time here in Apfelkuchen. And somehow, she sensed that everything would change. She and Trent would change. And maybe she wanted some reassurance that this new closeness they'd discovered wouldn't evaporate. She had no right to it, but it had become very precious to her all the same.

They were friends now. Please, let it stay that way.

CHAPTER THIRTY-THREE

Tyke lay on the couch, a microfiber blanket wrapped around him and his head on a pillow as he watched a *Sesame Street* episode. He had his plastic truck next to him upside down, and he absently thumbed a wheel to spin it. He looked so small under that big blanket, and Trent bent down and tousled his blond curls.

"Do you like this show?" Trent asked.

Tyke nodded, his eyes still locked on the screen. Big Bird was talking about the letter *A*—fascinating stuff for a toddler. A whole world was opening up for him with the alphabet, and Tyke had no idea everything waiting for him as he grew. Books, school, friends, sports... Kid stuff—the kind of childhood that Trent had enjoyed.

His life had changed so much in the last year. When Faith left, he'd never thought he'd be able to pull his heart back together again. But when Tyke arrived, he'd had a reason to get back on his feet emotionally—because Tyke needed it. There was no other option.

All the same, he'd always imagined raising a

child with his wife by his side. Heck, if he was going to be brutally honest, he'd imagined raising a child with Faith, and these last couple of weeks had started making him imagine that again.

Trent glanced down at the text he'd received from Faith. She had news, and she'd asked if she could come by and share it in person. Of course he'd said yes. The rumble of a car's engine drew his attention to the window. Faith's car was just pulling in.

He headed over to the front door and pulled it open, watching as she hopped out of the driver's seat and hit the fob to lock the door. That was a city habit—she had a few of those now. In Apfelkuchen, no one worried too much about a vehicle being stolen, it happened so rarely.

"Hey," Trent said, and he could feel the smile on his lips. "I'm glad you came by."

As she smiled back, he reached out and caught her hand, tugging her into the house. She squeezed his fingers and peeked into the living room.

"How's he feeling?"

"He's doing pretty good," Trent said. "He's glued to *Sesame Street*."

If Tyke were feeling better, he'd be bouncing on the carpet in front of *Sesame Street*—that was the difference. Trent nodded toward the kitchen.

"Do you want something to drink? Coffee? Tea? Coke?"

"A Coke would be nice."

They headed through the living room, and Faith ran her hand over the top of the couch on her way past, but she didn't disturb Tyke. Tyke did look up at her, though, wide eyes watching her pass by.

"Hi, sweetie," Faith said, and she fluttered her fingers at Tyke. He broke into a smile then.

"Hi! Hi!" Tyke said.

Trent knew that feeling, too. Faith could capture a guy in spite of himself.

Trent grabbed a can of Coke out of the fridge, cracked it open and poured it into a tall glass. If it were just for himself, he'd drink it from the can, but Faith had always liked things to be slightly more civilized. Women did that to men—made them take a step up.

"Thank you," Faith said, accepting the glass. Her gaze stayed locked on the fizzing cola.

She said she had news... Was it bad news?

"Are you okay?" he asked.

"Yeah, I'm fine." She looked up then, but her smile seemed forced.

"What's the matter?" Trent asked. Because he could see it all over her face—something was very wrong. "You said you had news."

"I do... I just found out a few minutes ago, actually." She shrugged. "Maybe I should have taken a bit longer to process it before I texted you. I'm sorry, I keep trampling normal boundaries."

"That's okay," he said. "I like you better without your proper boundaries, anyways."

He caught her eye and smiled.

"I got the bursary to open up my used bookstore in Philadelphia."

So that was it. She'd gotten her ticket out of here—her dreams come true. His first emotion was dismay, but he knew that was wrong. She deserved to be happy, even if being with him wasn't going to do that for her.

"You look ready to cry," he said.

Truthfully, he felt ready to cry, too, and he couldn't quite explain why.

Faith rubbed her hands over her face. "This is why I should have taken some time before I came pounding over here… I'm…surprised, I guess. I didn't actually anticipate getting the bursary."

"You applied for it."

"I know, but a lot of good people apply for these things. My chances were slim. They said that bringing a bookstore into a neighborhood with so many schools would be an advantage."

So she'd come over here to talk it out. But what did she want from him? She'd spent their entire marriage keening for just this kind of opportunity, and now she had it. Without his help, either. That fact stung just a little bit, too, because there was some small part of him that still hoped that even after their split he could one day give her something that no one else could…make up for the happiness he hadn't been able to provide in their marriage.

"That is great news, then," he said. "You wanted this, Faith. This is your own bookstore, and it sounds like the bursary makes it so that you can afford it properly."

"It does. It ticks all the boxes." She leaned back against the counter and he studied her for a moment.

"So why aren't you happy?" he asked at last.

Faith shot him a mildly irritated look. "I don't know. I might have dealt with things differently, if I'd known that I was going to be leaving again like this."

"Are you leaving?"

"I'll have to come back regularly to help run the shop here, but...yes. I'll be mostly in Philly."

"So what brought you over here today?" he asked, his throat tight. "Why are you here with me, and not celebrating with your sisters?"

"Because I'm going to miss you!" she said. "I don't know why I did this to myself! I knew it would be hard to see you again, and I knew I should have kept my distance from you."

Her words stabbed a little deeper than he anticipated.

"Kept your distance? You really think that was the right thing?"

"I don't know!" Faith turned to face him. "I feel foolish even admitting this, but seeing you again has...brought up old feelings for me."

Trent reached out and caught her hand again, tugging her a little closer. She let him draw her in, and he had to stop himself from wrapping his arms around her completely.

"You want to explain that?" he asked with a small smile.

"This isn't a joke."

"I'm not joking!" he replied, dropping his smile. "Two years ago, in this very kitchen, you told me you wanted a divorce. And you walked away. I don't know how you did it, but you did. And the only explanation I could give myself was that I was out of sight and out of mind. You moved away, and you didn't have to see me anymore."

"You weren't out of my mind!"

"Then why didn't you come back and face me?" he demanded. "Not even to sign the divorce papers. Why didn't you come back?"

"Because I loved you!" she retorted. "You know I loved you, Trent. I loved you more than you ever loved me, and I couldn't live with that! I couldn't look you in the face knowing that I adored you, and you saw me as a step above a roommate!"

"Who says I felt that way?"

"I could tell!" Her eyes flashed fire.

"You were wrong!"

She was so close, and all he could see was that fire inside her—and he didn't know how to put all of this into words. He never could! So instead of wasting another second trying, he dipped his head and caught her lips with his.

He pulled her in against his aching heart, and he kissed her with all of that stored-up loneliness inside him. He didn't know what any of it meant, but she still filled up his heart, against all of his wiser instincts! He loved her, and he'd never stopped. Seeing her again hadn't put anything to rest. It had only stirred it up more.

Her lips were soft, and when he was breathless, he pulled back and she blinked up at him.

"I never stopped loving you..." he admitted gruffly. "Not for a minute, and I tried so hard to let you go."

She stared at him, her lips parted as if she were about to speak. She was the most beautiful woman he'd ever met, and she'd always be. She'd been his first love, and he was realizing now that no matter what he did, she was going to own a part of his heart.

"I love you still," he concluded.

"Still?" she whispered.

"Yes, still!" Loving her was never the problem. "That should not surprise you. A guy who isn't in love with you doesn't do everything he can—drive you all around the county—just to spend time with you. Okay? That's what guys in love do. They do the little things, try and take care of you, and sometimes they are monumentally stupid enough to try and hand you your life's desire. So yes. I love you."

"Me, too," she whispered back, and he felt a crash of relief.

She was stuck in this miserable, heartbroken purgatory, too. Good! He shouldn't be here alone. In fact, neither of them should stay here!

"What do we do?" he asked. "I love you. You love me... What's the next step?"

And just then, he heard a snuffling sound in the doorway. Trent looked down to find Tyke looking up at them with wide eyes, his plastic truck hooked under one arm. What was the next step when there was another small, fragile heart to consider besides his own?

"Up?" Tyke said, and he came over to where Faith stood and lifted his pudgy hands to her. "Up?"

"Hey, you..." Faith said softly, and she scooped him up. Her throat felt tight, and she swallowed hard against her own emotions.

Tyke smiled into her face and put his hands on her cheeks.

"I'm going to get this cold, aren't I?" she said with a low laugh.

"Probably," Trent said, but his smile was sad.

"Come here, buddy," Trent said. "Let's start you a new show. What about some *Paw Patrol*, huh?"

Faith passed the toddler into Trent's strong arms, and she watched as he carried the boy out to the living room again. She loved Trent. That was the problem, wasn't it? She had fallen in love with her ex-husband all over again. Or maybe she'd just dug it back up again from where she'd attempted to bury it. How on earth had she not realized this sooner?

There was something so endearing about watching Trent with that little boy. He was so gentle with him, so patient. Trent got Tyke settled on the couch again with his blanket and his truck, and then he took the remote control and started up a different show for him. Tyke watched Trent with big, adoring eyes all the while.

"There you go," Trent said, putting the remote down on the side table.

He didn't turn back toward her right away, instead watching Tyke as the little boy wiped his nose on his arm again and settled in to watch his show. When he did look back at her, she saw the change in his face. He'd come to a decision.

He walked up to her and pulled her into his arms, wrapping her in a tight hug and resting his cheek against her hair. She leaned against his solid, warm chest, and she could feel his steady heartbeat. Oh, how she'd longed for this...

But something had been missing back then—something she couldn't quite identify. Had she loved him? Desperately! But somehow that hadn't been enough...and she wished she could explain it. Because it hadn't been a bookstore.

"Trent..." Faith pulled out of his arms, but she saw the pain in his eyes. He was feeling it, too.

"I don't know if we can do this," Trent said quietly. "We tried this before, and we loved each other then, too."

She nodded mutely, tears lodged in her throat.

"The thing is," he said, "if it were just me, I'd take the plunge. But I've got Tyke to consider. He's lost his mom already, and he's falling in love with you... If it didn't work between us again, it would crush him."

She nodded, tears filling her eyes. "I understand that. You're a good dad, Trent."

"I'm sorry..."

"No, you're right. It's not just you," she said. "Love wasn't enough for us then. I needed something more, and… I still need to know what that is. I owe it to myself."

Before she broke a good man's heart again, and before she did the same thing to a little boy who just needed a stable, loving home that he could trust. She needed to figure it out for her own peace of mind, so that she could understand herself, too.

"Is it your bookstore?" he asked quietly.

And in her mind's eye she saw Bumblebee Books, the shelves laden with story after story, and the potted plants that lent an air of exotic adventure. She thought of her plans for Second Chance Books, with the European feel of used books crammed onto shelves, stacked in piles and filling up both a little shop and her own wayward heart. It was both comforting and terrifying at once! It was her dream for so long now, and it was finally within reach.

"Maybe, but I don't know," she admitted. "I need to figure that out."

Trent reached out and tugged her close again. He pressed his lips against her forehead in a lingering kiss, and she rested her hands against his warm chest, his heartbeat trembling against her fingertips.

"I love you," he whispered raggedly. "I don't think that's ever going to stop."

A tear rolled down her cheek. "I love you, too."

Now Faith knew that love could be real and true, and still not enough to build a life on. But oh, how she wished that it was! For the second time since meeting this man, she was forced to walk away with her heart in tatters.

She hadn't meant to fall in love with him again. That had been both foolish and completely outside her control!

Faith took a step back and wiped her face with her fingers.

"I need to go," she said.

Trent nodded, and she gathered up her purse again and headed through the living room. Tyke had fallen asleep in front of his TV show, and she paused to brush his hair away from his face in one tender touch.

Because she'd miss this little boy, too… She'd fallen in love with both her ex-husband and Tyke, and it was going to take a very long time to heal from it again.

A very, very long time.

CHAPTER THIRTY-FOUR

FAITH PULLED TO a stop along the street a stone's throw from Amish Antiques. She sat there, her hands on the wheel, taking deep breaths. What she wanted to do was just sit here and cry, but she knew too many people in Apfelkuchen to do that. Someone who knew her would be alarmed to see her sobbing out her heartbreak in her parked car. In Philly, she could have. Here? She had to hold it together until she was truly alone.

The street was surprisingly busy this time of day, and she watched as a teenager attempted to walk a puppy on a leash for what looked like the first time, because the puppy kept winding the leash around the girl's ankles. She eventually gave up, picked the puppy up and let the leash hang.

The girl looked to be in her late teens...about the age when Faith first met Trent. Back then, he'd been a cute guy in jeans and cowboy boots, his hair kind of scruffy underneath a baseball cap. She'd fallen headlong in love with him. When he'd looked at her, it was like his heart just shone through his eyes, and there had been no going back.

And now? Now there were a few more barriers between them. They weren't kids with nothing but time anymore. They were adults with wounds and hearts that had been through too much. They were more hesitant now, and they knew just how much it hurt when things didn't work out. They'd lost their "it'll never happen to us" mentality, and she wished they still had their naive cocksure attitude, but they'd grown up.

Another figure trotted down the sidewalk—this one more familiar. An elderly lady wearing a long floral dress that fit her loosely, pulling a shopping wagon behind her. She was petite, and her long white hair was pulled back in a bun at the back of her head. She paused at the front of the store and leaned closer to the glass to look inside.

Faith pushed open the car door and got out. She paused while a pickup truck rumbled past, and then circled around her car. The air was full of the scent of flowers today, mingled with that familiar smell from the bakery.

"Mammi?" Faith called.

Trudy Lantz, Trent's *mammi*, turned and smiled. "Hello, dear! I've dug up some more books for you. It's the box here in my wagon, if you want to grab it."

"That's kind of you," Faith said, and she attempted to push back her own sadness.

Faith picked up the box that seemed a little heavy for Mammi, and she opened the front door and led her inside. Hope and Elaine weren't in the shop right now, but she could hear some footsteps overhead, so they must be upstairs.

"Come in and see what we've done with the place," Faith said.

Mammi looked around as Faith took a quick peek inside the box. There were some books of poetry, a nonfiction book about Amish country and a stack of Amish romance novels.

"Mammi, do the Amish women read these?" Faith asked, lifting out one and waggling it for Mammi to see.

"Not that they admit to, dear," Mammi replied. "But full disclosure—I got those from my Amish cousin's stepdaughter."

Faith smiled, and moved a few more books aside. At the very bottom, there was a book titled *You Promised: Taking Care of Your Marriage after the Vows*. She paused, then pulled it out. It looked like it had been read a few times because there were dog-eared pages and a bookmark stuck in the middle.

"Oh, please don't take that one amiss," Mammi said. "It's just one of those books that have been popular for married couples in our family. I tossed it in there thinking that maybe you could sell it. That's all."

"Any great insights in this book?" Faith asked.

"Many!" Mammi replied. "Everyone thinks that the wedding day is the end of the love story, but it's not. It's just the start. Nurturing a marriage takes forethought and intention."

Faith dropped the book back into the box. A

book could only tell her so much, but she had an old woman who was a fount of knowledge right in front of her.

"Can I ask you something?"

"Sure." Mammi squinted at her.

"What is the secret to making a marriage last?" she asked.

Mammi was thoughtful for a moment, her lips pressed together. "Putting each other first is important. So is honesty, integrity and never toying with the trust your spouse has in you. But sometimes... Sometimes it comes down to realizing that there are phases in a marriage. Sometimes it's harder than others. Sometimes you want to strangle him. Other times are wonderful and happy. But you keep moving forward, learning lessons, getting better at being married to each other. And then when you've been married forty or fifty years, you look like experts."

Faith nodded. "I'll remember that for next time."

Mammi stepped closer and put a soft hand on Faith's arm. "Are you all right, dear?"

Tears welled up in Faith's eyes and she wasn't able to blink them back this time. Her chin trembled.

"I love your grandson, but it won't work for us, Mammi," she said.

"Do you want me to talk to him for you?" Mammi asked. "I can sort that boy out!"

"No, no..." Faith said. "We've tried this once and we weren't happy together."

"And exactly how happy are you apart?" Mammi demanded. "Marriage isn't about being happy!"

"Excuse me?" Faith stared at her. "I think it is."

"Oh, happiness is a by-product, yes," Mammi said. "But marriage is about learning and growing and becoming a team. It's about nurturing something that is bigger than you—being part of a family tree. There are times when you have to call it quits if there is abuse or infidelity—I fully agree with that. Don't stick around if you're going to be treated like that. I'm not saying to stay married at all costs. But marriage—even the best of them—is like the army, my dear girl. It's hard. It takes determination and grit and a firm belief in what you're fighting for. And in the end, you have a husband by your side who is knit closer to you than anyone else—someone who has been through the trenches with you. And that kind of satisfaction and happiness—" she thumped her chest "—that goes deep. That goes down to your bones."

Faith met the old woman's stare, her breath bated. Then Mammi blushed slightly and shrugged.

"That's my two cents, at least," Mammi said. "Take it or leave it."

It was a beautiful sentiment coming about two years too late. There was no marriage to save now.

"I think you're very wise," Faith said. "And I appreciate these books. I'm starting up a used bookstore in Philadelphia, so they will be part of my collection there."

"In Philadelphia…" Mammi murmured.

"Yes." Faith firmed her voice. She was already close to breaking, herself, and she had no more energy to argue facts with anyone else.

"Well..." Mammi gave her a pointed, gentle look. "When you come back and visit Apfelkuchen, you stop by my place, and I'll have more books for you. I always pick them up when I see ones I think you could use."

Even with a divorce. Even with all of the history between Faith and Trent... The Amish didn't deal well with divorce. They didn't know how to accept it, or to face it. It wasn't part of their culture, and even though Mammi had left the culture to marry her late husband, she didn't seem willing to let Faith go, either.

"Thank you, Mammi," Faith said. "I really do love you."

"I love you, too, dear," Mammi said. "And I wish you the happiness you long for."

But if Mammi was to be believed, that kind of happiness didn't drop in one's lap—it came from hard work and determination. It certainly gave Faith something to think about, because the next time she took those marriage vows, she wanted to make sure she had it right.

Except right now, she couldn't imagine being married to anyone but Trent, so it would take a long, long while. Still, she could recognize age-old wisdom when she heard it.

CHAPTER THIRTY-FIVE

TRENT SCREWED THE last light switch plate onto the switch box and wiped it off with a cloth. He'd slept terribly the night before, and he hadn't bothered taking lunch today. He just wanted to finish the job so that Faith could send the form to her insurance provider. Half of him yearned to spend a little more time here—closer to the woman he loved in spite of it all—and the rest of him wanted to get away. Either way it hurt, and pouring himself into his work was the only mild respite he had.

Faith was working downstairs, and it was like he could feel a magnetic pull through the floor. He missed her already. He missed her still. People said you eventually got over a woman—he'd been on his way to that place of healing, and then he'd gone and fallen for her all over again.

He slid his screwdriver back into the slot on his belt. Eddie was late back from lunch—very late. They'd both been miserable this morning—two guys who'd had their hearts handed to them. Eddie had been quiet—he wouldn't talk about Sarah, although Trent could tell that Sarah was all the younger man was thinking of.

Trent, on the other hand, was just grumpy. He wished he could suffer with a little more dignity, but there it was.

"I'm an idiot," Trent muttered.

He heard Eddie's boots coming up the stairs. About time.

"Hey, Eddie," Trent said as the door opened.

Eddie came inside, looking lighter and happier than he had all day, and he had a private little smile on his face. He handed Trent a paper bag, oil-stained on the bottom. Trent looked inside. There was a doughnut.

"It's from Marta's Bakery," Eddie said. "I figured you could use a pick-me-up."

"And you're also an hour late," Trent said, casting Eddie a dry look. "I know you've had a rough few days, but a job is a job. It takes priority. We can drown our sorrows in on our own time."

"I know, and I'm sorry," Eddie said. "I have a good excuse."

It better be a phenomenal excuse. An hour late was irresponsible and showed a general disrespect for the job, and in the mood Trent was in this morning, he had no patience for it.

"Care to enlighten me?" Trent asked curtly.

"I'm getting married."

The words jolted Trent out of his mood. *Married?* Trent frowned. "What? To who?"

Eddie rolled his eyes. "To Sarah! Who else?"

"Sarah's leaving the Amish life?" Trent's stomach dropped. Her parents were going to be crushed. He could see it now—the tears, the grief, the silent attempt to accept something so heartbreaking to everyone who knew and loved her...

"No, I wouldn't ask that of her," Eddie replied. "She loves her family and they love her. Besides, we'll need family support starting out. I'm not a complete fool."

Trent just looked at him. "It's not adding up, man."

"I'm joining the Amish," Eddie said.

"You're—" Trent exhaled a pent-up breath. *"What?"*

Trent prided himself on being moderately more eloquent than this, but he was stunned. Eddie, his electrical apprentice, was going to join the Amish and live without electricity, without a gas-powered vehicle, would drive a horse and buggy and follow the strict Amish rules?

Eddie seemed to find Trent's shock amusing. "Yeah, I'm going to get a lot of that. I guess I'd better get used to it. Here's the thing—I admire the way they live. I think they're right—we need to get back to the basics. They focus on what matters most, and Amish men make their wives and kids the center of everything. They work hard, and they develop a depth of character that most of us can only imagine. I want to join the Amish and marry Sarah."

"You're an electrician!" Trent said. "Has anyone said you can join them?"

Eddie shrugged. "I won't be an electrician for much longer. I'm sorry if that means I've wasted your time, but I'm going to farm with Albrecht, if he'll have me."

"Have you talked to Sarah about this?" Trent asked.

"She met me for lunch. I asked her if she'd marry me and teach me to live Amish, and she said yes." Eddie grinned. "And with an Amish girl, her word is as good as a ring."

Eddie was right—their word was what mattered. The Amish didn't use wedding rings or engagement rings. They simply said yes or no. If Sarah had said yes, they were well and truly engaged. Even if her parents wouldn't be thrilled with the idea, it was Sarah's choice, and Sarah's word.

"Does she think they'll let you join?" he asked.

"She thinks they will. I'll have to prove myself, but she thinks her parents will support it because the other option is Sarah leaving. Obviously, I'm not asking her to do that, but she thinks that they'll see the logic of it."

"What now?" Trent asked.

"We're going to talk to her parents tonight about it. With all the worry over Sarah leaving, I'm hoping they'll see the value in what I'm proposing."

"You'll have to take classes—learn about their faith, learn their language…" Trent said. "You'll have to learn how to take care of horses, and drive a buggy. There are tricks and methods they use in farming, too. It's not just sticking a seed in the ground, you know. I mean, you're going to be learning everything from scratch."

"I know." Eddie didn't look daunted.

"Wow..." Trent murmured. "I have to tell you, I didn't expect this."

"I didn't expect to meet a girl I loved this much," Eddie said. "She's worth it. And I'll prove myself to her family and community, too."

Eddie loved Sarah Yoder, and he was finding a way. It was both utterly wild and admirable, too. He loved her and he was moving heaven and earth to be with her. There had been what seemed like an insurmountable obstacle between them, but Eddie was willing to turn his life upside down to make a life with Sarah possible.

"You really do love her," Trent said softly.

"Heart and soul," Eddie said, sobering. "I'll be true to her, I'll work hard and I'll make her happy. I promise you, Trent. Your cousin will always be happy with me."

If only it were that easy. If Trent could have willed Faith into happiness with him, he would have... But still, Eddie's determination was infectious. If Eddie could find a way of his own, was there a way for Trent to have a life with Faith, too? It gave him a dangerous tickle of hope.

"Congratulations," Trent said, forcing a smile to his lips. "I'm happy for you."

"Thanks." Eddie glanced around. "What are we working on now?"

"We're done. I finished up," Trent replied. "You

might as well take the rest of the day off. I have a feeling it's going to take some time to talk all this through with my aunt and uncle."

"Will you support us in this?" Eddie asked.

"Of course."

"Would you talk to your uncle on my behalf?"

"Nope." Trent laughed softly then. "What you are proposing is a very personal transformation. You're the only one who can talk to Albrecht about this and prove to the community that you're serious. This is incredibly rare. People don't just up and join the Amish. I mean... Sometimes they try, but I've never heard of it sticking. So this will be an uphill climb for you. Before the bishop will agree to marry the two of you, he's going to have to be convinced that you're going to stay Amish."

Eddie nodded. "Okay, well... Today I'll start the process."

"What about your family?" Trent asked.

"They'll think I'm making a huge mistake, of course," Eddie replied. "But who cares? I'll be Wild Uncle Eddie who went Amish. They'll tell stories about me for generations." He shot Trent a grin. "I'll go down in history in my family lore."

"The Amish are very against pride," Trent said with a low laugh. "So stop enjoying your future infamy."

Eddie shrugged. "Nothing is going to stop me from taking this step. Some people won't believe I'll stay. Others will think I'm foolish for doing it. But time is the proof, right? They'll get used to it—both sides. And I'm going to just keep on loving Sarah."

That was good to hear. Let love win this time around.

"Well, good luck to you both," Trent said. "Tell Sarah I'm happy for you."

"I'll pass it along." Eddie stuck his hand out. "I'll give you proper notice before I quit."

"I appreciate it." Trent shook Eddie's hand with a firm grip.

May those two have better luck than Trent had had... But as he watched the younger man head for the door, a spring in his step, his mind was already spinning. Eddie had taken an impossible situation, and he was making it possible...

Was there a way for him and Faith? Maybe there was a key to this he was missing somehow. Maybe he just needed to think outside the box. Because if he could find a way to keep Faith in his life and in his arms, he was willing to do just about anything.

CHAPTER THIRTY-SIX

FAITH LOOKED OVER her shoulder as Eddie headed back out the front door of the shop, the bell tinkling overhead. Eddie looked at his watch as the door swung shut, and she got a glimpse of his smiling profile. He'd gone from a miserable, moping young man this morning to this bouncy, hopeful version of himself this afternoon, and Faith wondered what had happened.

Were he and Sarah back together again? In a place this size, she'd hear soon enough. A local electrician dating an Amish woman was going to make the gossip rounds.

She glanced at the ceiling overhead. Trent was still up there, finishing up the wiring. He'd promised to complete it today, and Faith glanced at a clock on the wall. She hoped that he would be done—for the sake of their opening day and for the sake of that insurance. But it would mean seeing the last of Trent for a while. Maybe a very long while.

Faith fought back the lump rising in her throat. She'd known better than to fall in love with her ex-husband again.

She watched as Hope pulled out her phone for the hundredth time and looked at the screen.

"He'll call you," Faith said with a sigh. "I know you hate this waiting, but he's on his way, right?"

"His flight is leaving in twenty minutes, and he isn't answering his phone," Hope said.

"Maybe he's rushing!" Elaine said. "Maybe his ringer is on silent, or he's powering through security right now. He's on his way, Hope. Relax."

"I have a bad feeling about this..." Hope slipped her phone back into her pocket.

Faith looked over the shop, her heart heavy. She was going to be saying goodbye to a lot of things when she left to start up her Second Chance Bookshop. Of course, she'd come back and work here too, but it wouldn't be the same. And within a year, they'd sell this cozy little shop in the town where she'd grown up. She'd be leaving behind this newfound sisterly bond with Elaine and Hope...the memories in this dusty store. And she'd be severing her connection to Trent all over again. Except it would happen slowly—a year's worth of tearing apart.

Trent came into the shop next, and his dark gaze searched her out immediately. There was something about the way he looked at her that tugged her from across the room. Somehow, Trent still felt like hers. Faith put down the books she'd been shelving and she headed over in his direction. Things would be easier when there was more physical distance between them. Her sisters both turned away so quickly that she knew they were trying to afford her a bit of privacy, and she appreciated it.

"We're done with the rewire," Trent said. "I can sign the papers for the insurance company for you."

"Thank you." Faith grabbed the form from the till and handed it over.

As Trent worked slowly, methodically to complete the paperwork, she tore her eyes away from his familiar, strong hand. Trent had been more than her weakness. He'd been her first love, and it was like he was tattooed on her heart. There was going to be no erasing him...just somehow moving on without him.

He handed the paper back, pocketing his pen.

"Thanks..." she murmured again, and she pulled a check out of her pocket for him. He accepted it with a nod of thanks.

For a moment, they were silent.

"Eddie's asked Sarah to marry him," Trent said quietly.

"What?" Faith whipped her gaze up. "What did she say?"

"She said yes," he replied, and a small smile tugged at his lips. "And before you panic on Mary and Albrecht's behalf, he's going to become Amish."

"You're kidding!"

"I don't joke about marriage proposals." His gaze met hers, and she felt some heat touch her cheeks. Now was a miserable time to flirt.

"Are they really getting married?" she asked.

"I think so. I mean, the bishop will have to be

convinced that Eddie is serious, but given that he can stick with the Amish life for a while and take the classes, yeah. They're getting married."

"She found her way." Faith smiled at that, and found herself feeling a little misty at the thought. "She loves him, you know. I mean, she really loves him."

Sarah loved Eddie the way Faith had loved Trent... the way she still loved Trent. Why couldn't things be less complicated?

"Yeah, he feels the same." Trent's voice caught, and when she looked up at him, she could see the depth of his feelings in those dark brown eyes.

"If I'm invited to the wedding, would it be wrong of me to attend?" Faith asked.

"Of course not. You'd have to come."

"Would it be weird between us?" she asked.

"Everything is going to be weird between us." He reached up and touched her cheek. "There's no avoiding that."

"I already miss you," she whispered.

"Me, too." He swallowed hard and dropped his gaze. Then he caught her fingers and twined his through hers. "Why couldn't our situation be simple, like you being Amish?"

She smiled at his humor. "So simple, huh?"

"They found a way," he said. "It does make me think."

His words tugged at her heart almost painfully—like there was a barely healed wound being stretched apart again. But false hope wasn't going to help. She didn't have the emotional energy for it. She pulled her hand back.

"You have Tyke now," she said firmly.

He nodded. "Yeah, I do."

They had reasons—reasons she'd gone over again and again in her mind ever since yesterday. They had reasons that kept them apart, but whenever she got in the same room as this man, they seemed to flutter away.

Trent gave her a sad smile.

"I'd better head out," he said. "I guess I'll see you when I see you."

"Bye, Trent," she said, and she felt her chin tremble.

He headed out the door and she stood stoically there until the door swung shut, and then she felt Hope's arm slide around her waist, and Elaine caught her hand. That was when the tears started to flow. Oh, how she loved this man, but there just didn't seem to be a solution for them!

They'd tried this once…there was Tyke to consider…and she didn't know why a love like this one hadn't been enough for her. But it hadn't! She'd been the one to leave. Maybe she deserved this.

When Faith finally wiped her eyes, she found her sisters watching her with tears standing in theirs.

"I've loved Trent for so long that I don't even know how to stop," Faith said.

She'd explained herself to her sisters often enough, and they knew why this wouldn't work.

"You have us," Hope said. "We're here for each other for life."

"For life," Elaine murmured.

This was what sisters were for. They might bicker at other times, but when it mattered most, they pulled together and were each other's support. She wasn't alone—she knew that. With Hope and Elaine in her corner, they'd volley between comforting her and bossing her right back into shape.

"I'll get over him," Faith said, more to convince herself than anyone else. "I will eventually."

"You will," Hope agreed. "But it's okay to not be over him just yet."

And that was a good thing, because Faith's heart was in tatters.

CHAPTER THIRTY-SEVEN

AFTER SUPPER THAT EVENING, Trent washed Tyke's hands and let him splash under the tap water a little bit. Then he turned it off and dried him off again. Tyke was over his cold now. Trent had picked Tyke up early from the day home, so they'd already had a few hours together before supper, and Trent was emotionally exhausted. All he could think about was Faith, and he'd been trying to use logic to come to peace with things as they were. His emotions were not cooperating.

He had a lot going on inside him, but Tyke still needed constant love and reassurance. A child's needs didn't stop just because Trent's heart was crushed.

He put Tyke back on the floor and the little guy beelined for his train tracks.

"Tain!" Tyke hollered. "Tain!"

He still couldn't say his *r*'s, and Trent wondered if he'd miss it when Tyke finally figured them out.

His cell phone rang, and he saw his grandmother's number, and he picked up the call.

"Hi, Mammi," he said. "How are you?"

"I'm doing all right, dear," Mammi said. "There are no plumbing issues at present."

"Good." He smiled. Was Mammi just lonely and needing to talk? Because Trent wasn't sure he had much small talk inside him tonight. "What can I do for you, Mammi?"

"Well, dear, Albrecht and Mary asked me to come to their place tonight. Mary called me herself, and if she's tramping out to the phone hut before she's even done her supper dishes, you know it's important," Mammi said. "It's a long drive for me to do alone, and Mary suggested I get you to pick me up."

Of course, at her age, no one wanted Mammi driving by herself on all those back roads at night.

"What's happening?" Trent asked.

"Well, that's the fun news. Apparently, our Sarah is getting married!"

So Sarah and Eddie had sprung the news of their engagement, and now the family was being gathered. The Amish kept engagements a secret until they were ready to publish the banns at church, so only the closest family members would know about it this soon. And they were including Trent. It was an honor, and he'd deeply offend the people he loved if he didn't show up tonight with Mammi.

"I can pick you up and bring you over there," Trent said. "It'll give Tyke something fun to do. He'll sleep better tonight."

"Thank you, dear, I do appreciate it," Mammi said. "I'll go get into some visiting clothes. I'm all grubby from the garden right now."

"Okay, I'm on my way," he said, and as he hung up, he headed over to where Tyke lay on the carpet with his wooden tracks. "Come on, Tyke, we're going visiting."

"Okay!" Tyke said, and he got to his feet. He liked going visiting. Everyone gave him a lot of attention, and he normally got cookies.

Okay. It looked like his evening was cut out for him. No time to wallow in his own pain. Maybe it was for the best.

Half an hour later, Trent had Mammi in the passenger seat and Tyke in the car seat, and they headed out in the direction of Amish farm country. Mammi was dressed in some pastel blue pants and a matching cardigan. He filled her in on Eddie while they drove, and Mammi listened gravely.

"When I married your grandfather, I had to leave the Amish life," she said quietly. "It wasn't easy, but I wasn't part of the church yet, so I could make that choice without being shunned. But if I wanted to marry the man I loved, I had to leave. We didn't even consider the possibility of him turning Amish, and no one suggested it."

"Have times changed?" Trent asked.

"Not with the Amish," she said wryly. "I've never heard of an Englisher becoming Amish and having it stick. Not once."

"He's pretty determined," Trent said. "And he loves Sarah and her family."

"I guess we'll see," Mammi murmured. "The risk is that Sarah will marry him, he'll start out Amish and then he won't be able to hold to the strict way of life. Then she'll really have a choice on her hands."

"Was it hard for you to leave the Amish life?" Trent asked.

"Very hard. It was everything I knew," Mammi replied. "My family, my friends, my view of the world...everything. When I left, I was trusting your grandfather with my whole life. And it wasn't easy to adjust. I was always a little odd—a little different than everyone else. Your *dawdie* didn't mind a bit, but it was hard to find my place. It will be hard for young Eddie, too. This is not an easy path for him."

"Did you ever regret leaving the Amish life?" Trent asked.

Mammi shook her head. "No, your *dawdie* was worth it. I never regretted choosing him for a minute. I hope that both Sarah and Eddie will be able to say the same thing when they're old and gray like me."

That was what they were all hoping on behalf of this young couple.

When Trent pulled into the Yoder drive, the sun was low, and he noted that there weren't any other vehicles there besides the Yoder buggies parked and unhitched beside the stables, and Eddie's truck next to them. It looked like it was going to be a very private meeting, indeed.

Trent helped his grandmother out of the vehicle and then opened up the back door to unbuckle Tyke. He lifted the toddler out of his seat, noticing that the little guy had been growing. He was heavier these days.

The side door to the house opened, and Albrecht stood there waiting for them, a serious look on his face.

"Come in," he said, as they approached the steps. "*Danke* for coming. Hello, Aunt Trudy."

"How are you, dear?" Mammi asked. "I thought we were happy about this."

"We are, but there are bumps still to smooth out. That's why we asked you here. We're going to need your input."

"I'm happy to give it," she replied, and she cast Trent a wary look.

Albrecht gave Trent a nod, and they both came inside. The kitchen table was cleared and washed, and Sarah and Eddie sat side by side, elbows resting on the surface. Sarah looked worried, but Eddie seemed pretty calm. Trent gave the younger man a nod.

"Hi, Tyke," Sarah said with a smile, and Tyke squirmed to be put down, then pounded over to Sarah's side with his plastic truck held aloft.

"Can I get you some tea, or anything?" Mary asked. "Aunt Trudy, have a seat. Make yourself comfortable. I have pie?"

"No, no, dear," Mammi said. "I understand this is a serious time. Don't fuss over me. Let's hear it, now. What's going on?"

Family meetings were long events, and this particular family meeting had been kept small in order to keep the secret about Sarah and Eddie's plans to get married. Mammi and Trent had been asked over for their Englisher perspectives, Trent realized. Marriage was not something taken lightly among the Amish.

They discussed the seriousness of those vows. They asked if Eddie could be trusted to stand by his vows to the community—to stay Amish for his whole life. They asked what Mammi thought of an Englisher's ability to cross to the other side of the fence and be content. They listened very closely to everything she had to say.

They discussed learning the language, and learning their ways of life. There was much to talk through very frankly, and Trent watched Eddie's face the whole time. He stayed serious and focused, and not once did he look daunted. Trent had to admit that he was impressed.

"Trent, what do you think of Eddie's character?" Albrecht asked at last.

Trent sucked in a slow breath. This was his cousin's future being discussed, after all, so he had to give a considered response.

"He's a hard worker," Trent said. "He's honest, and he has integrity. He's never been the type to date around much. He isn't a flirt, and when he's serious, he's serious. Whether he can stay the course and stay Amish, I can't say. But I believe he'll try."

Albrecht and Mary exchanged a long, somber look. Across the room, Tyke rumbled his truck along the wooden floor.

"What is the next step?" Trent asked. "I know Eddie's wondering, and I'm wondering, too."

"If he wants to join the Amish, he'd better start now," Albrecht said. "I'll let him work with me. He'll have to keep driving his truck for the time being, since he will not be staying under this roof until he's well and truly married."

"We'll have to get him into some classes with the bishop," Mary added, "and he'll have to start learning our language right quick. Baptismal classes are how any of us join the faith, but the bishop might make some adjustments to make Eddie's in English."

"Maybe," Albrecht said. They exchanged a sober look.

Trent felt a smile tugging at his lips. This all sounded very serious and matter-of-fact, but it meant that they'd accepted the engagement.

"I think he should start wearing our clothing now, too," Albrecht said. "It's good for character to stand out a bit, and it'll give him ample opportunity to discuss this very serious decision with his own family."

"I'm happy to do it," Eddie said. "You're right—it will help me to change my mindset. Thank you for being willing to teach me, Albrecht. And for giving me a job on your farm. I'll prove that I can work hard and learn your ways. You'll see." He looked over at Sarah and gave her a warm smile. "This is the life for me."

"Then, I'll take you to speak with the bishop," Albrecht said.

"*Danke*, Daet," Sarah said softly, but her eyes shone with happiness.

"*Danke,*" Eddie added, using the Pennsylvania Dutch word.

Tyke crawled up into Mammi's arms next, and he leaned his head against her shoulder and reached over to touch the soft, wrinkled skin on her neck.

"Tyke—" Trent started.

"Oh, he's fine," Mammi said. "He looks tired. If you leave him be, he might fall right asleep. I have more than a little experience with two-year-olds, you know."

Mammi rubbed his back slowly, and Tyke's eyes did look a little bit heavy. Albrecht turned to Eddie to discuss farming chores and what his responsibilities would be—after he gave his two weeks' notice, of course. But it seemed clear enough to Trent that tonight was Eddie's official notice.

"Trent?" Mary said. "Would you help me carry in a crate of potatoes?"

Mary nodded toward the outside door.

"Sure," Trent said. "I'd be happy to."

Mary led the way outside, and headed around the side of the house toward the vegetable garden. Sure enough, there was a milk crate sitting on the grass next to the garden, full of new potatoes.

"Just a moment..." Mary said softly, putting a hand on his arm.

Ah. So this wasn't just a request for him to carry

things for her. He looked down at his aunt's earnest face, and she reached into her dress pocket and pulled out a small, yellowed piece of paper. He recognized it—the note written in Pennsylvania Dutch that had been with the recipe cards that Faith had texted to him.

"My daughter showed me the recipe cards my grandmother wrote. And she seemed to think this little note was from the same time."

"Is it?" he asked.

Mary shook her head. "Have you seen it?"

"Faith showed it to me. I don't speak Pennsylvania Dutch."

"It says, *'I miss you. I'm so sorry.'*"

Mary turned then and marched toward the fence, farther from the house. It overlooked a field of waist-high wheat, still green and rippling in the breeze. She leaned against the top rung, and Trent joined her.

"I have agonized about telling you this," Mary said quietly. "I don't like to tell this story—it's private. But I feel that I might have an experience that will help you."

"Help me with what?" he asked.

"With Faith." She turned and met his gaze. "This note is from Albrecht. He wrote it to me."

"When you were courting?" he asked.

"After we married. After I left him and went home to my *daet* and *mamm*."

Trent blinked. "What? You left him?"

"Marriage was very difficult for us," she said.

"He hurt my feelings constantly. I hurt his, too. We didn't know how to communicate properly with each other. We didn't know how to make a marriage sweet."

"You obviously got back together again," he said.

"*Yah*, we did. You know well enough that for us Amish there is no divorce. If there were that option, we might have taken it, though. But marriage is long. There's time to sort things out if you just stick with it."

"She left me, Aunty," Trent said.

"Do you love her?"

Trent shrugged. "Yes. Of course."

"Does she love you?"

He nodded.

"Trent, I know what it is to feel like there is no future with someone. And I know what it is to try again and finally find that core we were missing before. And I know that you and Faith struggled a great deal. But I've seen you two together, and I remember feeling exactly like you two seem to feel. It was back when Albrecht slipped me this note during a Service Sunday." Mary dropped her gaze to the note. "I kept this little piece of paper to remind myself how much I loved my husband. I didn't want to get so caught up in an argument again that I lost sight of what mattered most. I'd forgotten about it, though. And when Sarah brought it home, it got me to remembering."

"Can I ask your advice?" he asked quietly.

"Of course."

"Faith left me after three years of marriage. She didn't stick it out. She felt like I wasn't giving her enough. But now... Tyke adores her. If he gets attached to Faith—if I let myself get attached again—and she leaves us... It would be bad. Really bad. I need to avoid that."

"And if she doesn't leave you?" Mary asked.

"How do I know she won't?"

Mary smiled, then. "Here is where I think our Amish way is much better, and I'll tell you why. There is no other option for us. Once you marry, you can't just find someone else. As long as that person is living, they are yours. You are theirs. What you make of it is up to you. Once we've said those vows, it might be a risk to trust, but... What other choice do you have?"

"And you think I should take the risk?" he asked.

"Eddie in there—that young man is a risk," Mary said, pressing her lips together. "A big risk. And yet you spoke for him. Why?"

"Because he loves Sarah," he replied. "He adores her."

"So he's not so big of a risk, considering the depth of his love," she said.

"Exactly."

She spread her hands, and looked at him meaningfully.

Trent sucked in a breath. He and Faith loved each other even after two years apart, and he was terrified that she'd walk out again. But what if she didn't? What if he was simply giving up a chance at growing old with the woman he couldn't stop loving? She'd felt misunderstood in their marriage, and he'd had no idea. But he knew what the problem was now. They needed more open communication. They needed to be able to talk things through and really listen to each other. He had to stop bounding ahead and wait until she was ready to do something. Maybe he could fix that—talk to her more, figure out what she needed to feel the love that he already had for her.

"The potatoes are there—when you're ready to bring them in," Mary said, and she smiled, then turned back toward the house.

The Amish way could be difficult. It could go terribly wrong, and sometimes it did. Life wasn't perfect, and the rain fell on the Amish and English alike, as Albrecht liked to say. But the Amish ways could also foster long, close, united marriages that lasted in a way that most Englishers could only dream of.

What if Trent took a page from their book and made Faith his only option?

Could they have the kind of marriage that flourished in these Amish farmhouses? Because he loved her so much that he knew he'd never be able to set her aside, even if he never saw her again. He'd keep on loving her. Maybe it wasn't a matter of choosing to make her his only option... She already was! Whom was he fooling? Apparently, not Aunt Mary. He just needed to accept it, and do something about it.

Trent picked up the crate of potatoes and headed back toward the house. He would do something about it. Eddie wasn't the only one capable of moving heaven and earth for the woman he loved.

CHAPTER THIRTY-EIGHT

FAITH PASSED A bag of potato chips over to Elaine, and her sister took a handful, then leaned back into the couch. The sisters had gotten together that evening after dinner, and it felt good to be all in one room again. There was comfort in being with her sisters. When everything else fell apart, they always had each other's backs.

Faith was heartbroken for a second time over her ex-husband, and Hope was still eyeing her phone in irritation. Peter hadn't texted her or answered her calls all day. The flight time had come and gone. If Peter was going to arrive, he would have by now. Faith and Elaine had said everything they could to soothe Hope—that Peter must be held up somehow. He'd have a good explanation. He loved her... But her mind was going in other directions.

"Is he leaving me?" Hope asked for the hundredth time.

"It doesn't make sense to just disappear, does it?" Elaine asked. "He could just tell you."

"Unless he's a coward," Hope muttered.

"It doesn't seem like him," Faith countered. Although the longer it went, the more Faith wondered. Wouldn't he find some way to call his pregnant wife and let her know what was going on?

Hope put her phone back into her pocket and reached for the chips.

"If he tells me that he got caught up with work, I won't believe him," Hope said. "No one just gets caught up with work and forgets to take a flight!"

"He hasn't said that, though, has he?" Faith said.

"I'm preparing my reaction," Hope said.

"Sweetie, I don't think you can do that," Faith said. "I mean, you'll feel what you feel when you find out what happened. You can't prepare yourself for some awful news that hasn't even come yet. He might have a good excuse. Maybe there was a big accident that blocked the airport and his phone died. I mean… He might be walking down the side of a highway with no cell phone battery right now."

"He'd better be," Hope muttered, and she pushed a chip into her mouth.

"I always liked Trent, you know," Elaine said suddenly. "I was crushed when you two split up."

"So we're moving on to me, are we?" Faith asked wryly.

"Sure are," Elaine said.

"It didn't work…" Faith leaned her head back against the couch. Their marriage hadn't worked, and that fact would never stop hurting.

"He still seems to love you," Elaine said.

"And I love him, but he's got Tyke to consider,

and we're both scared that loving each other won't be enough for a second time."

"What went wrong?" Hope asked, turning toward them again.

Faith sighed. "That's what I've been trying to figure out. We fought constantly, it felt like. But what got us there? I felt so distant from him, and I don't know why. It was the loneliest feeling. He was kind. He loved me. He'd do nice things for me, but I felt like he never really saw me. So I'd be unfulfilled and lonely, and I'd be irritable, and he'd be irritable, and no one knew how to push each other's buttons like we did. He'd try and fix things, like by getting that store lease, but he never talked to me about it. We were living separate lives in some ways."

"Do you still feel that way?" Elaine asked.

"No, but... I guess I'm afraid it'll come back once we're comfortable again. Right now, we're filled with longing and heartbreak. That's powerful stuff. But why did I feel such a distance between us?"

Elaine shrugged. "I don't know. I've never been married. So instead of what went wrong, what did you want your marriage to be like?"

Faith smiled wistfully. "You know when you see a couple walking together, and they're completely connected? Or sometimes you see them with their kids and they're working as a team, getting the kids settled in a restaurant, or keeping them safe on the sidewalk..."

"You mean the Amish families," Hope said, pulling her phone out again.

"Maybe," Faith admitted. "I hadn't connected it to the Amish before, but they seem to have the closeness I wanted."

"You aren't Amish, though," Elaine said. "They have such a different lifestyle than the rest of us. We have to deal with a lot of different pressures that they don't. In Amish families, the mom is at home taking care of things. She's there when the dad gets back from work. Or they work a farm together. It's different. For us, you've got two people with different focuses on different careers away from home. It's just...not a fair comparison. We have to do things differently."

"Maybe adjust a few expectations?" Hope said quietly.

Faith was still working over the connection to the Amish families, though. Amish couples worked together on a farm, or in rearing children, or in facing all the Englisher differences when they went to town... Always together, shoulder to shoulder. That was the unity she'd wanted. What was the secret there?

"I don't want to live an Amish life, so maybe what I want is a family business," Faith said with a low laugh, but as the words came out of her mouth, they didn't sound so ridiculous.

She turned and looked up at Hope.

"Do you?" Hope asked. "Is that it?"

It all seemed to be tumbling into place now... what it would have looked like if she and Trent had been united the way she longed to be.

"When my shop went under, I wanted him to care as much as I did," Faith said slowly. "I wanted him to be as invested as I was. He got me the lease, and then his part was done. I was back to working on my own to keep that place afloat. I wanted it to be ours—not mine or his. Ours. I could have survived the disappointment if we'd both been crushed... I wanted that sense of shared work, and shared destiny. And somehow, we got lost in petty arguments."

"Did you tell him that? Ask him to join you in running the shop?" Elaine asked.

"No..." She hadn't. She'd never spelled it out, had she?

"So maybe the thing that went wrong wasn't so impossible to fix," Elaine said.

"Maybe it wasn't." Faith's heartbeat sped up in her chest.

Was this what she'd needed in their marriage—a joint venture? A family business like this antiques shop she was running with her sisters? It was amazing what a joint venture could do for three women who seldom saw eye to eye. And it had only been a week, but this last week had been more satisfying than her bookshop had ever been. The difference? She wasn't alone in it. Was it as simple as that? Was this actually something fixable for her and Trent?

The hope that surged up inside her almost rocked her. They loved each other... And maybe there was something she could do about that. Except it didn't fix Trent's concerns about Tyke and his own faith in their relationship.

The downstairs buzzer pulled Faith out of her thoughts. It was the doorbell on the street, and Hope's face lit up.

"That's probably Peter," Faith said.

"I'm still mad at him!" Hope said, but she headed out the door, leaving it open a few inches, and her sandals tapped down the staircase. Faith and Elaine both went to the door—curiosity stronger than Hope's right to privacy.

When Hope pulled the door open at the bottom floor, though, she froze. There was no hug, no kiss...no Peter. It was a Pennsylvania state trooper looking for Mrs. Hope Taylor.

"Yes, I'm Hope Taylor..."

Their voices were loud enough for Faith to hear clearly.

"Can I come upstairs?" the trooper asked.

"Just tell me!" Hope said. "What is this about?"

Then the trooper started to talk, his voice lowered compassionately, and Hope sank against the doorframe. Faith couldn't hear the rest of the news, but she and Elaine hurried down the stairs.

"What's going on?" Faith asked.

"He's gone," Hope whispered. "Peter... He..."

And Faith wrapped her arms around her sister, the reality of the situation slowly sinking in to them all...

"There was an accident, a big pileup on the highway on the way to the airport," the trooper told the sisters. "Peter Taylor died at the scene. I'm so very sorry."

CHAPTER THIRTY-NINE

THE REST OF the night passed in an unreal blur of tears and shock. The next morning, Faith and Elaine didn't know what to do. Faith made tea—on TV, people made tea when there was a big shock, and at least it was something concrete she could do. Elaine got a lap blanket and put it over Hope's legs.

Hope kept pulling her phone out.

"Why do I keep expecting him to text me still?" Hope sobbed. "I keep thinking Peter will text me and say he's sorry he's late."

"It's shock," Elaine said. "You're in shock, Hope."

"Could there have been a mistake?"

"No, sweetheart."

"Maybe it was someone else, not him."

"They double- and triple-check everything before they come find a family member," Elaine said. "This isn't a mistake. I'm so, so sorry, Hope. I'm so sorry…"

Faith brought a mug of hot tea into the room and set it on the side table next to her sister.

"I'm on my own!" Hope said. "I'm having a baby, and I'm completely on my own!"

"No, that's where you're wrong!" Faith said firmly. "Hope, you are not on your own. You have us. We're here for you always. Your baby is going to be loved very deeply by his mother, and by his two aunts. By Mom and Dad, too. You are not by yourself, and you never will be."

Hope leaned her head against Faith's shoulder and exhaled a shuddering sigh.

"It's my fault..." Hope whispered.

"No—"

"It is. I wanted him to come back and see me. I wanted him to prove he could choose me over work. I was so stupid! He was rushing for *me*!"

"You are not stupid!" Elaine said fiercely. "He was coming back for his pregnant wife. Some things are worth the rush—*you* are worth some rushing!"

Faith leaned her head against her sister's tangled hair, and tears misted in her own eyes, too. Poor, poor Hope. And poor Peter, who had been heading home for his wife and baby in utero.

If only Peter had been given more time on this earth. Faith was positive these two would have worked things out.

But time wasn't always on a person's side. And while she'd been focused on her sister for the last twelve hours, for the first time since they'd heard the terrible news, Faith's thoughts went to Trent. How much time had they wasted already? She'd been holding back, afraid of being hurt again, but some things were worth a risk, and worth taking a bold step. And Trent was one of them, she realized. Trent was worth some rushing! She loved him with everything she had, and she was willing to take a leap, so long as he was taking it with her.

Faith couldn't just leave her sister right now, but when the time was right, she needed to talk to Trent about their relationship. If this changed nothing for him, she'd make her peace with that. But she had to at least tell him what had changed for her.

CHAPTER FORTY

WITH A TIRED toddler fussing in the back seat of his truck, Trent drove Tyke to Abigail's day home. He had another job starting—fixing some faulty wiring in a local house. He couldn't put off the work he'd scheduled, but he needed to talk to Faith. She hadn't called him, or texted... He'd hoped she would. Maybe if she reached out, she'd be ready to think about options.

Did she not miss him? Or had she made up her mind for good? Had he messed this up all over again?

Aunt Mary's advice was still echoing in his head. There were risks that were worth it, and while he wanted to make sure that Tyke had a stable, reliable childhood, Faith would make a loving mom, too. She was so patient with Tyke, so warm and affectionate, and Tyke had fallen for her hook, line and sinker. So had Trent... And a family of three was looking a whole lot more possible in the soft, golden light of a Pennsylvania morning.

Tyke fussed in the back seat, that wordless whining complaint of a tired kid who could have used another hour in bed. Trent couldn't just go by Faith's place like he longed to do, and he couldn't very well ask her to come to him. This was one of those conversations where he needed to man up and go to her. If he was going to show her that she could rely on his love never changing, and that he could be as present in their relationship as he was with Tyke, then he'd better be the one to show up on her doorstep, not call her to his.

So Trent dropped Tyke off at the day home, but before he drove away again, he texted Faith.

Can I come by tonight when I'm done working? I really need to talk to you. I also got the story behind that little note you found.

She didn't reply right away, and he headed out to the house to get started. For the next few hours he wondered if Faith really was done with him. Maybe her heart had moved on. Maybe she couldn't handle any more emotional roller coasters right now... Maybe she was upset about how much he'd said already. Maybe their relationship was over—well and truly—and he wouldn't get another chance.

He wasn't going to be put off by an unanswered text. If this was the end, then he wanted her to tell him to his face. He needed that much just to start the process of letting go all over again, and he determined to go to her shop at the end of the day.

But then just before 5:00 p.m., she texted him back.

Yes, please come by. We do need to talk. Peter was killed in an accident, and I'm taking care of my sister right now. Can you come by tomorrow? She needs me.

Trent stared down at his phone. Hope's husband was dead? Every cell in his body wanted to jump in his truck and rush over there, but she'd asked for space. If she needed a little more time, he'd give it to her.

Poor, poor Hope...

He texted back: I'll come by tomorrow after work. If you need anything—and I mean anything at all—I want to be your first call. I'm here for you. Okay?

Her reply was a phone call.

"Thank you, Trent," she said, and there were tears in her voice. "I love you. I really do."

"I love you, too. That's not going to change. But right now, take care of your sister," he replied. "I'm not going anywhere. We'll talk tomorrow when I'm done working. But I mean it about letting me know if you need anything."

"Thank you," she said. "Tomorrow?"

"Tomorrow."

And for the rest of his life, if they could finally find a way.

CHAPTER FORTY-ONE

Faith and Elaine decided it was best to put off the soft opening for another week or so. Hope needed their support, and there was no way they could give the store their focus right now. So Faith taped a sign to the glass of the front window saying they were closed until further notice because of a family emergency.

Hope was asleep upstairs after another awful night and a long day of tears, so Faith was puttering in the shop when she saw Trent's truck pull up to park right in front of the shop, and she felt such a crash of relief she could have cried. It was half past five.

Faith headed out the front door and locked it behind her. Trent hopped out of his truck, circled around and clasped his arms around her without a word. She leaned into a musky, warm neck and exhaled an exhausted sigh.

"Hi," she whispered, muffled against his neck.

"Hey…" He pulled back and looked down at her. "How are you doing?"

"Not great," she admitted.

"How's Hope holding up?"

"She's not…"

They fell in beside each other and walked slowly down the sidewalk as she explained about the accident and the trooper's visit. Then how Hope had just crumbled, and how she and Elaine had done their best to take care of her while she came to grips with the horrible reality.

"I wanted to talk to you about us, our future," Trent said. "I have a feeling this isn't the right time, though."

"It's better timing than you think," she said softly.

"Yeah?"

"Time isn't always on our side," Faith said, looking up at him. "That's what I realized when the trooper came with the news about Peter. No one was ready for this. Everyone thought he had decades left, but life is so short, and so fragile and precious. I don't want to waste another minute of it."

"So… We can talk about this?" he asked.

She nodded. "I think we should."

Trent looked wary, and she understood. But maybe she needed to talk about this right now—put it out there. Because life came with ups and downs just like this one, and they could either pull together, or not.

"I know that Tyke complicates matters for you," she went on, "but I need to tell you how I feel, Trent."

"And how do you feel?" he asked softly.

An Amish couple pushing a stroller ambled down the sidewalk toward them. They were young, so much younger than even Faith and Trent had been when they first got married. And they walked close enough to each other that their arms brushed, and the Amish man had the wispy beard of the newly married. Faith moved aside to let them pass, and she watched them as they carried on together—in a whole world just the two of them and their new baby. It was the life she'd wanted so badly.

"I love you." That really seemed to encapsulate it all. "That's it. I love you. And I figured out what I needed when we were married. It was Elaine who noted that it's just like Amish marriages. You and I were always pointed in different directions. You had your company, and I had mine. You had your dreams, and I had mine. I wanted a baby, and you wanted to wait… We were never quite on the same page. It was lonely."

"Can we work on that?" Trent asked.

She nodded. "Yeah, I think we can. The silly thing is, it's probably pretty simple. I don't want to run a bookstore by myself."

He frowned. "What?"

"I want a family business. I don't want it to be my bookstore, I want it to be ours. And I don't even want to go to the city! I want to stay here. I don't want to sell the antiques shop. I want to let that be a family shop we all work in and keep afloat, and I want to start that bookstore, but I don't want to do that alone."

"You want to run it together?" Trent asked.

She nodded. "A family business. I want to hire

our nieces and nephews. I want to make all those decisions together. It doesn't mean you can't have your electrician business, too, but I want everything to be ours together. I don't want any more yours and mine. I want to work together, sink or swim together. And if something sinks, I want us both to be crushed, and then carry on together."

"I could do that..." A smile spread over Trent's face. "I can absolutely do that."

"I don't want to do it in Philly... Is that reckless of me?"

"We have a community here," he said. "We have family on both sides, people who love us. Community is important, too, you know. It's part of what makes Amish people so content. They've got relationships."

They stopped in front of a flower shop, and Faith looked up at him. "But what about Tyke?"

"Well... I had a good chat with my aunt about what makes Amish marriages last, and it turns out it's not so magical after all," Trent said. "They just choose each other for life—no matter what. And what else will they do but fix things when they need fixing? For them, there is no other choice, Faith. And I realized that it's not about Amish rules. For me, there already isn't any other choice. I love you. It's not going away. For me, it's you or bust." He winced. "I guess that wasn't very romantic."

"Trent..." She wrapped her arms around his neck and pulled him down into a kiss. She felt his strong arms lock around her waist, and when she pulled back, Trent looked tenderly down at her.

"I want us to raise Tyke together," he said softly. "I want to have more kids, too. I want to run your bookstore with you, and I want you to help me with my electrician business. Maybe you'll take care of the accounting for me? And... I know I'm always jumping at things and doing stuff too fast for you, but—" he gave her a hopeful half smile "—I want to get married again. I want to belong to each other, come what may."

"Are you sure?" she whispered. "Because before you were worried about—"

"Hey, forget before," he said. "Life is always a risk, but it's not so risky when you love someone as much as I love you. Just promise never to break my heart again."

"I can promise that. It's you and me, no matter what," she said. "And Tyke, too, of course. I'd love to be his mom..." And tears welled up in her eyes at the depth of that honor. She could love both of them with everything she had, and she and Trent would pull together, shoulder to shoulder.

"It's not too rushed for you?" Trent asked.

"Some things are worth the rush, Trent," she said. "*You* are worth the rush."

And Trent gathered her up onto the tips of her toes as he kissed her all over again. And in his strong arms, she felt like she'd finally come all the way home.

EPILOGUE

THE NEXT COUPLE of months were busy, full of meaningful moments. There was the funeral for Peter, and Trent made sure he was there to support Faith and her family, too. Her parents came back for the funeral and the whole clan all pulled together to support Hope during this terrible time. Aunt Mary and Uncle Albrecht pitched in as well, bringing casseroles and desserts to Faith and her sisters as they adjusted to everything. Mammi and Faith's mother got particularly close, too. Trent didn't fully understand what was happening there, but it looked to him like Mammi was being the mother that Faith's mom needed, too. Everyone just gave what they had from the heart.

Trent and Faith organized a small wedding. They didn't want anything big this time around, but they did want to mark the occasion with as much ceremony as they could. Because this was the last time they were doing this—it was the wedding for a lifetime.

So, on a hot August afternoon, Trent and Faith stood in front of a judge, their hands clasped tight.

They'd dressed Tyke up in a little suit they'd borrowed from a friend, and Trent wore a new suit he bought in the city. He hadn't had time to get it tailored, but Aunt Mary had done some expert nipping and stitching until the suit fit like a glove.

Faith bought a new wedding dress—it was actually a sundress from an upscale boutique in the city, but it was just what she wanted, she said. And Trent could not complain. It didn't matter what she wore, but the dress she chose was simple, white and truly beautiful on her. The best part was that she smelled of her favorite perfume, and he couldn't wait until she unpacked all those bottles and vials onto the top of his dresser again. She'd move in right after the wedding. They'd made an offer to the current owner to see if he'd sell it to them, and he'd agreed.

Elaine and Hope attended the ceremony, as did Aunt Mary, Uncle Albrecht and Mammi. Faith's parents were there, too, of course, and before the ceremony, her mom gave Trent a spontaneous, teary hug. They loved him, and he knew it. So they had all squeezed into the judge's office in a happy, chattering muddle. Trent and Faith might have wanted to keep this small and low pressure, but this was as small as absolutely possible.

The judge looked up from reviewing all their documents and he gave them a smile.

"Are we ready, then?" he asked.

Trent and Faith both nodded.

"We are here to witness the marriage of Trent Lantz and Faith Fairchild. Marriage is a legal union before the state of Pennsylvania that unites this man and this woman together for life…"

Trent never did remember the vows that the judge had used. Love, honor, cherish, protect, stand by… He'd do it all. Faith said she would, too, and then by the power vested in that judge, they were pronounced husband and wife.

Again. At last. And Trent's heart had encircled Faith with a strength that surprised even him.

She was his wife, and when he pulled her into a kiss, it felt like everything had finally come back into place. Tyke came running up, having escaped whoever had been holding him, and as Trent broke off the kiss, Faith scooped him up.

"We're a family, Tyke," Faith said with tears in her eyes. "That's Daddy, and I'm Mommy, and you're Tyke."

Tyke put his hands on her face, and she kissed his forehead.

A family. That was what this feeling was—Trent had a family of his own now—and he turned to face their extended family. He couldn't be happier to claim them all as his. This was a new start, and this time around, he was holding his wife close and they were going to make it. With the way his heart loved, Faith was his only choice.

And that was just the way he liked it.

* * * * *

*Don't miss the next book
in Patricia Johns's miniseries
An Amish Antiques Shop Romance,
coming March 2026
from Harlequin Heartwarming*

Harlequin® Reader Service

Enjoyed your book?

Try the perfect subscription for Romance readers and get more great books like this delivered right to your door.

See why over 10+ million readers have tried Harlequin Reader Service.

Start with a Free Welcome Collection with free books and a gift—valued over $20.

Choose any series in print or ebook.
See website for details and order today:

TryReaderService.com/subscriptions